DARK DESIRES

DARK DESIRES

A collection of twenty erotic stories

Edited by Miranda Forbes

Published by Xcite Books Ltd – 2011
ISBN 9781907761706

Printed and bound in the UK

Cover design by
Madamadari

Contents

Animal Attraction
by Lucy Felthouse

As soon as I saw the sexy naked guy lying on the ground, I knew this was going to be no ordinary day.

I approached him with caution, just in case he lashed out. After all, who doesn't feel at their most vulnerable while naked? Certainly in the woods, anyway. And I should know.

I touched him on the shoulder, which I couldn't help but notice was broad and muscular. My eyes then just happened to glance lower and catch sight of his rather glorious bottom. Hell, if he hadn't been in a foetal position, I'd have checked out his crown jewels, too. Come on, could you blame me, the guy was gorgeous!

And he was just waking up. Obviously having no idea where he was, he turned over, giving me a full-frontal view of aforementioned genitals. I averted my eyes, though not without a struggle.

The man's eyes flicked open momentarily, then closed again. He obviously hadn't been satisfied with what he saw the first time round. Which, looking up I could understand. I didn't have trees or blue sky on the ceiling of my bedroom, either. Trying again, hot guy opened his eyes. Frowned. He started to sit up, then caught sight of me standing there and opened his mouth to speak. Before he could, though, his brain must have caught on to the fact that he was naked.

Looking down, he immediately reacted by pulling his knees up to his chest, covering up his bits. Then he tried speaking again,

'OK, what the fuck?'

I couldn't help it. I laughed, causing the poor guy to look even more out of sorts. Walking up to him, I said, 'I'm sorry, I was expecting something a little more traditional to come out of your mouth, like "Where am I?" or "What's going on?" You just took me by surprise, that's all. I'm Rayne.'

I held out a hand. Pulling his legs in tighter, Mr Naked reached up and shook my hand.

'I'm Claude. So, should I ask the more traditional questions now? What's going on?'

'Well,' I said, removing my sweater from around my waist to hand to him, 'I'm not exactly sure. I was just out running. This is my usual route home, but today you were lying starkers by the side of it! I'm as surprised as you are.'

By now he'd taken my sweater gratefully, though he now seemed to be struggling with the dilemma of what exactly to do with it.

'It's fine, just tie it around. It'll wash, it's an old one anyway.'

Holding the garment gingerly over his crotch, Claude stood. His face flamed and he obviously didn't know where to put himself. Suddenly remembering my manners, I turned my back, allowing him to sort himself out.

Seconds later, he said, 'Um, OK. I'm kind of decent.'

Turning to face him again, I had to stifle a grin. As I said before, this guy was broad, so my little sweater didn't cover much, just the most important bits. He'd tied the sweater on backwards, and I strongly suspected you'd be able to see his bottom in all its glory if you were behind him.

'Do you want to come back to my place and sort yourself out? It's only a few minutes away and I'm sure I can dig out some sweatpants and a T-shirt for you.'

'Um, are you sure? I mean, thanks, but why are you helping me? I could be anyone. A serial killer, anything.'

'True. If you are a serial killer I have to give you points for your original way of snaring me. But to me you look like a seriously confused guy who needs help. And I'm the only one here. Come on, I'm a big girl, I can look after myself.'

A little while later, Claude was sitting on my sofa sipping a cup of tea. I'd given him some of my ex-boyfriend's clothes to wear. I'd always known they'd come in handy.

'Right. Now we've got you clothed and watered, let's start from the beginning.'

I already had a pretty good idea of what was going on, but wanted to get more information first, in case I was barking up the wrong tree. Blurting out my conclusion would just freak the poor guy out and probably make him think I was a raving loony.

'I don't know what to tell you. I went to bed last night as normal. When I woke up, I was naked in the woods and you were there. That's literally all I can tell you.'

'No strange dreams? Anything weird happen to you lately?'

'I don't normally remember my dreams.' He paused, and a thoughtful expression crossed his face. 'Actually, I vaguely remember something about dogs.'

'Dogs?' Now we were getting somewhere.

'Yeah. I guess it's my subconscious playing tricks on me, something to do with when I got bit.'

Jackpot.

'Bit? By a dog?'

'Yeah. A couple of weeks ago I was on my way home from a night out with the lads and this huge dog started chasing me. I tripped over something and bumped my head. The next thing I knew I was in A&E being patched up and given a tetanus shot. Weird thing is, though, it's gone.'

I knew, but I asked anyway, 'What's gone?'

'The bite. The beast was massive and it could have really messed me up, killed me even. But it only bit me once, then

3

left me alone. And now the mark has gone. It's like it never happened.'

'So you were bitten by a dog and the mark has now disappeared. You dream about dogs, then wake up in the buff in the woods.'

'I know it sounds mental, but that's how it happened.'

'It's not as mental as you think. You see, I have a theory.'

'You do?!'

'Yes. Can I show you something?'

I figured it would be easier to make him believe me if I presented him with evidence. If I just told him straight out, he'd think I was crazy. He might anyway, but I had to take the chance. Claude needed to know the truth.

Once in the basement, Claude had a little trouble controlling his emotions. I'll give him his due, he'd remained calm and quiet when we went through the pin-coded door beneath my stairs and headed to this hidden basement. But what he saw now was obviously a step too far. He looked stunned.

I couldn't blame him. The place resembled some kind of kinky dungeon. There were heavy duty chains hanging from the walls, the ends threaded through the bars of equally hardcore cages. Handcuffing people whilst they were inside cages? I was surprised he hadn't bolted.

He was obviously brighter than I'd given him credit for, though. Walking up to one of the cages, he peered through the bars, studying what was inside.

'These are no ordinary handcuffs.' Claude said, resting his head against the bars. By now, he must have clocked the scratch marks covering the floor and bars of the cage.

'No.'

'I think I know what's going on here.' He turned, his back against the cold metal of the cage, and slid to the floor. I rushed towards him and knelt down in front of him. I said nothing, just rested a hand on his knee.

4

'Am I ... a werewolf?'

He looked at me then, and I thought my heart would break. Claude's face was awash with feelings. Hurt, confusion, worry. I couldn't think of anything to say to make him feel better, so I did the only thing I could think of to do – I moved next to him, slid an arm round his shoulders and pulled him to me. He didn't resist; he snuggled into me like we'd done it a million times before.

He didn't cry, rage or scream. He simply lay in my arms silently, his mind no doubt buzzing with thoughts. I don't know how long we sat there, but eventually he sat up and looked at me.

'How long?' He didn't need to finish the question.

'Fifty years.'

'Fifty – but you're ...'

I put my fingertips to his lips to shush him.

'Claude, there's so much you need to know. Don't worry, I will tell you everything. We'll get through this, together.'

'But, why are you helping me? What's in it for you?'

'I'm helping you because there's no one else. There was nobody to help me. I had to figure it out on my own, and it was the hardest thing I've ever had to do. I wouldn't wish that on anyone. And as for what's in it for me, well, that's up to you.'

'What do you mean?'

'It's a lonely existence when nobody else knows what you are. You can try to carry on as you did before but soon enough people will notice your disappearing acts and start asking questions. Can you imagine having to tell the people you care about that you're a werewolf? They'd be on the phone to the men in white coats, first chance they got.'

'I guess so. So what are you saying? I shouldn't go back home?'

'Only you can decide that. I don't want to influence you either way. Just know that's there a home for you here if you want it. I'd be glad of the company.'

He didn't say anything then, he just looked me in the eyes. I hadn't said much, but Claude had obviously read between the lines and seen how desperately lonely I was.

I looked down. The eye contact was making me feel like he was exposing all my innermost secrets. He reached out a hand and put it beneath my chin, raising my head and forcing me to look at him again.

He opened his mouth as if to speak, but said nothing. Then he leaned toward me and gave me the most toe-curlingly blissful kiss I'd ever experienced. I was startled at first and didn't respond. But when I felt him start to pull back, I didn't want him to. I slipped a hand behind his neck to stop him escaping and pressed my lips to his more forcefully.

I had no idea what the kiss was about – whether it was passion, comfort or what. And at that point, I didn't much care. I slipped my tongue into Claude's mouth and slid it against his. I felt my body start to respond to what was happening; my nipples hardened and I felt a pleasant warmth between my legs.

The heat was obviously starting to get to Claude too, as he pulled away, breathing hard.

'I'm sorry, Rayne. I never should have ...'

'No, you've nothing to be sorry for. We're both adults here. But there's one thing you need to know before anything else happens.'

'What's that?'

'Sex will be ... different, from now on.'

'Different, how?'

'Well, once things start getting hot and heavy, you'll feel different to how you used to. Sure, you'll be horny and your body will do all the normal things. But you'll also feel something else, something inside. Your wolf will awaken.'

'What! Getting horny will turn me into a werewolf?'

'Let me finish,' I said, giving him a stern look. 'Your body won't change, but your wolf, which is normally

6

dormant, will awaken. His consciousness will merge with yours and he'll also crave what you're aiming toward; climax. Just be aware that he'll have an influence and make you more, well, animal.'

'Um, OK. Does it work that way for you, too?'

'Yes. So just be ... aware.'

Claude seemed lost in thought, probably processing all I'd told him. But I hadn't had sex in quite some time, so my woman *and* my wolf were ready. Oooh so ready. I took his hand and slipped it around my waist. We kissed again, and this time there was no going back.

Soon, things went from hot and heavy to molten lava. Claude had me pressed up against the bars of the cage, kissing me hard. He pulled back, only to tug my T-shirt and bra off. Then he was back, his tongue invading my mouth once more, before trailing his lips down my face and neck and heading for my breasts.

My nipples were already as hard as pebbles, so when his hot mouth enclosed one of them, I gasped at the sensation. A jolt of arousal zipped to my pussy and I could feel my juices pooling in my panties. Claude worked his mouth over both sensitive buds in turn, time and time again, until I couldn't take any more teasing. It appeared he couldn't, either. Soon, he pulled away and ripped off his own T-shirt, tossing it on the floor.

We hadn't found him any underwear, so his erection had nothing to hold it in check. It was making quite the tent inside his tracksuit bottoms and I reached out to stroke it, eliciting a growl from him. I had no idea whether it had come from his man or his wolf and I didn't much care. All I knew is both parts of me wanted to wrench noise after noise from him, until we were both sated.

I stood, only to undo my trousers, wrench down my panties and yank off my socks. Claude removed the tracksuit bottoms, leaving him entirely naked. Of course, it wasn't the first time I'd seen him in a state of undress, but this time I had no intention of being polite or averting my eyes. He was a stunning looking man and I wanted my hands all over him, never mind my eyes!

After a pause, we stepped towards one another once more. Claude, tall as he was, bent down to kiss me, and wrapped his arms around me, pulling me to him. His hard cock pressed into my tummy and I slipped a hand between our bodies to touch it.

Wrapping my fingers around his shaft, they barely touched around its girth. I could feel my pussy juices coating my thighs, warm and sticky. The thought of that thick cock stretching and pounding me just made me hotter and wetter. I squeezed him in my hand and began stroking up and down as our tongues fucked each other's mouths. He groaned, and before I had chance to increase the pace to tease him further, he reached down to lift me up.

Hitching me up so my legs wrapped around his waist, I felt tiny in his arms, like I weighed nothing. He'd obviously been a fit guy before his transformation, but the new genes in him made him stronger and fitter.

He moved towards one of the cages, and pushed my back against one of them, causing me to squeal as the cold bars touched my heated skin. Claude laughed, and pushed me harder against the bars, obviously enjoying the way I was writhing and wriggling in his embrace. I dug my nails hard into his biceps, which cast a dark look into his eyes. Most women would have been frightened by that look, but I knew what it was.

His wolf. Peering out at me through Claude's eyes. I repeated the action with my nails, and it was a done deal. Claude's lips crushed mine, kissing me bruisingly hard. I stretched my arms up and behind me to grasp the bars of the cage to give me leverage and lifted myself up a little. Claude took the hint and pulled back a little, just enough to take himself in hand and stroke up and down his rock hard shaft a couple of times. I looked down to see the shiny purple head of his cock seeping precome, and I wanted it. Now.

Tilting my hips toward him, I growled. Claude – and his wolf – needed no more invitation. Guiding his cock to my slick pout, he lined himself up and plunged into me, deeply and without hesitation. He slid in right to the hilt, I was so wet and ready. Grasping my hips hard, he took advantage of the fact I was using my arms to hang onto the bars of the cage by rocking me forward and back onto his prick.

He was fast and furious and I loved it. Sliding one hand between our bodies, Claude pinched my clit between thumb and forefinger. I screamed with the pleasure/pain, my pussy grasping tighter around his cock. He continued to manipulate my swollen bud as he fucked me relentlessly, until I felt my climax approaching.

My head lolled back as I felt the tingling of orgasm grow inside me. I grunted and groaned as he pumped into my pussy, my woman as wild with desire as my wolf. Then another flick of my clit caused my climax to hit, like smashing glass. My cunt spasmed wildly around Claude's cock and the knuckles of my hands went white as I gripped the bars of the cage so hard it hurt.

Feeling my vaginal walls clutching around his prick tipped Claude over the edge, too. He slowed his pace and leaned his head against my shoulder. He dug his teeth into my skin as he came; not hard enough to draw blood, but enough to leave a mark. His cock began to twitch and jump, emptying his balls inside me.

After what felt like for ever, our orgasms abated and we slumped together. I let go of the cage and wound my arms around Claude's neck. His head rested on my chest, and my head on top of his, his thick dark hair soft against my skin. I rubbed my face against it playfully as he sighed contentedly into my ample cleavage.

Nice as it was, the position we were in became uncomfortable, so Claude put me down gently. In the absence of anything comfortable in the room, we sat on our discarded clothes, holding one another. Though the silence was far from awkward, I broke it anyway.

'Well,' I said, grinning from ear to ear, 'that was certainly a different use for the cage!'

Claude chuckled. 'I guess it was. Now I suppose we should talk about what they're really for, shouldn't we?'

'Mmm,' I said, stroking a hand idly up and down his abs, noting that his cock was semi-hard again, 'we should.'

I disentangled from our embrace and pushed him flat to the floor, straddling his hips. 'But there's plenty of time until sundown. And I know just how we can fill it ...'

Familiar
by Sommer Marsden

My mother was the practising witch of Clara County. Folks came to her for healing and assistance – normal and paranormal. My father was an average guy with no supernatural talents beyond an amazing chicken dish he seemed to make out of thin air and sheer will. His name was Joe and he died of cancer. He died in August. My mother gave into her own heart condition four months later in December. Two days after Christmas, three days before my twenty-fifth birthday.

On my twenty-fifth birthday my own powers were to take hold. I often asked her why twenty-five, it just seems so *old*. She told me it only seemed old because I was younger than twenty-five which was too damn young. Then she said 'Sarah, it's twenty-five because you're too stupid to have power before that. And twenty-five is still iffy.' And then she kissed me on the nose.

When mum died I inherited enough money to not worry that I'd miss rent or starve, her little yellow Spitfire that had been her prized possession and her familiar, a red cat named Cyrus. And when I say red, I mean it. He's a red baked brick sort of colour and has eyes that look like uncut emeralds shot with topaz. He won't eat anything but steak and cheese. He's an expensive cat.

So here I sit, on my birthday, waiting for my powers to take hold. Only there's no one here to help me, I'm pretty

11

much an orphan and I don't give a good goddamn about my witchy ways. I miss my mother, I miss my father and I am officially alone in the world.

I could be a country song for all intents and purposes.

So I do what any smart girl my age does. I drink a bottle of wine and go to bed. Cyrus winds himself around and around me until I feel like the room is spinning and I pin him under my hand. 'Listen, cat, find a place to settle down or you're getting the boot.'

He curls himself into a comma of red fur and starts to purr against my side. I get one sandpaper lick from his tongue and then I'm fast asleep. My body going limp second by second as sleep sucks me under.

Two hours later I wake in the dark with a jolt. A hand has grasped my ankle and the warmth of a human palm presses to my skin, making me sit up. There's a flash of green eyes, absinthe coloured eyes that seem to pin me. I'm paralysed, I'm stuck, I'm panicking. And then the paralysis breaks and I hit blindly into the darkness, waving my hands and striking out hoping to hit whatever it is by sheer accident.

And then Cyrus prances over my lap with his tiny hard paws and my head feels fuzzy and I feel that whatever it was – *whoever* it was – is gone.

'Fuck,' I say to the cat and he nuzzles my arm. 'What was that? Is this what powers are like? If so, I'd like a refund.'

Cyrus says nothing (duh) and I flop back pushing my hands into my long messy hair. I twirl a thin strand around my finger and then let it go. I do this over and over again – the grown up version of sucking my thumb – until sleep comes back with greedy claws and snatches me down.

The hands are back not long after but my head is lazy and heavy and I feel like I'm made of warm syrup and sunshine. 'Whoozat?'

I hear nothing but what I think is Cyrus purring as the hands, big and warm and strong from the feel of them, part

12

my ankles. The fingers stroke me and my skin pebbles with goose bumps at the soft attention. '*Hellooooo*?' I sing out because for whatever reason I am very much unafraid.

A soft tongue follows the firm hands and against my better judgment I sigh with contentment.

'I am dreaming,' I tell myself. 'I must be.'

There is no anxiety this time, only anticipation. Who is this person starring in my dreams? And why do I feel so very alert and so very surreal at the same time? I wiggle a little, the sheets feeling soft and entirely real under the backs of my thighs. The hands that have whispered their way up to my knees also feel truly real. And the lips that press a warm kiss to the inside of my right calf feel like very tactile bits of heaven on my skin.

'It's a doozy of a dream.' Somehow, I seem hell bent on talking aloud to myself through this very real waking sort of dream. A sexy one, judging by the way it's going. 'And here I am saying something else to myself,' I say and snicker.

The laughter rumbles through my belly. I'm feeling very lucid, and yet, I go slack and soft for the ministrations of my unseen dream lover. 'I haven't had sex in nine months, one week, three days and umpteen hours,' I say. 'But who's counting?'

Another kiss lands and it's above the knee now. A wet stroke of the tongue over tingling flesh and I hold my breath as one of the hands closes around my wrist. I shiver, giving in to the pleasure of his weight, his touch. 'Aren't you going to at least say something, dream-person who is making the moves on me?' I whisper. Another kiss falls on my waiting skin and he's only an inch or so below the good stuff. Ground zero. The sweet spot where I want so badly at this point for his mouth to be.

'Shhh,' comes the answer.

'Well that is something. A noise at least,' I babble. But when his mouth presses to the front of my panties, for I'm sleeping in nothing but panties and an oversized T-shirt, I shut the fuck up.

I listen for any sound of Cyrus. The thought of my mother's familiar watching me get it on, even in a dream, is kind of freaky. I don't hear him and I'd left the door open. Maybe he's sauntered his red ass out into the living room.

I wiggle and I shake and when big sturdy hands pin my hips I feel what some might have described, once upon a time, as the vapours. The world seems to move under me and when he hooks his fingers in my panties and tugs, I bite my tongue to sharpen my mind. Dreaming is one thing, this is almost an out-of-body experience.

I reach out and find a bicep, a forearm, a head full of thick hair. A chest, the indentation of a navel, a hipbone. My hand closes around a cock and my fingers thrill at the contact of hot flesh with mine. 'This is the best dream ever,' I say.

There's a dark chuckle in the blackness. Not even street light or ambient light from the alarm clock. My room is in utter darkness thanks to a stint on third shift at a convenience store. I'd invested in blinds that would block out the flash from a nuclear detonation. But that is neither here nor there because he's pressed chest to breast with me and I can feel the steady pounding of his wild dark heart.

'You're not some robber? You haven't broken in here to rob me of my … virtue?' Even I have a hard time pushing the word virtue over my lips. Though I've had a long dry spell, virtuous is not an adjective I'd pin to myself.

I swear I hear him smile. Then he drops me a single word, like a trinket flying from a Mardi Gras float. 'No.'

'Good.'

His lips brush mine and his hands tangle in my hair. He tugs just enough for the flash of pain to rocket through me to my heart, my belly, and lower. I arch up and kiss back, wishing so much that the soft lips and warm tongue and tender kisses were real and not a figment of my drunken freshly twenty-five-year-old mind.

'Please don't torture me any more. With my luck, you'll get right to the good part and I'll wake up.'

He mumbles something but I can't hear and I don't care because he's flush to me. The smooth steely head of his cock is nudging my wet opening and I hold my breath seeing little flashes of white light in the dark. I'm not getting enough air. I have to breathe. I might go blind, black out, lose it … but funny, I don't care.

He grabs hold of my hips and slips into me one solid inch at a time. My body taking in the heated pulse of his cock, his heartbeat seemingly slamming through every bit of him.

'This is my birthday gift to me,' I tell him. He's pushed my T-shirt high around my neck and his lips close over my nipple. He follows suit with his teeth. I wrap my legs around him, holding him deep as he thrusts. I've heard talk of dream guys, dreamy guys, man of your dreams … I've found mine.

Outside a car door slams, sounding oh so real and oh so improbable in a dream. I touch him – hot skin, thundering heart, stubbled jaw. His lips close over my finger and he sucks it deep. I feel the resounding erotic tug in my tummy, my pussy. My mind reasons that I should stop but when he dips his head, gives me a gentle kiss and then nips my bottom lip just hard enough to trigger the pleasure pain thrill of approaching orgasm, I push my rationale away.

'In for a penny in for a pound.'

I tug at him, desperate to yank the good feelings in my body closer. To grip my impending climax tight and ride it like some wild thing. But he laughs softly, his breath feathering across my face. 'Patience is a virtue, Sarah.'

He licks the tip of my nose and though I think it strange, he's rocking his hips in a back and forth motion that's touching off every single needy swollen nerve deep inside of me. I touch his face, stroke his hair, hold him close and at that last moment, he pushes my arms high above my head and holds me there – pins me to my own pillow. He pounds into me, thrusting hard, breathing fast, I catch a flash of absinthe green in the dark, my eyes are half closed, and dream dude dips his head and bites my shoulder just enough. The perfect, spectacular amount I need.

I'm coming, spiralling down into the rich wave of pleasure, fighting his hands just so I can hold him, touch him. But he traps me fast and his sounds are harsh and loud as he comes right behind me.

I wait to wake up. I wait for him to go poof. And I wait …

His head is resting on my shoulder, his hands travelling along my sides, his heartbeat a steady thing trapped between my chest and his. 'Happy birthday, dear Sarah.'

I let out what feels like it will be a horrid horror movie screech but instead sounds like a wheeze or a tyre deflating. 'Oh my God. Geddoffmegedoffmegedoffme.' I rear back and shuffle scootch backwards on my ass. I flip the light on.

I get a fast flash of a huge hunky man with nice abs and jet black hair. Flashing green eyes and a slow curling smile. And then … Cyrus!

'Oh my god, this is illegal in all states!'

He gives me a slow even blink and stares pointedly (for a cat) at the light. I turn it off.

'Now listen to me and do not panic.'

'Cyrus!'

'Sarah I …'

'Oh my God. I've had you for ever. Not known. *Had*. You've been in my house. You were my mother's pet!' I know this is wrong but I say it anyhow.

'We grew up together, in a way. And a familiar is not a pet …'

'I know, I know!' I hiss. 'Is this because of my birthday?'

'Yes and I…'

I flip the light back on.

'… meow,' he finishes.

Meow? Shit!

I flip the light off.

'Stop doing that.'

'Am I drunk?'

'No. This is part of your powers,' he says. I feel his strong hand on my ankle, patting me. Patting the crazy lady.

I flip the light on. A paw is where the hand should be.

I flip the light off. 'I have the power of hallucination and insanity?' I ask him, my words thin and high like I'm full of Helium.

'No. You can perceive the true nature of anything. Even a shifter like me.'

'But I thought you were a familiar.'

'I am. But a shifter by design. I chose to help your mother.'

I humph. 'Well, what do I do with it? In the dark you're all yummy and manly. In the light you are … A Cat.' I growl at him. I'm getting sort of pissed.

'Focus,' Cyrus says and he plays one big manly (in the dark) finger over my ankle bone. The shiver works from foot to knee to ankle, to girly bits and I hold my breath. I focus on the image of him as a man. The naked, firm, perfect image of him as a manly, studly just-rocked-my-world guy and then I flip the light on.

There he is. Solid and ripply and smiling. Black-black hair across his forehead, his brilliant green eyes looking into my soul it seems. 'Why are you here?'

'I'm your family. In a way. But I also …' He dips his head, looking shy and annoyed with himself.

'What?'

'I love you,' he says to my ankle.

'Me!' I snort it out and then feel bad. And very unladylike.

'I have for ever.'

'Did my mother know?' I ask, feeling shocked and a bit off balance. He's a cat. Or a man who can be a cat. He is a cat-man and he loves me. Something in my belly warms,

17

something in my chest follows suit.

'Yes. She told me that I couldn't tell you until ...'

I lose my focus and when I shake my head to clear the cobwebs he says, *meow* because he's a fucking cat again.

'Damn. Hold on.' I go through the whole thing again until he's a man. 'Until what?'

'Until you could give consent. Understand, which meant you had to perceive me on your own. For when you could maybe love me back and consider being my mate.' His fingers close around my calf; I recall the fireball of an orgasm.

'Did I give consent?'

'All the *oh gods* sort of did it.'

'I need time.'

'And you have it.'

'Will you help me? With my witchy-ness?'

'It's why I stayed. I was never beholden. I was free to leave whenever.'

'I'm not alone,' I say to him as if he doesn't know.

He touches my hair and kisses me softly. 'Nope.'

'But my someone is a cat,' I sigh.

'About that human thing, I can be human whenever I want. You needed to learn to control your perception for when it's not a shifter you're dealing with. That was a test to see if you could hold me in human form. I don't need you to keep me that way. But you, Sarah, can see the inner workings of any soul. That is a gift. A big one.'

'Are there more? Powers, I mean.'

'There are more. Reading intent. Conjuring. Conversing with elementals ...' He smiles.

'I'm scared.' And I am. Saying it aloud to someone other than myself is nice. He kisses me, nods, doesn't say anything but his fingers stroke soft circles on my skin until I feel looser and soft and then I kiss him.

'Oh God,' I say and laugh.

'Cyrus will do.'

'Your hair isn't red.'

'I chose that colour.'

'Dear goodness, why?' I take him in hand. Feel his body respond to mine.

'Your mother liked it. She said it matched the kitchen colour scheme.'

I laugh but feel a blip of sadness. 'That sounds like Mum. She was super skilled. She was talented and humble and loving. I'll never be great like her,' I say. 'I feel so inept.'

'You're great too, Sarah,' he says. 'You just need a little help.'

'You'll help me, you'll help me,' I chant and his lips are warm on mine. 'But after we do this again,' I say and guide him to me. I wrap my arms to his neck, hold him close, feel him slide deep and move in small rocking motions that make me hopeful and somehow brave.

I have someone. Someone who loves me. I'm not alone.

'You're not alone,' Cyrus says, reading my thoughts somehow.

'Did you just …'

'Maybe. We'll talk later. We have a long time to figure it all out.'

'Right.' I tip my body up to take him in. I ride the warm waves of pleasure until I can't stand it any more and I come.

Cyrus says in my ear, 'Happy birthday, Sarah.'

I smile.

Then … *meow*

I freeze. Horrified.

'Just kidding,' Cyrus laughs and then he's groaning out his own release, holding me tight.

'So I guess this job comes with a built in familiar?'

'Only if you want him.'

'One request?'

'What is it?'

'Black hair? It is *fierce*.'

'Done and done,' Cyrus says.

I wind myself around him, letting my heartbeat synch up with his. 'And a hot pink leopard collar with a bell,' I say, grinning, waiting.

'Don't press your luck,' Cyrus says.

When he gathers me in hugs me, I'm grateful for my powers. I'm grateful for a guide in this process. I'm grateful to be twenty-five and I'm grateful to have a legacy to carry on.

'That's good,' he says.

'You can totally read my mind, can't you?'

'Maybe just a little.'

Séance
by Mary Borsellino

We found the planchette first: an elongated triangle of dark wood, almost a heart. A little smaller than my palm and lacquered shiny and smooth from years of touches. It was tied on to the same piece of fraying string as the keys to the old woodshed, having been mistaken for some kind of nondescript ornament.

'It's a planchette,' Louisa explained to me, recognising it for what it really was. 'That's French for "little plank".'

Her own set of keys – for the rental car, and the front door of the main house, and our own flat back home in the world beyond a fortnight's holiday among mist-wreathed country fields – was attached to a pocket knife. She sliced the rotting string apart easily.

'It's almost an old-fashioned cursor, like on a computer screen,' Louisa explained to me, passing the little object over so that I could get a better look. 'It's what ghosts use to spell out words on Ouija boards. I wonder if there used to be séances here, when the house was lived in properly.'

'The board might be down in the cellar. The landlord said there were a few old trunks down there,' I suggested, turning the planchette over between my fingers. The wood was heavy and warm despite the clammy chill of the outdoor air. We'd gotten a cheap rate because of the vibe of general disrepair around the place, but Louisa and I both found the idea of a little dose of gloom rather romantic. A few weeks shivering under bedclothes in a drafty house is much less depressing when there's the prospect of a return to central heating at the end of it.

Louisa had been the one to suggest the whole adventure, of course. She's always been the creative, impulsive one – I often explain the differences between us, to those who ask, by pointing out that in our respective bands she's a lead guitarist, while I play rhythm. Flashy, brilliant, showy, versus reliable regularity, the two of us working in complement to make the music of a life together.

But for now the touring season was done, our crowds of fans back at school and busy with exams, our band mates holed up in their own seclusions just as we were in our damp little hideaway.

Despite some idle discussion of looking for the board which matched the planchette, we forgot our discovery soon enough after wandering back to the house. We left the trinket and Louisa's keys on top of the strewn newspaper still covering the sturdy wooden kitchen table, where we'd been cheerfully arguing over the crossword answers before going for our walk.

We ended up on one of the soft worn couches in the living room, the balding blue velvet shiny under Louisa's smooth olive skin and dark curls of hair as I pulled her T-shirt up over her head. Her breasts were heavy swells inside the flimsy black lace of her bra. I sucked wet kisses against the fabric, nipping lightly at the pointed nubs of her nipples. My hands worked swiftly to open the buckle of her belt, to ease the buttons of her jeans open, to slide down the zipper and slip my fingertips inside. Louisa stopped wearing panties when her band first started touring – one less item of clothing for her to pack and wash – and the habit stuck.

My fingers, still bearing their guitar-string calluses, brushed against the slick folds of her cunt, making her buck up against me with a strangled sigh.

'Shit, Benny,' she gasped. 'Quit with this girly foreplay

stuff and fuck me already.'

There was a condom in the pocket of my jeans – I'd been Louisa's boyfriend for long enough, by that stage, to know that it was best to always be prepared – and after a few fumbled moments I had it rolled on and was pushing inside her. Louisa's sex-laugh, throaty and breathless as I pulled back and then sank in deep again, was just the same as her concert-laugh. Music or lovemaking, her joy was equally palpable.

There was a gust of cold air, infiltrating the room through some unseen crack, making our skin prickle up into goose-bumps as we approached climax. Hot flesh and chill wind, clashing as we writhed and groaned, clutching at one another in the shocky little deaths of our orgasm.

Later, when we were rumpled but re-clothed, we went back into the kitchen to make ourselves lunch. Toasted cheese sandwiches, tinned tomato soup, and black instant coffee – when two rock stars end up in a relationship with one another, culinary mastery is rarely found in their household's skill set.

Louisa went to clear the table, pausing with her hand over the planchette atop the newspaper and making a small surprised sound.

'Benny, come look at this.'

The circular cut-out shape in the centre of the planchette had landed over part of a headline, the letters HI visible in the circle.

I shook my head, hoping my smile didn't look condescending. 'That's just where your hand happened to put it down when we came back from our walk. It doesn't mean anything,' I told her.

'But that's how these things work,' she said, insistent, picking up the planchette and turning it over and over in her palms. 'The spirits push your hands this way and that, moving this thing around, so they can spell a message. What if someone – some*thing* – pushed me just that little bit as I put it down, so that it could say hi to us?'

'And what if you happened to drop it there by pure coincidence in your hurry to go have a quickie on the couch?' I countered teasingly, even though I could tell from her expression that Louisa wasn't going to be persuaded away from her version of events any time soon.

Sure enough, after a few seconds of thinking she went over to her knapsack and rummaged inside, pulling out a notebook and a thick black pen.

Tearing an empty page free from the pad, Louisa sat down at the table and started to write out the alphabet in neat capitals.

'The name *Ouija board* comes from the words for "yes" in French and German, you know,' she said to me as she worked, adding "yes", "no" and "goodbye" beneath her rows of letters. 'Right, that should do it. Come sit down; we should both put our hands on it to work everything properly.'

I suddenly felt oddly hesitant. I shook my head. 'This is a silly game. Let's go out and explore the grounds some more.'

'Come on, just sit down. Don't be a killjoy,' Louisa demanded, pointing imperiously at the empty chair where she wanted me to sit.

'This may not be a good idea,' I insisted, holding my hands up in front of me and taking a step backwards. 'People are always saying how dangerous Ouija boards are. We shouldn't do this.'

'So which is it, dangerous or silly? It can't be both,' she teased. 'I'm sure it's safe, Ben. They said "hi" to us, after all. That's more polite than most of the record executives we've met.'

I snorted. 'Well, that's true.' Her joking had made me realise just how silly and superstitious my reservations sounded, so with a shrug I nodded and sat down, resting my fingertips on the planchette beside Louisa's.

'OK, uh,' I said, addressing the empty air. 'Hi there, whoever's listening.'

We waited, trying to keep our hands still in the long seconds of silence.

When the planchette jerked suddenly under my hands, I was looking directly at Louisa. She seemed just as surprised as I was.

N... O... the planchette began to spell. *T ... L ... I ... S ...*

'Not listening,' I said aloud when it was done. 'Watching.'

I swallowed, forcing a weak laugh. 'OK, kind of creeped-out now.'

Now it was Louisa's turn to snort. 'You spend half your life on stage, yet the idea of being watched gives you the shivers? You might be one of the quiet ones, Benny-boy, but I know you're an exhibitionist.'

The planchette began to move again as she finished speaking.

D ... I ... D ... N ... T ... M ...

'Didn't mean to be creepy,' Louisa translated as it continued to spell, the little wood heart moving so fast beneath our fingertips that I was half-concerned that it would slip away from us entirely and fly across the room. 'I only wanted to see. I miss ...'

We waited, hardly breathing. Eventually the planchette moved again.

W ... A ... R ... M ... T ... H.

'I miss warmth,' Louisa repeated softly.

'Who are you? What's your name?' I asked.

N ... O ... B ...

'Nobody now,' I read along as it spelled. 'But my name used to be Gabrielle.'

'Gabrielle,' Louisa echoed. 'Hey, Gabrielle. Nice to meet you.'

I ... W ...

'I was 20, my second cousin Rudy was 17. We were very

much in love,' I read out for Gabrielle. 'But we held off marrying until Rudy returned from the Great War. He did not return.

'After a year of grief, I bought an Ouija board. It's in the cellar now, along with all the other relics Rudy and I left behind. I tried so many times to speak to him using the board, but with no response. He'd moved on to whatever it is that comes next after this life.

'When I fell ill with pneumonia the following winter, I did not struggle very hard. It seemed that fate was going to reunite me with Rudy. But when I died, I stayed here, still waiting. Always cold.'

By the time Gabrielle had finished her message, the strange sensation in my arms was too strong to ignore any longer. It was as if thin tendrils of the chill in the air had infiltrated my skin, threads of invisible willpower wrapping themselves around my bones and muscles, directing the movement of my hands. The sensation was alien but not at all unpleasant.

Louisa gave a small shiver, clearly feeling the same thing. She had her lazy, troublemaking smile on her face, which always meant she had some scheme in the works.

'Just a moment,' she said, addressing me and Gabrielle both, and got up from the table. She went back to her knapsack, searching its pockets and finally brandishing the small foil envelope of a condom packet.

'Come on,' Louisa ordered me, nodding in the direction of the living room and leading the way in. She pointed at the couch. 'Sit.'

'Lou … I started, then sighed. It was rarely worth the battle to go against Louisa's wishes, and usually they turned out to be worth going along with. I sat.

'I think Benny's still a little worried,' Louisa told the empty air around us. 'So I'm going to kill two birds with one stone, if you'll pardon the expression. We'll give you warmth, Gabrielle, if you touch Ben like you were touching me in there.'

Louisa pulled her jeans off, lifting one of my hands to touch her and feel how wet and plump and ready she was. Apparently ghosts were an aphrodisiac for my whip-smart, impulsive girlfriend.

'Really?' I asked teasingly, rubbing my thumb over her clit as I started to harden.

Louisa simply smirked. 'You'll see.'

A few minutes later, I did. With Louisa across my lap, her thighs straddling me as she sank down onto my cock, a light tickle began to trace up my spine to the nape of my neck. Not like threads or wind, this time, the touch was a prickle like the ozone that fills the air before a storm. Electrified and elusive. Higher and higher it went, raising the hairs on my scalp as my back arched involuntarily and I groaned aloud. Down through the shell of my skull it went, into the meat of my brain.

Lightning. Crackles of pleasure, nerve ending all over my body alight with the icy, otherworldly presence of Gabrielle's being. I couldn't tell if I was shouting, sobbing, or completely silent. I was lost within pure sensation, my body jerking like a rag doll under the onslaught of it.

Warm, my bones seemed to sing. *Warm.*

When I eventually came back to myself I was lying on the couch, sprawled and wrecked. Louisa's cheeks were flushed a hectic red, her eyes blown dark and glittering with amusement as she climbed off me.

'I'm going to go see what's in the cellar,' she said, pulling her jeans back on before leaning in for a happy, sated kiss. 'Come down and join me when you're ready.'

Then I was alone in the living room, just me and the ghost.

Come With Us
by Landon Dixon

Colonel K slammed his riding crop down on his desk and muttered, 'Blast it all! I must get more recruits for the front! Where have all the young men gone?'

Miss Anna pulled the Colonel's cock out of her mouth with a wet pop, gasped, 'That's what I'd like to know.' She grinned cheerfully up at the grey-haired military man, from between his legs, beneath his desk.

The Colonel grunted, placed a large, authoritative hand on his busty secretary's blonde-pleated head and redirected her attention back to his ramrod straight cock. 'You've got a dirty mouth, Anna,' he mused. 'That's what I like about you.'

The simple country girl began eagerly sucking on the Colonel's cock again. She gripped his muscled thighs through his black worsted uniform pants and boisterously bobbed her head. Colonel K absently pumped his riding crop through the circled forefinger and thumb of his opposite hand, unconsciously imitating his secretary, urging her on to even more vigorous efforts.

The tall, bluff career Army officer had more on his mind than Miss Anna's comely mouth and figure, however. His command was homeland G sector, his responsibility as Provost Marshal to round up – by recruitment, if possible; conscription, if necessary – young, able-bodied men between the ages of 18 and 34 for the war effort. Both his

28

specific task, and the overall war effort in general, were not going well.

The Colonel knew there were still plenty of men in the rural valleys and woods and villages that made up his sector, who weren't in uniform. If only he could find them. Otherwise, he might find *himself* in a trench by Christmas.

He suddenly bucked, like back in his cavalry days, as Miss Anna took an extraordinarily deep pull on his pulsating cock, her deft fingers fondling his tightened balls. He looked down at her again, anxious for the return of the staff officer he'd sent out to assess the missing men situation (and who, himself, had been missing for over a week); anxious now, as well, to come. He gripped Anna's head with both his hands and pumped his hips in his fine leather chair, fucking her plump, pleasing face, as she sucked.

'Oh, no you don't, Colonel!' the woman squealed, abruptly jerking her head back, banging it on the oaken underside of the Colonel's expansive desk. 'You're not spouting off in my mouth,' she reproached him.

He grimaced. 'No one wants to swallow my orders any more.'

Colonel K shoved his chair back and got to his feet, helped Miss Anna to hers. He briefly fondled her ripe breasts, popped them out of her embroidered peasant blouse and took a quick pull on each of her cherry-red nipples. Then he cleared a space for her up on his desk, brushing aside the maps and population charts he'd been studying.

He held Miss Anna's hand, and hip, assisting her on to the desk, on to her back. She pulled her ankle-length skirt up to her waist, revealing the dense tangle of matted blonde fur in between her shapely young legs. 'Oh, Colonel K!' she moaned, as the man probed her furry pussy for an opening with the shining tip of his sword.

He found it, plunged through, driving his steel-hard length deep inside Anna's dripping wet sex. They both groaned, sounding sexual union.

Miss Anna hooked her slender ankles onto Colonel K's broad shoulders. He leaned forward and recaptured her breasts in his hands, shunting his cock back and forth in her cunt. The desk creaked, flesh slapped briskly against flesh, Miss Anna cooed, Colonel K puffed; a young man clad in a ragged uniform stumbled inside the office.

'Captain Yannsen!' Colonel K ejaculated.

'Oh, Captain Yannsen!' Miss Anna cried.

The dishevelled officer staggered up to the desk, gasping for breath. His spectacles were knocked cockeyed on his long freckled nose, his cheeks, normally red as his flaming hair, were a ghastly white, drained of all colour. 'I've found the missing men, Colonel ...'

'One moment,' Colonel K stopped him, holding up a hand lifted from a plush, trembling breast. 'One thing at a time.' Many battles, military and bureaucratic, had left the commander unflappable.

He returned his attention to Miss Anna, his hand, fucking her faster now. He banged into the woman with parade ground precision. She darted a hand down to her cock-pistoned cunt and rubbed her hair-trigger clit.

She shrieked, he grunted. She shuddered, he jerked, the pair coming in a heated gush of mingling, squirted juices. As Captain Yannsen straightened his glasses and pulled his tunic together, regaining some level of military composure.

'I'll hear your report now,' the Colonel stated brusquely, pulling his cock out of his secretary and sheathing it back in his pants, buttoning. 'That'll be all, Miss Anna.'

Anna demurely raised her blouse and lowered her skirt, getting up off the desk. She smiled at Captain Yannsen.

'I found almost a hundred military-age men stretched out flat on their backs underground – in the caverns along the west bank of the Josporus River, 20 kilometres south of Woormas,' the Captain reported.

Colonel K gripped the slickened edge of his desk. 'What!? Dead?'

'No. Half-dead. Too weak to flee or fight, all but drained of their spirit. I know. I was one of them for a time!'

Colonel K's iron-grey eyes widened. 'Who's holding these men captive? The enemy?'

Captain Yannsen smiled wanly. 'Of a kind, yes sir. An enemy of life. But not our current military enemy.' The man suddenly swayed, swooned, collapsing down into the chair Miss Anna rushed to his backside.

'Water! Water, Miss Anna!' Colonel K ordered.

He took a great gulp out of the glass his secretary handed him, then passed it on over to Captain Yannsen. 'You're tired,' he observed, some measure of concern in his rugged voice. 'But I must have your report – quickly. So we can act. A hundred men could mean the difference between victory and defeat at the front.'

Captain Yannsen drained the glass of water, gave it back to Miss Anna. Her warm, caressing hand on his shoulder seemed to do him just as much good as the cool liquid. 'My report,' he spoke.

'I was on the road out of Woormas, feeling dissatisfaction at finding not a single service-eligible man in the village. Only worried, frustrated, tight-lipped women. It was midday, warm and sunny. When a woman suddenly emerged from out of the woods alongside the road.

'She was one of the strangest creatures I've ever seen: short, well-fed, with large breasts and sturdy arms and legs, thick wide knees. Her long blonde hair was almost white, large pale eyes almost milky, and her creamy skin seemed just about translucent. She was wearing a simple white dress, see-through, and as she walked up to me on the road, I became hypnotised by her unblinking opaque eyes, mesmerised by the cloying scent she exuded, the utter lush redness and juiciness of her lips and mouth.

'She said nothing. Simply looked me in the eye, then the crotch. I followed her gaze, and was astonished to see that my cock was strikingly erect in my trousers, aroused so quickly I hadn't even realised it. She dropped to her knees in the middle of the road, at my blatantly erect penis, relieved some of the pressure and added much more, by taking it out of my pants and into her mouth.

'The glide of her overfull lips down my shaft was divine; her velvety mouth pure wet heated heaven engulfing my cock; her sliding tongue a silkily sublime instrument of otherworldly pleasure. Or so I thought at the time. Only later, did I come to know that that mouth and those lips and that tongue had more fallen angel than exalted angel about them.

'But, right then, I revelled in the woman's wondrous cocksucking. She consumed my full throbbing length, sucked back up, stroked forward again, blowing me soft and supple and sensuous as the hot, humid summer breeze blows the trembling leaves on their hard wooden branches.'

Colonel K and Miss Anna exchanged glances.

'I'd never experienced a finer fellatio,' Captain Yannsen went on, a strange shining light in his myopic blue eyes. 'I just stood there in the open road, under the burning sun, looking down at the ethereal woman, feeling her eternally erotic suck and lick and tug all through my exposed, wildly pulsing body and soul.

'Then I climaxed, suddenly, overwhelmingly, uncontrollably. Flooding her mouth. And she swallowed! Drank in my heated jack with a willing, voracious appetite, her milky eyes gleaming up at me, throat working with fearsome intensity. That was when I truly realised that this was no ordinary country-kin woman – for they may suck, but nay do they swallow.'

Colonel K raised his eyebrows at Miss Anna. She crossed her arms under her breasts.

'My suspicions, and fears, were confirmed when she led me deep into the woods, down to the Josporus River, then below-ground, into the caverns. That's where I saw the other men – scores of them – lying on the ground, naked. Tending to them, turning them erect at the groin and then sucking and swallowing, were a dozen or so women just like the one who had led me astray.

'It was all so weird, so eerie, down in those dimly-lit caverns. The laid-out men, the women servicing them. Just the sound of rapacious slurping, the weak grunts of climax, the eager gulping and gulping and gulping!'

Captain Yannsen sprang to his feet and grabbed onto the desk. 'They were feeding on their bodily fluids, don't you see! Those men were being sucked of their very lives!'

He dropped back down into the chair, exhausted. 'I was laid out and tended to like the others, hour after hour initially, then more sporadically, as I became more drained. I was held fast at first by the irresistible eroticism of the women, by what they were willingly doing to my over-receptive cock. And then, when it was too late, I was too weak even to get up – except for *it* now and then.'

Captain Yannsen buried his face in his hands, shuddering at the memory.

Colonel K and Miss Anna stared at one another, their own faces drained of colour by the disturbing report.

'Who ... what are they, Colonel?' Miss Anna breathed at last. 'These oral whores?'

Colonel K sat down in his chair and folded his fingers together. 'I don't know,' he admitted. 'We've all heard the legends of vampires roaming the countryside – but vampeters ... I've never heard tell before. Craving protein instead of plasma? The life-blood of young men who should be dutifully serving their country at the ...'

He suddenly sprang to his feet and wheeled around his desk, fastened his capable hands onto Captain Yannsen's slumped shoulders and violently shook the man. '*You* escaped their cocksucking clutches! How did *you* get away!?'

The Captain looked up into his superior's glaring eyes, taking strength from the other man's rough treatment.

'My ... friend Karl rescued me. He's a homosexual, so he wasn't caught in the vampeters' velvet-lined trap. He beat the bushes looking for me when I failed to appear at a scheduled rendezvous with him, found me and dragged me out of there.'

Captain Yannsen glanced nervously from the Colonel's grim face to Miss Anna's even grimmer visage. 'I'm, uh, bisexual, you see.'

'Not if I can help it,' Colonel K muttered. 'But that provides me with a strategy – for getting those men back and up to the front where they belong. A-tten-tion!'

Captain Yannsen and his friend Karl guided the squad to the spot along the riverbank where a narrow path led through the thick brush to the underground caverns. Colonel K was at the head of what he'd dubbed, "the sissy brigade", 25 men selected for their flagrant homosexuality; unfit for regular service, but ready-made for this special duty.

The Colonel, himself, wore a gas mask, the glass of which was deliberately distorted to prevent clear vision. Thus, he was protected from the seductively intoxicating sight and scent of the sucking women.

'I want an orderly evacuation,' he told his men, his voice as distorted as his eyesight by the gas mask. 'First, we'll secure the women. Then the men.'

There were moans of protest at the ordering, but Colonel K and his brigade charged down into the caverns. As Captain Yannsen beat a hasty retreat back through the woods to the road.

On the road, was lined up a column of motorized troop carriers. Under the blackout canvas stretched over the rear of the last truck in line, was a steel cage, capable of holding a dozen or so prisoners. The men manning the vehicles all wore gas masks similar to the Colonel's.

The women rushed at the invaders, as they stormed into the caverns. There were twelve women, all told, a comely

34

dirty dozen alike in milky-white appearance. They fell at the booted feet of the squad, dexterously drew cocks out of trousers, throatily sucked.

But their salacious counter attack was met with stunning indifference. Cocks stayed soft; Colonel K's, locked up for good measure in an iron chastity belt, secure.

The assault was repelled. The women staggered to their feet with creamy expressions of terror. They fought hard against their capture, however, their strength almost equal to that of the slightly feminised men under the Colonel's command. But sheer numbers, and Colonel K's indomitable will, soon turned the battle. He clapped irons onto the wrists of the vampeters, as his soldiers held them tight.

Ninety-eight men were taken barely alive and bodily-fluid-drained out of the caverns. To be rehydrated and rested. Then shipped to the front.

Miss Anna glanced up from the Colonel's erection. 'But what will you do with those – those vampeters?' she spat out, on to Colonel K's cock.

He shuddered, as she resumed sucking. He stroked his riding crop contemplatively. 'They will have to be destroyed,' he said with a sigh. 'Our scientists are working on a special "rod" which ejaculates a toxic chemical when sufficiently heated and wetted and pulled upon. It's a shame they …'

'*They* should be the ones sent to the front,' Miss Anna pouted, teasing a drop of precome out of the Colonel's slit and slurping it up and swallowing it down. 'Not all those handsome young men.'

Colonel K looked down at the woman squatting beneath his desk. Then he bolted even more erect, to his feet. 'A capital idea!' he roared. 'We'll send the vampeters to the front as part of a prisoner exchange with the enemy – two hundred of our captured men for twelve of *their* captured women. They'll wreak havoc in the enemy trenches!'

He stood tall, both vertical and horizontal. Miss Anna gripped his shining cock with delight. 'The war will be over by Christmas,' Colonel K pronounced.

Circle in the Sand
by Elizabeth Coldwell

The beach was completely deserted as Aidan and I strolled along it, only the odd gull wheeling overhead to break the illusion there was nothing left in the world but us. Waves rolled gently on to the shore and the sky was a rich, clear blue, unbroken by clouds. It was possibly the most romantic setting I'd ever found myself in, yet all I could feel was a simmering resentment which had started the moment we boarded the cruise ship.

When Aidan had told me he'd booked us on a summer cruise, I was delighted. We'd always had very different ideas of what made the perfect holiday. I was never happier than when I was lying on a beach in the skimpiest of bikinis, nose buried in a trashy paperback novel and a jug of sangría close at hand. Aidan, on the other hand, preferred city breaks, mixing a dash of culture and the cool interior of a bar or two. With his red-gold hair and pale, Celtic complexion, the sun was never going to be my husband's friend.

Somehow, despite being diametrically opposed in our tastes, we managed to reach a compromise. We would take it in turns to choose a destination. At first, it had worked pretty well. Two years ago, Aidan had taken us to Amsterdam for a week. He'd loved the museums and the brown cafés, and I had taken advantage of our apartment's tiny sun trap of a balcony to work on my tan. The following summer, I'd rented us a villa in Cyprus, giving Aidan the chance to explore the island's ruins while I luxuriated by the side of our pool.

So, this year, Aidan didn't even need to show me the brochure before he booked our trip. I was sure he would instinctively know what would please both of us, and pictured us cruising the Mediterranean in style. There'd be a stop-off at somewhere historic, like Pompeii, which he would enjoy, and the rest of the time I could lie on the sun deck, sipping a refreshing cocktail or two.

Except Aidan had other plans. 'A cruise of the Scottish islands?' I asked in disbelief when the tickets arrived. 'Are you kidding me?'

'You'll love it, Amy. The Hebrides are really beautiful. We'll be able to take long walks on the beaches, and the food on board ship is supposed to be exquisite. We might even get the chance to dine at the Captain's table.'

I bit back a reply, barely able to hide my disappointment. Instead of bikinis, I knew I'd be packing sweaters and hiking boots. Not exactly my idea of a dream holiday.

As the date of our departure drew near, I did my best to convince myself it wouldn't be as bad as I thought. Maybe my horizons were too narrow. There was every chance I could be seduced by the combination of stunning scenery and fine cuisine Aidan described.

That's what I continued to think until the moment we stepped off the train at Oban station, after a three-hour journey from Glasgow, to see rain beating down from a heavy grey sky. There was no sign of a taxi, and even though it was only a relatively short walk to the pier where the *Hebridean Queen* departed, by the time we reached the ship we were soaked through and on the verge of a volcanic argument.

It was hardly the ideal start to our holiday, and even though our cabin was beautifully cosy and the food just as good as had been promised, with a generous glass of 12-

year-old malt as a most welcome nightcap, I was still too mad at Aidan to really appreciate it.

The weather barely improved over the next couple of days. Nor did my mood. I hardly said a civil word to my husband and spurned the chance to take the organised walking tours, preferring instead to skulk in our cabin with a magazine and my MP3 player.

In the past, a holiday had been our opportunity to enjoy long, sensuous sex sessions, rather than the frantic fucks which were all we usually managed to find time for, given our busy routines. Now, however, when Aidan reached for me in the middle of the night, his hand seeking to mould to the curve of my breast, I moved away, or pretended I was so deeply asleep he couldn't rouse me.

We would have carried on festering like this for the whole week, doing who knows how much harm to our marriage, if we hadn't woken on the fourth morning to see that the clouds had lifted.

'Sun's shining,' Aidan commented brightly, before going to take his morning shower. I caught a glimpse of his taut arse cheeks as he padded across the cabin barefoot, clutching a towel in front of him. If I hadn't been sulking, I might have been tempted to join him in the shower cubicle. I'd been so snowed under with work in the last few weeks that I couldn't remember the last time Aidan and I had enjoyed a really good fuck. We could change all that right now. There was just enough room in the shower for two, and I knew he wouldn't object when I sank to my knees and grabbed fistfuls of those glorious cheeks while I sucked lovingly on his cock...

I snapped out of the fantasy quickly, before I could seriously think about putting it into action. Now the weather had improved, I no longer had an excuse to avoid going ashore. Once Aidan had finished in the shower I quickly took my turn, before dressing in jeans and a thick top. I supposed I had to at least show willing, even if there were a hundred things I would rather be doing than tramping through the dunes on some barely habited island.

The *Hebridean Queen* docked in the harbour on Berneray just after breakfast. We were given the choice of taking a guided tour, which would include a stop-off at the island's tea shop and a dedicated seal viewing spot, or exploring on our own.

'Let's not do the tour,' Aidan suggested, hefting his back pack over his shoulder. 'The beaches on the other side of the islands are supposed to be the ones that are really worth seeing.'

I didn't argue with him, even though I quite liked the idea of watching seals basking on the rocks. Much to my surprise, now I was on solid ground for the first time in days, the urge to go exploring was hard to resist.

We must have walked for a couple of miles and seen no one apart from a farmer who waved to us from his tractor as we passed and the odd placidly grazing sheep. At last we saw the sea, and within minutes we had rounded the dunes and reached the most breathtaking stretch of unspoilt white sand.

'This is amazing,' Aidan said, speaking in hushed tones as though not wishing to disturb the peacefulness of the surroundings. 'Really worth coming all this way.'

I muttered something non-committal in reply, then my eye was drawn to something that appeared to be buried in the sand. It glittered where the sunlight hit it. When I examined it more closely, I realised it was a bottle, and it looked like it had something inside it.

Fumbling with the cork that had been firmly wedged in the neck to keep the contents safe and dry, I finally wrenched it open. I tilted the bottle and a rolled-up piece of paper slithered out into my palm.

'Wow!' Aidan was right behind me, the point of his chin resting on my shoulder. 'A genuine message in a bottle. What does it say?'

'I don't know.' I felt strangely shy about opening it up, in case the contents turned out to be a love letter or something equally private.

'Whoever put that thing in there meant it to be read,' Aidan pointed out. 'Perhaps it's a cry for help from a shipwrecked sailor.'

'Who could have been dead for hundreds of years.' Even though the bottle had piqued my curiosity, I still couldn't resist sniping at Aidan. 'I mean, how often does someone come walking along here? But if it keeps you happy...'

I carefully unrolled the paper. If it was as old as Aidan suggested, there was a chance it might crumble away if I handled it too roughly. Whatever I'd been expecting, it wasn't the screed of tiny, copperplate writing that was headed, 'To bring back what you are in danger of losing.'

'So, what is it?' Aidan reached for the scrap of paper, but I held on to it.

'It seems to be some kind of spell,' I said incredulously. 'There are instructions telling whoever finds this to draw a circle in the earth, then stand in the middle of it and recite the words that follow.'

'Well, we don't have earth, but we do have plenty of sand...' Aidan reached for a piece of driftwood that was lying close by his feet and rapidly sketched a circle about a metre in diameter.

'You're taking this seriously?' I could hardly believe what I was seeing. Aidan was the most rational, sceptical man I knew. He'd once mocked the suggestion I made on a day trip to Brighton, early in our relationship, that we should visit a gypsy fortune teller to find out whether we had a future together. Now he was preparing to perform what appeared to be a centuries-old spell.

'Come on, Amy. You saw what it said about bringing back what you're in danger of losing. You can't tell me that doesn't apply to us, not after the last couple of days.'

I was genuinely surprised by his reaction. I'd been

deliberately cold to him, but I fully intended to thaw out again ... When? I asked myself. Back home, with all the stress of work deadlines and commuting and keeping on top of my finances? Suddenly, I realised how easy it would be to let everything slide, to gradually find myself too tired for sex, too busy to show Aidan how much he really meant to me. Here I was, too concerned with scoring points and wallowing in self-pity to notice I was neglecting what was really important in my life.

'OK.' I stepped into the circle, still feeling a little foolish, and together Aidan and I spoke the words on the paper.

'I ask the gift of second sight

To see the past, to set things right

And grant to me a future bright.'

I looked round. Nothing seemed any different. 'I don't think it's working.'

'Let's try it again.' Aidan took hold of my hands. 'Close your eyes and really wish hard, like when you were a kid and you blew the candles out on your birthday cake.'

So I did. We recited the spell again, then once more for luck, and that's when it happened. I seemed to feel the blood fizzing in my veins, and a surge of heat where my fingers were linked with Aidan's. I opened my eyes to see that the air between us appeared to be shimmering. I blinked hard, but the illusion didn't vanish. If anything, it appeared to grow brighter, as though I was looking at a TV screen.

Just as with a TV that's being tuned in to a channel, the picture moved from white snow and fuzz to something more solid. Two figures seated at a restaurant table. I recognised them instantly, and their surroundings. Aidan and me, on our third or fourth date, in a little Italian place close to where I worked. There was no sound, but whatever Aidan had just said had caused me to laugh and blush a little. He reached for my hand, caressing my palm with his thumbs in slow circles. I remembered exactly how that had felt at the time. I'd started to get wet at his touch, knowing I was being

42

deliberately seduced by him and not caring in the least. This was the night we'd fucked for the first time, finally giving in to the sexual attraction that had been raging between us since the moment I'd been introduced to him by one of my colleagues at a press launch.

The vision changed. Now we were on the way back to my place, walking through the park close to my home. Aidan pushed me up against a tree so we could kiss, tasting each other properly for the first time as my fingers tangled in his silky hair and his hand gently kneaded one of my breasts through my top. From what felt like a strangely long way away, even though he was still holding hands with me, I heard Aidan give a soft groan, caught somewhere between nostalgia and lust. We'd done more than kiss against that tree; he'd eased up my skirt and rubbed me through my panties till I came, not caring that we might be seen by anyone passing. I'd bitten his shoulder to stifle my cries, loving his wicked streak and his ability to make me come without ever making contact with my bare skin.

Now the vision was showing us the messy flat Aidan had lived in before we'd married and moved in together. We were lying on his bed in the middle of the afternoon. If I recalled rightly, we'd both phoned in to work that day claiming to be sick, simply so we could spend the whole day fucking. I was wearing nothing but a black lace bra – something Aidan had always found more sexy than if I was entirely naked and something, I now realised, I needed to put back into my repertoire of sex moves. I was crouching over him, grasping his cock and slowly licking along it from base to tip. As I did, I was gazing into his eyes in my best porn star fashion. We were having the kind of dirty, horny fun that seemed to have completely disappeared from our lives in recent months. How, I wondered, did we let that happen?

Just as I was beginning to really enjoy the sight of Aidan's cock disappearing into my mouth, the scene changed yet again. Now we were looking at our honeymoon suite. I was in Aidan's arms as he carried me to the bed, the white lace of my skirts frothing around the two of us. He set me down carefully, wrapping an arm around me as we lay together on the satin quilt. We'd been so tired when we'd reached the room we hadn't done anything more than fall asleep in each other's arms, but we had felt so incredibly close that night, so full of love for each other.

'We could lose so much if we're not careful,' I murmured. I'll never know whether it was my words that broke the spell or whether we'd been shown all we needed to see, but the vision suddenly dissolved.

'So what do we do?' Aidan asked.

'Well, first I apologise for doing my best to ruin this holiday, then ...' I raised myself up on tiptoes so I could kiss my husband, fingers laced together round the back of his neck. He pulled me hard on to him so I could feel the bulge in his crotch. Clearly he'd got just as turned on watching those hot, romantic snippets from our shared past as I had.

A little awkwardly, as both of us were reluctant to break a kiss that was becoming increasingly passionate, he lowered me to the sand. Our bodies pressed together; we could feel each other's excitement even through all the cumbersome layers of clothing.

I fumbled with Aidan's sweater, pushing it over his head, anxious to see him at least partially naked. Between us, we stripped each other of everything but Aidan's T-shirt and my bra. When he reached to undo that, I shook my head, thinking back to what I'd just watched. Instead, I encouraged him to pull my breasts out of the cups so he could lick my nipples into tight peaks.

As we writhed and grappled, we were erasing the marks Aidan had made in the sand, but that didn't seem to matter. The magic wasn't just in the circle; it was in us, all around us. As I lay back and spread my legs, ready to be taken, I was acutely aware of the fine sand beneath my back and arse, the breeze that ruffled Aidan's hair, the soft hiss and drag of the waves. I had never felt so at one with nature, so in tune with my husband's rising desire.

He shimmied down my body to plant his head between my legs. His hot mouth latched on to my pussy, sucking on my long, frilled lips for a while before turning his attention to my clit. When we'd first been together, he'd loved to lick me like this for as long as I could bear it, but as time had passed it had become something else that had been largely bypassed in the race to the finish line. We'd have to stop making that mistake, I thought, arching my back in pleasure as he hit a particularly sensitive spot.

'How long have we got before we have to get back to the boat?' I asked.

Aidan broke off from what he was doing. 'Who cares? They can sail away without us, as far as I'm concerned.'

We changed positions, me climbing on top of him so I could straddle his hips. His cock reared up at me and I guided it into my cunt, the breath catching in my throat as he filled me. I paused for a moment, relishing the hot, solid feel of him inside me, then started to rock.

'Oh, that's good,' Aidan sighed. 'Just like the first time...'

He was right. Somehow it did seem as though we were getting to know each other all over again. I was listening more intently than I had in a long time, tuning into his sighs and gasps, those little clues telling me I was stimulating all the right places. As I rode Aidan lazily I stroked my own clit, not just for the pleasure it was giving me but to see how much it turned him on.

I could have carried on making this slow, stately progress towards orgasm, but Aidan decided he needed more power, more friction. He grabbed me by the hips and started thrusting up hard, taking me with him as he raced towards the summit of his orgasm. Eyes closed, toes curling against the sand, I felt the tension build to the point where I almost couldn't stand it any more. Then something seemed to shatter, sending countless shards of sensation rushing through my body. Together, Aidan and I screamed our ecstasy to the deserted landscape, knowing no one could hear just how much noise we made as we reaffirmed the love and passion we felt for each other.

It was quite a while before either of us had the strength to reach for our scattered clothes. Despite Aidan's comment about letting the boat leave without us, I knew we'd have to make a move soon, or risk the wrath of the captain for returning late and delaying everyone. I didn't want to ruin our chances of being invited to dine at his table, after all.

Having finally struggled back into my jeans and boots, I watched as Aidan retrieved the scrap of paper containing the spell. He rolled it up and stuffed it back into the bottle once more. 'What are you going to do with that?' I asked, as he hammered the cork firmly into place with the heel of his hand.

'Throw it into the sea, let fate take it to whoever might be in need of it, just as it brought the bottle to us.'

He heaved it into the waves, and we watched it bob for a moment before the current carried it away. Who knew where it would be washed up, and how long it would be before someone else found it. And when they did, would they trust in the magic the way we had? Looking at Aidan's handsome face and feeling a fresh surge of desire for him, I really hoped they would.

'Come on,' he said, taking my hand in his. 'We've got a boat to catch.'

Making Lewis Hard
by Esmeralda Greene

This was the third morning in a row. A faint streak of *something* was on my skin. It was dry now, but clearly had been wet to start with. It was whitish, flaky, and washed away easily.

The first morning it had been on my belly. I figured I'd spilled something on myself before going to bed, and didn't puzzle over it too much. The next morning there was some on my forearm as well as my stomach, and it looked like some had pooled in my navel. What the heck? I wondered. A few possibilities occurred to me: I could have drooled some toothpaste froth, or maybe a squirt of liquid hand soap had flown out of the dispenser at an odd angle. That night I remembered the little mystery as I was getting ready for bed, and gave my torso a careful looking-over before lying down. Nothing.

This morning it was streaked across and between my breasts. 'There's just no way I went to bed with that amount of goop on my boobs,' I mused. I gathered up some of the dusty flakes on a fingertip and, hesitating a moment, touched them to my tongue. Mostly tasteless, but ... maybe, just a little bit, it tasted like ...

I spat into the sink. It tasted like come. 'This is fucked up,' I said aloud. Not that I talk to myself; I was speaking to my cat Chicklet. Chicklet had no response, preferring to stare contemplatively at the empty bathroom doorway.

That night, instead of sleeping naked as usual, I put on a T-shirt and sweatpants. Then I took the sweatpants off, put panties on, and put the sweats back on over them. I tucked the T-shirt into the waist of the sweatpants. I checked that the front and back doors were locked, and locked the windows too, although my condo is on the third floor with no fire escapes. I wedged chairs under the doorknobs of the front and back door. I took a third chair into the bedroom with me and closed the door, wedging the chair under that doorknob. I opened the closet and poked at the blouses and skirts, kicked at the shoes. I left the closet door open. Then I unwedged the chair, opened the bedroom door and went to fetch Chicklet. While I was doing this I checked the locks on the front and back door again.

With Chicklet and me sealed in, I got into bed, leaving the overhead light on. I sat up with my back to the headboard and opened a book, not really intending to go to sleep.

Ned, my boyfriend of two relationships ago, was brushing his cock against my face. Lightly, gently, he moved it to my lips. I opened my mouth for him, but he pulled away, teasing. He started jerking it, inches away. I could hear the sound of his hand, his heavy, irregular breathing. I smiled, watching as his hand froze in place, waiting that exquisite interval between when his orgasm starts and the come appears. And then there it was, flying out of his cock, a thick, healthy, ballistic spurt of it, landing, wet and warm on my cheek, followed by another, against my nose, and another, on my lips, and another ...

My eyes snapped open.

It's an interesting experience, looking back on it, to scream. To truly scream, not with any deliberation or thought or control, but to scream because my body, some primeval part of my brainstem, decided I *must* scream. Now. Loudly.

In addition to screaming, I scrambled out of bed. Like the

scream, this was a completely visceral action, and completely uncoordinated. I was trying to keep my face toward the whatever-it-was as I put distance between me and it, but my feet were tangled in the sheets and I fell. My bottom hit the floor and the back of my head hit the bedroom wall at the same instant, and everything came to a halt. Screaming and scrambling clicked off like a switch, as a fuzzy, sparkling darkness swam in front of my eyes. I'm dead, I thought. I'm lying here stunned and I can't move and he's going to kill me. I was sure there was a "he" involved, though I couldn't see him. I couldn't see much of anything except fuzzy sparkling darkness.

'Oh dear!' a voice said. 'Oh dear! Oh good heavens! Are you all right?' The voice was deep, a little throaty; very masculine despite the effeminate phrases.

I tried to focus my eyes. Then I tried again, closing them tight and opening them. On the third try it seemed to work pretty well; the bedroom settled into focus. The bed, the walls, the bright overhead light all became reasonably sharp and stopped moving around. That's better, I thought.

Only it wasn't really better, because the bedroom was empty. The door was closed, the chair jammed under the doorknob, the window – I turned my head to look – closed and unbroken. Chicklet looked at me from the bed and made a puzzled 'Mm-rarr?' I reached up to the back of my head. It hurt, but wasn't bleeding. I rubbed a hand over my face, and it came away wet with a thick, gooey substance that made strings between my fingers.

I started swearing. I started with 'What the fucking ...' and went on from there. Still swearing, I scrunched my body down so I could look under the bed – nothing. Still swearing and holding my come-sticky hand away from my body, I struggled to my feet. With my back to the wall and the closet door open, there wasn't a square inch of the bedroom I couldn't see. I looked at the come dripping from my hand again and went on swearing, though I'd long ago run out of

49

unique words and was having to repeat myself.

'Madam, *please!*' a voice said. The same voice.

I stopped cussing, but left my mouth open.

I stood there for a while. The remaining come on my face started to itch and tickle, but I didn't wipe it away. I didn't want to acknowledge that it was there. I didn't want to move at all. Eventually a glob of it dripped off my chin and landed on my T-shirt. Keeping my head still, I strained my eyes downward to look at the wet stain over my left tit.

Then Chicklet got bored with me. He hopped down off the bed and walked over to the far side of it. There he raised his tail and made a happy little purring sound, rubbing his head against... against ... against ... I squinted, trying again to focus my eyes. When that didn't work I tried un-focusing them, the way you do to look at one of those annoying hidden 3-D images. There! There it was! A leg. Chicklet was happily rubbing his head and neck against the faint, transparent shell of a man's leg.

'You're a fucking ghost!' I said to the leg. I tried to make it sound like an accusation; like something more exasperating than frightening.

'Well, yes, actually, I am,' the voice said apologetically. 'Evidently.'

'OK.' I took a deep breath and let it out. 'I can deal with that. I've seen ghosts before, when I was little, in my Gram's house. I can deal with a ghost.' I hoped I sounded more sure of that than I felt.

Working to keep my eyes in the same not-focused state, I started scanning up the leg. The foot and calf were bare. Upward, a bare knee. Then a bare thigh, heavy and firmly muscled. Up a little further, and ... Um, wow. It wasn't fully hard, but drooping down in a long graceful curve. Reluctantly I continued scanning upward. Flat stomach, hard, tight chest. His face came into wavering view: Wide jaw, a long bent nose, high cheekbones. An old-fashioned haircut, and deep set eyes that were frowning with concern.

50

'Are you sure you're all right?' he said. Then before I could answer, 'Wait, you can see me? Oh, my.' He dropped his hands to his crotch. He had big hands, but they weren't big enough. 'This is quite remarkable. No one has ever been able to see me before.'

My nose itched at that point, reminding me of something. 'Hey, goddamnit! What the fuck is the fucking idea of jerking off onto me the past four nights?' I pulled the front of my T-shirt up and used it to scrub off my face. 'You think that just because you're a ghost you can be a fucking pervert too?'

His face looked pained. 'Madam, really. Such language! And from a fine, sophisticated young lady such as yourself!'

'Oh, can that Victorian crap, mister. What's your name, anyway?'

'Lewis, ma'am. Lewis Williams at your service. I happen to know your name is Juliet Regan. May I call you Juliet?'

'You fucking damn well may not. Now talk. What's with shooting your come on to me the past four nights? Is that your goddamn pervert way of haunting this place?'

'Ah, well,' he said. It was getting easier to see him. I could look away for a few seconds at a time now without having to cross my eyes to get his image back. He sat on the side of the bed with his legs angled away from me, hiding his formidable cock. Chicklet hopped onto the bed and curled up next to his hip. 'This is most embarrassing, Miss Regan, and I do humbly beg your forgiveness.' He looked down at Chicklet and petted him. His hand passed through the fur without disturbing a hair of it, but still the cat purred contentedly. 'You see, it never occurred to me that you would ever know – that you would ever be able to see me.'

'How could I not know?' I shouted. 'You squirted half a cup of jism in my face!'

He winced at the word "jism", but thankfully didn't reproach me for my language again. 'Yes, but ... you see, I'm a ghost, as you pointed out.' He waved an arm behind

51

him, and it disappeared into the wall. 'I'm quite insubstantial. So it's most remarkable and unexpected that you could sense my, uh ...'

'Jism? Come? Spunk? Spooge? Nut juice?'

A series of little winces. 'Yes.'

I looked down at the wet stains on my T-shirt, noting with some annoyance that my nipples were rigid and sticking out. 'Yeah, that is weird. If you're a ghost, how come your come is ... you know, real?'

'Yes, exactly,' he said. 'And this is a recent development, you see. I didn't realise until just this night that I'd started ... uh, leaving evidence behind. It's quite remarkable, Miss Regan.'

'"*Started* leaving evidence"?' I mulled over his words. 'So you're telling me that you've been jerking off onto me for longer than the past four days?'

'Ah ... well ... yes.'

I gritted my teeth. 'Just. How. Long.'

'W ... well, since you moved in here. Four months now, isn't it?'

'Every night?'

'Y ... yes. Miss Regan, you must try to appreciate how few opportunities there are for a person in my ... situation to get any sort of sexual gratification. The last person to occupy this space was an extremely elderly woman. Before her there was a man – an *invert* – most distasteful. And then ...' He held his hands up, the palms inward as if he was holding something delicate and precious. 'Then you appeared! So wonderfully beautiful! Such an exquisite vision of young womanhood! Such a strong, healthy figure! So graceful, so poised, so ...'

'Awright, awright, get on with it.'

'Yes, well ... And then there were your activities at night ... walking around nude after you bathed, sleeping naked, and your, uh ... unbridled, joyful, enthusiastic fondness for ... um ... shall I say, pleasuring yourself?'

'Fucking pervert,' I said, but I didn't say it with much conviction. The anger was draining out of me. I couldn't deny that Lewis had a point. We all need to get our jollies somewhere.

I looked at the clock. 'Listen, Lewis. I have to start getting ready for work in two hours, but I don't think I'm going to get any more sleep tonight. Can we go into the kitchen and have some coffee?'

We went into the kitchen. Lewis pulled a chair out from the table to sit down, but the chair didn't move. Instead a phantom, translucent duplicate of the chair pulled away from its real-world copy, and that's what he sat on. I poured him some coffee, and the same thing happened when he picked up the cup. He sipped phantom coffee and said, 'Ah, lovely.'

He told me that my condo building had been a bordello in the nineteenth century, and that he'd "suffered a fatal apoplexy while enjoying the company of one of the young ladies". I tried to get him to tell me what it was like being a ghost, but he claimed there wasn't much to tell. Instead he talked about his life, about the old Philadelphia streets he remembered, people he'd known. Somehow I found myself telling him about my job, about my previous cat who'd died last winter, about my father's alcoholism and the art teacher who told me I should become a painter. It seemed no time at all before dawn was lightening the windows and birds were beginning to sing. I showered (Lewis swore to me that he never set a ghostly foot inside my bathroom) and got dressed for work.

'You'll be here when I get back?' I reached out to touch my fingers to the back of his hand, but of course there was nothing touchable there. He smiled and nodded. That's a really stupid question to ask a ghost, I realised.

I got through the day's work in a hazy stupor. I was desperately eager to get home, and then terrified to go in the door. What if he wasn't there? Would that mean the whole thing was a hallucination? That four months of sexual deprivation had made me literally, certifiably, committably, crazy? What if he *was* there? Would that be better or worse?

I went in the door and closed it behind me. 'Lewis?'

'In here,' he called from the kitchen.

For some reason my heart did a little somersault in my chest. I ran the few steps down the hall to the kitchen, then jerked myself to a stop in the doorway. 'Lewis,' I said again.

He was sitting at the kitchen table, where I'd left him that morning. He was still naked; during our talk last night he'd told me that he'd died naked and been that way ever since. He stood up and took long, eager strides toward me, stopping when his face was inches from mine. 'Juliet,' he said.

'J … Julie. P … People call me Julie.' My lips seemed to be trembling. Maybe talking to a ghost does that to me.

'Juliet.' He lifted his hand, holding it so the palm was hovering over my cheek, almost touching me. Without thinking I leaned my face into his hand, closing my eyes.

And thumped my skull against the doorframe. Ow. His hand was still there, apparently embedded in the middle of my face. He snatched it away.

I chuckled, embarrassed. 'You look so real. More visible than you were last night.' I reached a hand to his chest and it passed through him with no sensation at all. Just air.

He looked down at the floor. 'I'm sorry.'

I started to ask what he was sorry about, but didn't. I sat at the table and we shared cheese and crackers with wine. He watched me eat, his eyes never leaving me. I bent down to give a piece of cheese to Chicklet and saw something that made me linger. 'Jesus, Lewis, I didn't know they made 'em that big back in your day.'

He blushed. I didn't know ghosts could blush, but they can.

We talked some more. This time we got on to the

catastrophe of my senior prom and the 10K race I finished on a broken ankle.

'It's getting towards my bedtime,' I said.

'Yes, Juliet. You needn't worry; I'll stay out here. Perhaps Chicklet will keep me company.'

I paused, not sure why. 'OK,' I said, and went to my bedroom, closing the door. I got undressed and into bed and turned out the light. And turned the light back on again and got out of bed and went out of the bedroom and into the kitchen. I watched Lewis' eyes on me as I walked up to him. I stood in front of him for a while, and then made a little nod of my head in the direction of the bedroom. 'C'mon,' I said.

It was nice. Watching him watch me was nice; laying naked on my back for him was nice; touching myself was nice; the sight of him stroking himself over me was nice. We moved things along at a steady clip, and soon I was making funny noises and arching my back, working on my pussy with both hands. Lewis was breathing raggedly, his hand a back-and-forth blur on his cock. We worked together, our eyes glued to each other's bodies, climbing to that sweet precarious height that was our destination.

'Oh Juliet,' he gasped. 'May I ... I'm about to ... Would it be all right if I ...'

'Yes, Lewis. Yes. Right here.' I grabbed a nipple and pulled hard on it. 'On my tits. On my tits. On my tits.'

His come splashed across me, wet and heavy and warm. Warm almost to hot, body temperature, the temperature of life. I spread it over my skin, smearing some on my cunt lips and my clit. Then I came, doubling up on myself and shouting, knowing he was watching me, feeling his gaze on me like a covering blanket.

I dozed, and woke sometime after 2.00 a.m. Lewis was sitting beside the bed on a phantom copy of one of my kitchen chairs, a phantom book in his hand. He put the book down when he saw I was awake and we chatted for a while. Before long his cock began to straighten out and rise up from his lap. I started to ask him if he was this virile while he was alive, but decided not to. Instead I began masturbating again.

'On my face this time, Lewis,' I said when it seemed the right time to say such a thing. He moved close to my face, aiming his cock as he stroked it. It seemed completely opaque now. I could still see the walls and furniture through the rest of him, but the cock that loomed in front of my face looked solid. On an impulse, I opened my mouth, lifted my head upward and closed my lips.

Onto hardness. Onto the living, throbbing hardness of an erect cock. Lewis gasped, inhaling desperately, raggedly. Instantly he began spurting into my mouth. I whimpered with surprise and delight around his cock. I reached up and grabbed at his buttocks, but my hands closed around nothingness. Yet the part of him that was in my mouth was hard and substantial and very, very real.

I didn't want to release him from my mouth. We stayed like that for a while; he crouching over me, me on my back with my head raised, his cock in my mouth. I was looking up into his eyes; he looked down into mine.

Soon I felt him softening in my mouth. Not softening into flaccidity, but into insubstantiality. The in-between phase was something like cotton candy, and that was creepy, so I let go of him. Some of his come dribbled out of my mouth; the rest I swallowed.

'That was ... most ... remarkable,' he said.

'How long until you can get hard again?' I said.

Not very long later, we fucked. It was, to put it mildly, quite odd having sex with a man whose only corporeal part was his penis. I got on my hands and knees and he did me from behind. From time to time he'd push too deep and I'd yelp a bit, but pretty soon he got the knack of me. He pumped me with controlled strength, with graceful passion. Gradually, imperceptibly at first, something about the sensation changed. A realization crept into my

56

consciousness and I reached down between my thighs to confirm. 'Lewis, your balls,' I said between the gasps he was squeezing out of me.

'Oh, Juliet,' was all he said.

'Lewis, your balls are hard – I mean real – I mean – I can feel them.'

'Oh, Juliet, my Juliet!'

He was increasing his pace, his breath and his thrusts coming faster. I fondled his balls, rolling them between my fingers, bouncing them, tugging gently on them. He came extravagantly, making sounds somewhere between a grunt and a roar. He collapsed to the bed, and I lay down on my back, playing lazily with the fluid dribbling out of me. If I didn't have my IUD, I wondered, would I get pregnant? And with what – a half ghost, or a baby whose father lived over a hundred years ago? Lewis lay beside me with his eyes closed, his sculpted body shiny with incorporeal sweat, a beatific smile on his lips. I dozed again.

I awoke to a tingling, aching excitement radiating from my nipples. Lewis was on his knees beside me on the bed, running the hard, tight head of his cock over my right nipple, flicking at it, bumping it, pressing it into the softer flesh of my breast.

'I have spent three times tonight, my sweet,' he said, 'and you only once. We must try to correct this imbalance.'

I spread my legs for him and he knelt between my thighs. He slid his cock in, crouching over me and supporting himself on straightened arms. I kept forgetting and trying to touch him; to run a hand over his chest or wrap my legs around his hips. Once I tried to pull his face to mine for a kiss and ended up kissing the palm of my own hand. I laughed at my fumblings, but Lewis suddenly looked very sad. He sat back, leaving half his cock buried in me, but no longer fucking. He reached a hand toward my face, then pulled it away. 'This isn't right,' he said. 'This is no way for a man to make love to a woman – to be unable to touch you,

57

unable to caress your face, to kiss your beautiful mouth, to rest my cheek on your sweet breast. I can't do any of the things a man should do to show tenderness toward the woman he ...'

His voice trailed off, leaving me trembling for that final word. 'Oh Lewis ... please don't worry. It feels good for me, really,' I said.

He dropped his face and wouldn't meet my eyes.

'Lewis, you *are* making love to me. Your words make love to me. You've been making love to me all the time we've been together.'

Still he wouldn't speak or move. This sulking was starting to annoy me.

'Yes Lewis, you're right, those things would be nice. I'd love to kiss you and touch you and have you touch me, but one thing you *can* do is fuck me with your cock, and that's what I need right now. You understand? I need you to start fucking that big cock into my cunt.' I scooched downward, trying to get more of him inside me.

Lewis made an exasperated sound and turned away. 'Really, Juliet, I've asked you before to *please* mind your langu ...'

'Would you please fucking *fuck* me?!' I bellowed. Lifting up, I grabbed one of his buttocks in each hand and pulled him to me, digging my nails into his skin.

At the touch of my hands to his arse, he gasped and jerked forward, driving his full length into my distended cunt. It was a few moments before I could inhale to speak again.

'Lewis! Your arse! Your bottom! It's hard!' Keeping my hands where they were, I lifted my legs and wrapped them around his now-solid hips, hooking my ankles together. 'Look! I couldn't do this just a minute ago. Lewis, it's spreading! You're getting hard, all over!'

Lewis didn't answer, and I didn't want him to. He just started plowing me like a madman, slapping his belly against mine, driving me down into the mattress, then lifting up to catch me on the rebound with another pile driver plunge. I slowly moved my hands upward from his arse. At the small of his back he transitioned to that cotton candy texture and my fingers started to sink into him. I went back down to his hard, very hard butt, feeling the muscles flex and tighten under my clutching hands.

I have no idea how many times we had various permutations of sex that night. I do know that by the time I passed out, Lewis was firm, solid, living flesh from his knees to his chest and from his elbows down to his fingertips. His hands were the last part of him to make the transition that night. It was what he did with those hands that toppled me over the edge into unconsciousness and near-comatose sleep for six hours.

When I woke up Lewis was lying beside me, asleep and semi-transparent. My hand passed through the whole misty length of him. This was a disappointment, but not unexpected. Leaving him to sleep, I staggered into the kitchen to get something to eat.

When I climbed back into bed, Lewis looked like a man who was having a nice dream. I reached out a tentative finger, and sure enough, it bumped against something hard. Something that twitched and grew in response to my touch. By the time Lewis' eyes flickered open I had his cock in my mouth and his body was hard up to his belly button. 'You see,' I said when I'd emptied my mouth for a moment. 'It's faster this time. Each time we …' I paused to think of a term that wouldn't upset him. '… we do it, the effect is quicker and spreads faster.'

I called in sick to work that day and the next day was Saturday. By late Sunday night my body was sore and aching, but also tingling with the electric echoes of countless orgasms. I was plastered and sticky with preternatural quantities of come, his and mine. I lay in bed, on my back, all but immobile with throbbing fatigue and throbbing bliss.

59

Lewis' face appeared over mine, hovering close, closer, closer still. His lips pressed against mine.

'A small reward to give you for all your efforts, my love,' he said.

I touched my fingers to my own lips. How ghostly a thing a kiss is, I thought; you can't touch it or hold it, and yet when you find a real one, it is very, very real.

Demon
by Kathryn O'Halloran

He looks me over then does a double take, checking the name on the door. Yep, he's in the right office and yep, everyone does it. But *Clem Starr – International Demon Fighter*, that's me. That's what it says on the door and that's what it says on my driver's licence. Well it doesn't say International Demon Fighter on my licence but it definitely says Clem Starr. Well, OK, technically it says Clementine, but ick. What a damn stupid name.

I get the looks of confusion all the time. Mostly because I look like a 16-year-old but, trust me, you can add 10 years to that. It's my upturned nose and freckles and my fire-engine-red hair, but I'm damn wiry. I could kick your arse, you'd better believe it. Muscles and quick reflexes, that's what you need in this line of work.

I dunno what they're expecting – something like those guys from Ghostbusters maybe or some spooky-looking mystic chick. I sure as hell don't do that whole velvet and lace Stevie Nicks shit. You can't kick a demon's arse wearing a flowing skirt.

So anyway, this geezer takes a seat in my office and, before he says a word, I've figured it out. I've had a few of these cases before. Not to mention I'm the greatest expert on demons in … well, the world. I don't think that's too strong a take on it.

He slumps in the chair, grey and droopy with a face like

61

one of those St Bernard dogs. I'm tempted to cut to the chase and tell him, 'yeah, buddy, it's a cuckold demon ...' but if I've learnt one thing in this biz, it's to hold your tongue and let them tell their story. It's my smart mouth that's sent more clients running off to the second best demon fighter around, Harry McConchie. Second to me, of course. If there's one person I hate, it's Harry McConchie.

So I sit and pick my nails with the letter opener and let him talk. A textbook case and the textbook says:

The cuckold demon is summoned by the power of sexual frustration ... blah   blah   blah ... form   of incubus ... blah ... gains strength from the female orgasm ...

I know the whole textbook definition off by heart. I should. I wrote it. Also, sex demons are my specialty. See, you need more than fighting smarts and a knowledge of demonology and state of the art weaponry. To fight a sex demon you need a great set of hooters and that's something Harry McConchie will never have.

I grab my notebook and pretend to take notes. The punters like it when you do that. It looks like you're thorough but I'm drawing spiral and curls 'cause I only need to know two things about this case:

        1.His address.

        2.Can he afford my fees?

He's wearing some snappy Italian shoes so I take it that money's not going to be an issue but you can never tell. Sometimes the rich ones can be cheap bastards.

There is a third thing I need to know but he's not going to tell me that. I need to know if the relationship has been consummated. She won't tell him. What kind of wife is gonna say, "by the way, honey, I've been shagging a demon", over the cornflakes? But I'll know when I meet her. It's the difference between glowing like a cheap light globe and being lit up like Las-frigging-Vegas.

'Can you handle it?' he asks.

I lean back and crack my knuckles. He's going to call me girlie. I can tell. I hate it when they call me girlie.

I get my important person diary out of the drawer and flip through it. Truth is, demon fighting's been quiet lately and I could do with the cash.

'I'm pretty booked up at the moment,' I tell him and he looks distraught. 'I could clear a spot ...' he smiles, '... but it'll cost extra.'

'No problem,' he says.

I tell him the drill. He takes the missus for a weekend of lovin' meanwhile, I housesit. By the time they get back Sunday night, that demon will be dead meat. Not literally, of course. And thank God for that. I've got enough to worry about without disposing of demon carcasses.

Mr Droopy-Drawers hands me the deposit cheque. I have enough self restraint not to kiss it until *after* he leaves. Four days and I get the rest of this gorgeous money.

'OK, girlie, we'll give it a go.'

Arrggh, he had to say it.

I'm manicuring myself – you wouldn't believe the crap you get under your nails fighting demons – when Jack knocks on the door. I sigh. He's up for some hot action, wearing his blue cotton shirt that feels so soft against his hard biceps. He knows it melts me every time. And the cowboy hat – making him about 50 per cent more sexy. He's scruffy and unshaven and all lopsided grins.

OK, before I go any further, I think I need to tell you the pivotal fact about destroying the cuckold demon – and this is why I earn the big bucks. I have to fornicate with this hell beast, which isn't even the hard part. The most difficult part is that he has to come first.

That'd be fine and dandy if he actually were a hell beast during the shagging but, once he enters the house, he's flesh and blood. Usually hot, studly flesh and blood at that.

Then there's the other part to it. This is maybe, possibly even the worst part. To lure him out, I have to be totally, 100 per cent fuck-anything-that-moves frustrated.

Some folk think demon fighting is easy money but they are so totally and utterly wrong. I'll just reiterate in case you haven't quite got it. I have to be as horny as fuck, alone in a house with a hot man-beast who's 100 per cent focused on my sexual pleasure and I have to NOT come. Got it?

So, of course, Jack turns up out of nowhere.

'Hey darlin',' he says, squashing me in his arms.

'Wet nails,' I shake my hands.

He sits down, trying the puppy dog eyes. He thinks I'm a sucker for the puppy dog eyes but I'm only a sucker when I want to be.

I put on a movie. A passion-killing movie. Rocky. Only a sicko wants to make out during Rocky. I curl up on the end of the couch with a buffer zone between us.

As Rocky runs up flights of stairs, Jack encases my foot in his hand, stroking it softly. I know I should stop him but hello, who knocks back a free foot rub?

I relax, letting him knead my foot-flesh, not purring like a kitten at all. He runs his fingers down the arch of my foot and I pull away. It's a reflex because of the tickling but he grips my ankle tight.

'Stop it,' I tell him but with that giggly voice that means, "don't really". So he squirts lotion onto my foot. Then he rubs it between my toes and I sink down further into the cushions, feeling all whirly inside.

His thumb slips into the slit between my big toe and the next toe, while his fingers tickle over the sole of my foot. He works his thumb around the crevice and it sends heavenly ripples through me.

As his fingers spider down over my arches, I shudder and buck against the couch. Each tickle sparks a pussy twinge. He lifts my foot to his mouth and bites down on my toe, not hard but with just enough pressure.

Jack is so fucking hot. I don't think I told you that before but to illustrate how strong and self controlled and committed to the job I am, you need to know. It's not like I'm knocking back just mundane sex here. He's got rock star hair that knows exactly how to flop. He has steely arms and an unrelenting arse. He has grey-blue eyes that make my body hum with desire.

I can feel his cock under my foot. Oh boy, can I feel it. I want to unbutton his jeans and jump onboard, riding him like a tricycle. I want to fuck him until we both need surgery to remain intact.

After I kick him out, I try to sleep. I put mittens on my hands to stop myself from masturbating and add £50 to Mr Droopy-Drawers bill for mental and physical anguish. Three days until touchdown.

It's a slow week and I can't even distract myself with internet porn. I keep telling myself, "don't think about sex, don't think about sex." As you can imagine, that works a charm.

I mutter it under my breath on the train when the stranger with the wide shoulders rubs against me. He smells of kink – of leather and handcuffs and slow drawn out sessions of teasing. Like he'd make you frenzied and begging for it then finally enter you with just the tip of his cock while you squirm and call him a bastard.

I cross my legs and tighten my grip on the handrail, looking out the window and muttering louder until everyone moves away thinking I'm crazed.

Two days to go and an extra £200 to the bill for miscellaneous damages.

Finally, a job. I get to the house and the dude's in the shower. He opens the door in just a towel, body dripping with water and Irish accent dripping with sex.

It's a cosmic-fucking-conspiracy, I can go weeks, months

even without anything shaggable crossing my path – it's just me and Mr Buzzy – but as soon as I try to avoid it, it's raining men and there's no damn hallelujah.

I follow him through the house trying to think of unsexy things like global warming and cricket. I tell myself he's got a small willie and he's a premature ejaculator. He probably wants to talk about his "feelings" after sex. Not just his feelings, but his feelings about his mother.

I will not look at how the droplets of water glisten on his thighs, I will not notice his shoulder and that delicious, lickable indent. I definitely won't look at that round curve of arse pressing against the towel.

I make him put on some clothes while I snoop around in his roof cavity with my demon-locating torch. Like I thought, it's possums not demons. I'm not a bloody pest controller but I charge him my call-out fee and skedaddle to safety.

One day to go and the bill is adding up.

I can't get away from it. The weather turns hot and it makes me horny. The shops smell of mangoes and that makes me horny. I go for a run and the sweat on my skin makes me horny. My body becomes molten – all fluid and juices.

In the park, couples feel each other up. A boy has his hand up his girlfriend's skirt and I see a flash of red knickers. That's enough to have me juiced up, and thinking of red knickers all day.

I go to the gym, punching and kicking things for an hour, but that doesn't help.

The old man at the grocery shop suddenly doesn't look so bad. Even the ear hair isn't that off putting. I fantasise about removing his dentures and riding him while running my fingers through his comb-over.

Sam, the hellish housemate, decides to make me lunch and even the tin opener becomes loaded with sexual suggestion in his hands. I watch his burly farm-boy arms until he realises I'm drooling. The baked beans on toast take on erotic possibilities. I turn on the TV and they're advertising hot dogs! Hot dogs squeezing tight into buns, dripping with mustard.

I scream and run for the shower. Eight hours to go and I wonder if I'll make it.

I get to Mr Droopy-Drawers' house just before they leave for the weekend, enough time to check out the condition of his wife. She's carrying her bags out to the car and definitely looks un-demon ravaged. She even walks like she hasn't been laid in months. I go inside.

Finally the car backs out the driveway leaving me free to raid the fridge. They have caramel-crunch ice cream and chocolate sprinkles. Score. I fix myself a bumper-sized bowl and curl up to watch some cable. I've got a few hours before the demon reveals himself and, if I can't have sex, ice cream is second best.

I have no idea of the form he'll take – it'll be a projection of Mrs Droopy-Drawers' fantasy. He could be some emo poet boy quivering with angst or he could be a buff sex god – all cock and no brains. He might even be a chick. Hopefully it won't be too horrific but I don't trust her taste in men on account of the evidence – she married Mr Droopy Drawers.

Even bigger score – the wrestling is on. But sweaty men jumping on each other, that just makes things worse. My nipples rub against my bra and I'm painfully aware of the ache between my legs. If I sit up and squirm just right, I can pretend it helps but really it just reminds me that I have a wet, swollen, aching vagina and I haven't had an orgasm for four long agonising days.

I turn off the TV and look for something decent to put on the stereo to hide the pounding of my cunt. The Droopy-Drawers have the worst CD collection ever. Fleetwood Mac, Neil Diamond, Bob Dylan, I'd not even wish that on a demon. I find a *Best of AC/DC* hidden at the back and put that on, cranking it up loud.

This is the most nondescript townhouse I've seen. Tasteful and elegant, but so beige. Upstairs, the bedroom is so lacking in sexual charm, they may as well get twin beds.

I open Mrs Droopy Drawers' wardrobe. Man, she's got the hugest wardrobe I've ever seen. I walk in and keep walking until I wonder if I'm going to get to Narnia. I decide to try on some of her clothes. I could fool you into thinking I'm doing that to cleverly disguise myself in order to seduce the demon but the reality is I'm just bored.

Most of the clothes are as beige as the house but something red and glittery catches my eye. I pull out a ball gown. It's all swishy and girlie and almost the same colour as my hair. I slip off my jeans and T-shirt and put on the dress. A red strapless dress with baby pink bra straps showing – so wrong. It's too long and baggy on me and far too tight in the boobs, but what the hell?

As *Highway to Hell* comes on the stereo, I jump on the bed playing air guitar and singing. It's something I like to do when I'm in other people's houses – jumping on beds, I mean. I've never done it in a ball gown before though. I'm building up to my big finale when I hear a noise. I frigging hate being caught unawares.

I check him out and my jaw almost hits the ground.

Two thoughts fight with each other in my brain – the first is Mrs Droopy Drawers is a walking cliché. And my other thought is holy crap, I'm about to do it with a demon who's a dead ringer for Johnny Depp. This has to be my lucky night.

When he moves into the light, I see he's not quite Johnny Depp. Sure he has some Depp-like features but he's more like someone who gets told all the time that he looks like Johnny Depp.

We size each other up for a minute. If I look too eager, he'll know something's up. These demons get awful skittish when they think you're going to vanquish them. So I jump off the bed and make for the door, fully expecting him to pursue. He runs for the door at the same time. We collide in the doorway and I make sure I accidentally press my boobs against his arm. I hold his stare long enough for him to question just how accidental the brushing really is.

I wait for him to make his move. I feel the heat of him against my skin. He runs his finger along my collarbone. I don't make a move. I try not to react, but a tiny gasp of air escapes me. It's enough.

He has sensuous lips and dark, brooding eyes. More like a *What's-Eating-Gilbert-Grape* Johnny than a *Pirates-of-the-Caribbean* Johnny or, thank God, an *Edward-ScissorHands* Johnny.

I run my fingers down the tight black T-shirt, finding the buttons of his jeans. 'Be gentle with me,' I whisper, because I know it's not worth trying to be original.

'Not bloody likely,' he replies and pushes me up against the door frame, ramming his leg between mine and I'm thankful for the layers of red, swishy skirt because I'm so fucking horny that I need a barrier between me and my instinct to use him as a toy for my own pleasure.

But he bunches the skirt up and pushes my legs apart with his knee. We stare defiance at each other like the cover of some bodice-ripping romance until he slams his lips against mine.

There's no trace of sulphur like you sometimes get with demons, just cheap whiskey and cigarettes.

I'm jammed up against the door frame and he's kissing me so furious that the tulle of my skirt gets snagged in the door catch. The wooden frame cuts into my back and the heat of his body sears my front. Without removing his lips, he frees me from the ball gown and it falls into a puddle of froth and glitter at my feet.

He hoists me free of the dress. His fingers dig into my arse cheeks, inching into my crack. Mrs Droopy Drawers had better not be having anal fantasies because I don't care how much they pay me, it's front door action only. But he moves his hands down to my thighs, lifting me up and carrying me to the bed.

He's on top of me, hot and sweaty and holding me firm. I could take him right now, but I decide to act all girlie and weak, letting him think he's in control. When they think they've got you, they let their guard down - so I moan and gasp while he runs his finger under the lace of my bra. I squirm and giggle as he licks over the lace. Then his teeth tear through a hundred bucks of designer bra lace and he bites and sucks. My moans and gasps become real. I meld into the bed and I melt into the sensation of his tongue. For just an instant, I lose myself and my screams are loud enough to block out the vocals of Bon Scott turned up to eleven on the stereo downstairs.

I try to think of the money. The beautiful, crisp money.

His fingers play with the gusset of my panties and it's only the thought of those extra zeroes in my bank account that give me the fortitude to push them away. Instead he moves his mouth – licking and nibbling a line down to my belly button.

Without the weight of him on me, I break free and push him back on to the bed. I hold his hands down and straddle him. The push of his cock through the denim of his jeans rubs against my cunt and I want to just sit there, slowly rocking, feeling denim-encased cock against lace-sheathed pussy. But you don't get the job done looking after yourself.

He breaks into a slow, easy grin.

I undo his fly and yank his jeans down. No need for finesse. With free access, I can finish him off in seconds. I grab his hands and climb on top, holding them over his head and making sure my tits swing just inches away from his mouth. His tongue darts out to lick them but I move out of reach, swaying them in front of him. I know I'm tempting him; I can feel his hips writhe and his cock twitch. I hover

70

over him, my pussy not touching him yet close enough so that he can feel its heat. Take that, demon; you're playing in the big league now.

Then I make my finishing move. I turn around and he thinks we are going to 69 but I've got other plans. I pin his arms down with my legs and hold myself over him. He can smell my arousal, he can see my arousal but he can't touch it.

Ha, ha. I'm winning. I always win because I'm the best. The thought of my own superiority makes me hornier. Times like this, I like to picture myself on a winner's podium with my theme music, *The Final Countdown* by Europe, playing in the background and the cheers of the crowd deafening me.

I pause for a moment, letting him feel my breath on his cock. Tease them in the beginning and they blow all the faster. He bucks like a bronco. I flick my tongue out, lightly licking the head of his cock, just a little, just a teeny little taste.

Softly and slowly, I circle the head with my tongue then run it down the shaft. Victory will be mine.

I expect him to put up more of a fight. Doesn't he know I'm going to suck him to his own destruction?

I grab my fingers tightly around the base of his cock. His hips buck up to meet me and I take him all in my mouth. He's not nearly as big as Jack. I suck hard, swirling my tongue along his cock. It's not going to take long now. I think I can feel his every heartbeat. He's gasping and shuddering and muttering 'oh fuck, oh fuck.'

I move my hand and mouth in unison, faster and faster until I know he's going to explode and, as I feel his final thrusts, I brace myself for his disappearance and for me to tumble face first onto the bed.

I pull my head away as he shoots his load into the air, then …

Nothing.

71

He's still lying below me. I freeze. There's no vanquishing and it tilts my world on its axis, just for a minute.

I'm angry and confused and so fucking frustrated that I shake. I want his hands on me, I want my own hands on myself. I inch down my knickers. Images flash through my brain – Jack in his cowboy hat, kinky man on the train, towel wrapped buttocks and red knickers and mangoes and sweat. Everything dissolves into a blur. I'm bucking and moaning, charged like an electrical storm. I'm tangled in cotton sheets, focused on my cunt and my clit, hips bucking, seconds away from climax.

'That looks like fun,' says a deep voice from the doorway.

I ignore it. Don't fucking mess with me NOW.

But my lover jumps from the bed.

'Dude,' he says in a strangulated voice. 'She made me.'

Huh? I halt in mid-stroke.

My lover scoops up his jeans from the floor and bolts out the door. I've never known a demon to bolt before; but then I've never known a demon not to vanquish.

As he crashes down the stairs, I check out the dude leaning on the doorframe. He smells of sulphur and has a devilish gleam in his green eyes. He checks me out too, breaking into a wry grin, all angles and cheekbones. It takes a moment to piece it together, my brain slow and sex-befuddled...

On the Other Side
by Peter Baltensperger

Galen had always dreamed of living in an old house of his own, but he never expected his life to be changed as dramatically as it did when he was finally able to realise his dream. Growing up in an old farmhouse that had been in the family for generations, he always felt comfortable and secure in the ancient surroundings. As soon as he established himself in a career, he found exactly what he wanted: an old, well-maintained farmhouse in excellent condition in beautiful countryside. He felt the old feelings of comfort and security flood over him the moment he stepped into the house.

He was completely at home as soon as he moved in and spent the evenings decorating and familiarising himself with the house. After a busy week, he started spending his evenings more leisurely in his living room. It was then that some unexpectedly strange noises began to disrupt the silence of the house. At first, he thought they were just the usual creaking of dried-out wood and ancient plumbing characteristic of old houses, but there were other more disturbing noises as well.

One evening as he was sitting in his living room reading a book, he heard a persistent knocking against one of the outside walls, a knocking that seemed to come from outside but was also inside the house itself. He looked all around the house, but he couldn't find anything that could have caused such a noise. At other times, he heard loud thuds, as if large pieces of furniture were falling, but when he went to check, nothing was amiss anywhere.

And then he began to hear indistinct voices. He couldn't make out any words, but they were definitely voices, penetrating, it seemed, the same outside wall where the knocking had originated, and echoing faintly through his house. He walked up to the wall with trepidation and pressed his ear against it. The voices grew louder the more carefully he listened, but he still couldn't hear individual words.

A few evenings later, the voices were getting louder than they had been before. He went and pressed his ear against the wall again, and the voices were definitely more pronounced, agitated, it seemed to him, but he still couldn't figure out where they were coming from or what they were saying.

He was leaning against the wall trying to catch a word or a phrase when suddenly the wall beside him began to move. He froze in terror. All he could do was to stare at the motion and then, to his horror, an arm reached through the wall out into the room. It wasn't so much an arm as an arm-like protuberance pushing itself through the wall and elongating the wallpaper as if the wall and its covering had become pliable, expandable, alive.

He could clearly make out a hand at the end of the long tube of expanding wallpaper, a hand that was feeling around as if looking for something, a hand that was very much alive although it never broke through the paper and he never actually saw what it really was.

Panic-stricken, he grabbed the wallpaper arm with his hands, only to feel the hand grabbing his own arm and pinning him against the wall. He heard a rustling behind him and turned around to see a second arm worming its way into the room, pushing the transformed wall and its paper cover into the air behind him. Before he could react, the second arm grabbed him around the waist. He felt himself being pulled into the wall and through it in one continuous motion and found himself standing beside a strangely attractive young woman. The wall was completely solid again.

The room was eerily similar to his own living room, yet very different at the same time, almost a replica but not quite, larger and higher, with a long dining table and wooden chairs along the far wall. He was obviously in an old house much like his own, with a heavy door and windows on three walls. It looked all too familiar, yet strangely alien, warped almost, in an eerie kind of way.

The young woman was clad in a simple brown shift that covered her slender body from her neck down to her feet. She had a very pretty face, although her skin was very pale and her eyes unusually deep and black. The strangest thing was that she had no hair at all, not even eyebrows or lashes. She smiled at him pleasantly as if nothing out of the ordinary had just taken place.

'Who are you?' he asked, consternation and disbelief in his voice.

'I'm an Ugly,' the young woman said. 'Like you.'

'What do you mean, an Ugly?' Galen asked, perplexed and confused.

'Just what I said,' she replied calmly. 'We're the Uglies, you and I. The others are the Beautiful Ones. They rule the world. We're just being tolerated and used, and sometimes not even that.'

'You mean there are others?' Galen asked in disbelief.

'Oh yes,' the young woman answered casually. 'There are many others. Most of them live out in the woods, but I'm allowed to live here because my family is one of the Powerful Ones and their Uglies are always allowed to stay with them.'

'And what ...' Galen interrupted her, shaking off his terror and regaining some of his composure, '... does all this have to do with me? Why did you pull me through the wall?'

'Because you're an Ugly like me,' the young woman said lightly, nonchalantly. 'I was feeling lonely and I like you, so I wanted to have you with me.'

'That's all very flattering,' Galen replied, 'but you can't just pull me through the wall of my house simply because you want to. I have a career and a life and I want you to put me back right now.'

'I'm afraid I can't do that.'

'Can't do that?' Galen echoed. He was running out of patience. 'You just did it a few minutes ago!'

'No, I didn't. I brought you through the wall,' the young woman corrected him. 'But I can't put you back. It only works one way.'

'That's just great,' Galen snapped. 'I demand to be back in my own house.'

'As I just said,' the young woman replied in her quiet voice, 'that can't be done. You're here with me now. It's very lonely, being the only Ugly in the house.'

'Why don't you go and be with others in your own world?' Galen countered. 'You said there were many others.'

'I'm not allowed to leave the property. My family owns me and they're allowed to keep me and use me in any way they want.'

'I'm really sorry you're lonely,' Galen said sympathetically, 'but I don't belong here.' He banged his fists against the wall, only to wince in pain. 'Make it open, now!' he cried out in frustration.

'I already told you I can't do that,' the young woman said without emotion.

'But you don't know me at all.' Galen decided to try a different approach.

'I know you,' she said with a smile. 'I've been watching you ever since you moved into the house.'

'So now you can see through the walls, too,' Galen said,

his voice sharper than he intended it to be.

'Of course I can see through the walls,' the young woman replied. 'I just have to press my face against the wall and it goes right through to your wallpaper and I can see everything in your house.'

'I don't get it,' Galen sighed, reaching the end of his patience, but also of his arguments. 'At least tell me your name so I know what to call you.'

'I don't have a name. None of the Uglies do. Only the Beautiful Ones have names.'

'Well, I'm Galen,' he said.

'It doesn't matter,' the young woman said laconically. 'We're not allowed to have names.'

The large door on the opposite side of the room opened and a hideous creature came limping in. Galen shuddered. The young woman pressed herself against the wall, hiding partly behind him, as if trying to make herself invisible. 'Don't look at him!' she hissed. 'They don't like it when we look at them.'

Galen couldn't take his eyes off the creature, despite the warning. It looked sort of human, in a grotesque kind of way, misshapen and deformed. It was completely naked, with a large, almost conical head covered by long unruly hair and an equally long and unruly beard, and its body was covered with a light layer of hair. It wasn't fur, as an animal would have, as far as he could tell, but rather human hair, only that it covered the whole body except for the prominent genitals hanging between its legs.

The creature busied itself around the table, obviously getting it ready for a meal, then disappeared again without having paid any attention to them.

'What on earth was that?' Galen asked, totally bewildered.

'One of my brothers,' the young woman explained.

'You're kidding!' Galen exclaimed, taken aback by her unexpected reply. 'And they call you the Ugly? Are they all like that?'

'Of course they are,' the young woman answered. 'They are the Beautiful Ones. Couldn't you tell?'

'They should be called the Uglies,' Galen said. 'We're beautiful, you and I, not those creatures.'

'Don't talk about them like that. They're my family.'

'Yes, of course.' Galen caught himself. 'I'm sorry I said that. Don't they wear any clothes? You do!'

'Why should they? They're the Beautiful Ones; they don't have to cover themselves up the way we do. We'll get you a proper gown and get rid of all the hair you have on your body so you'll fit in.'

'You what?' Galen exploded. 'You can't do that!'

'Of course, I can,' the young woman replied. 'You belong with me now.'

'No, I don't,' Galen protested. 'I'll just walk out the front door and go back to my own life.'

'Can't be done.'

Their argument was interrupted by a group of the creatures filing into the room, one more repulsive than the others, all swaying on their deformed legs. The females were hairy and furry like the males, and all had large pendulous breasts. They were carrying bowls of food and putting them on the table. Then they sat down and began their meal, picking up and eating their food with their hands, talking noisily and smacking loudly. So those were the voices and noises he had been hearing in his house.

He started to say something, but the young woman silenced him with a gesture of her hand. 'They don't like us to talk when they're in the room,' she whispered. She slid down on the floor, wrapped her arms around her knees, and pressed her body against the wall to make herself as unnoticeable as she could. Galen crouched down beside her and watched the progress of the noisy meal. He couldn't understand a word anybody was saying, their voices garbled, their crooked mouths full of food. He just kept staring at them in disbelief.

The creatures finished their meal and filed back out of the room. As soon as the last of them closed the door, the young woman jumped up, grabbed him by the hand, and pulled him over to the table. She moved swiftly from seat to seat, gathering food with her hands and piling it on to a plate. Then she set the plate down, grabbed another one, filled it with food. She handed him one, grabbed one herself, and scurried back to the wall, crouching down and starting to devour the leftovers as rapidly as she could.

Galen watched in amazement as she stuffed the food into her mouth with her hands. He crouched down beside her, picked up some pieces of food, and put them tentatively into his mouth. It tasted quite good, he had to admit, after the first couple of bites. He realised that he was hungry as well and stuffed the food into his mouth more and more quickly as he got used to the new flavours and tastes.

They finished their meal in silence, then the young woman took his plate and carried it back to the table with hers. When she came back to where he was still crouched on the floor, she held out her hand to him. 'Time to go to my room,' she said. 'They don't want us in the room after we finish eating.'

She led him down a hallway to a small cell-like room. There was a kind of mattress on the floor, but no other furniture, and no window. The room was lit by a fluorescence that appeared to be coming out of the walls and the ceiling, although there weren't any light fixtures anywhere.

The young woman casually pulled her shift over her head. She wasn't wearing anything else. He looked at her in awe. She had a beautiful body underneath that shift, long, slender legs, solid round perky breasts with firm, pink nipples set in large, dark areolas. The only thing amiss on an otherwise perfect body was that she had a prominent third nipple between her breasts, almost like a miniature third breast. She had no pubic hair at all, giving her a freshly-shaven appearance with a nice protruding pussy partially revealed for him. Her whole slender body was a medley of visual delights.

Ignoring his stare, she stretched out on the mattress and spread her legs He took her pose as an invitation and quickly took off his clothes. Then he stretched out beside her and put his arm around her. She didn't move. She just lay there beside him, her head turned slightly away from him, her eyes shut tight, but she didn't protest. Emboldened, he put his hand on her blossoming breast and started to fondle it, delighting in the silky smoothness of her skin, the malleability of her globe, the firmness of her nipple. She remained completely motionless, completely silent, giving him no indication of whether she liked his caresses or not, so in the absence of any negative reactions he just assumed she did.

Feeling more adventurous and strangely aroused by her noncommittal attitude, he slid down along her body, made his way between her legs, and dove into her proffered pussy. Her labias were full and soft, morsels from the gods. She was dripping wet with the most delicious juices he had ever encountered, so strange and different, so unexpectedly unique, so much from a different world.

Her emanations were rich and plentiful and his mind was reeling from the deluge of delectable tastes and smells, the sweetness, the underlying tartness, the slightly coppery aftertaste, the luscious aromas. He rejoiced, licking and sucking, swallowing, inhaling, wallowing in the flood of the unexpected sensory impressions flooding his mind, titillating his lips, his tongue, his nose. After a while, he felt he should involve her as well, so he moved back up beside her.

'You can do things, too, you know,' he whispered tentatively.

She opened her eyes slowly, as if coming out of a deep

dream or a trance, then turned her head towards him and slowly focused her eyes. 'Do what things?' she asked.

'You know, touch me the way I touch you,' he suggested.

'I don't know how to do that,' she said.

He wasn't quite up to a lengthy tutorial in basic sex, and too eager to continue. 'I'll show you some other time,' he said, grasping her body impatiently.

Climbing on top of her, he entered her eagerly, his throbbing penis finding its way easily into her dripping cave. He put his hands on her breasts and rested his face against the delicious softness. He moved in and out of her very slowly until he couldn't contain himself any longer and gushed into her, moaning his delight into her breasts, squeezing them together against his face, inhaling the musky scent of her skin.

She still hadn't moved or said anything, so he climbed off her, put his arm around her again and tried to pull her close to him. She didn't budge, but she did turn her head towards him and opened her eyes. A transformed smile spread over her face.

'I liked what you did,' she said, much to his surprise. 'Nobody's ever done that to me before.'

'Did you have an orgasm?' he whispered.

'Of course,' she said, matter-of-factly, cryptically. 'I usually do.'

With that, she did let herself move a bit closer to him so he could feel her body against his, although she still didn't touch him or say anything else.

They had been lying there like that for some time, when the illumination in the room suddenly dimmed. He heard the sound of a bell from somewhere, and there appeared to be some commotion outside.

'What now?' Galen wanted to know, but before he could elicit an answer, the door swung open and one of the horrid males came limping into the room. The young woman detached herself from his embrace, turned her face away

81

from him, and closed her eyes. The creature headed straight for the mattress, climbed unceremoniously on top of the young woman, and started thrusting into her. Galen watched the proceedings in disgust. She deserved better than this hairy, deformed creature on top of her.

The creature bent over her and began sucking her third nipple. Then it thrust a few more times, grunted and bellowed, dismounted and left the room. A second male entered the cell, climbed on top of her, and sucked and thrust and grunted himself to an orgasm as well. Then a third came in and did exactly the same thing. As soon as the last visitor closed the door behind him, a bell rang again somewhere and Galen thought, and hoped, that it was signalling the end.

'Doesn't this bother you?' he asked.

The young woman turned towards him and opened her eyes very slowly the way she had done before. 'Bother me?' she said lightly. 'Why should it bother me? That's what we Uglies do.'

'But why?' Galen asked incredulously.

'It's the evening ritual,' the young woman explained. 'They believe they gain power and status from lying with us. And for us, it's a matter of honour and pride, to be selected by them like this. The more often the Beautiful Ones pick us for their ritual, the greater our status and our liberties.'

'And what …?' Galen began, but the door opened again and another creature stepped into the cell, this time one of the grotesque females with the pendulous breasts. She, too, headed towards the young woman lying beside him, then caught sight of him. Before he knew what was happening, the creature grabbed his penis with her gnarled, leathery hands, rubbed it to a fresh erection, and silently impaled herself on him.

The female started bobbing up and down, her hairy breasts swaying above him, her hideous face staring blankly down at him. She bent over him, and rocked herself to a moaning, groaning orgasm. Galen couldn't believe what was going on.

Just when he thought he couldn't stand it any longer, the creature climbed off him and left the room, holding the door open for a second female. Galen groaned in dismay, but the second female ignored him and headed straight for the young woman. She climbed on top of her and started rubbing herself against the perfect body, taking the young woman's breasts into her hands and kneading them and sucking on her third nipple until she too shook in a groaning orgasm, climbed off, and left.

The bell began ringing again, louder and longer this time, and the light in the cell dimmed to a glimmer.

'Is that it?' he asked, desperation in his voice.

'The bell, yes,' the young woman said tonelessly, coming out of her trance. 'Nobody else is going to come.'

Galen sighed with relief. He reached for her with his hand. Her body was trembling, her eyes wide open, staring at the ceiling. She was breathing heavily but didn't say anything else.

'Come,' Galen said, soothingly. 'Let me hold you.'

This time she didn't resist. She moved as close to him as she could and pressed her body against his while he wrapped his arms around her and stroked her until the trembling subsided and her body began to relax. Her breasts were touching his chest, her pussy his penis, her legs his legs, and he just held on to her, for her benefit as well as for his own. He felt warm and comfortable against her beautiful body.

'Who were those creatures?' he asked into the stillness of their togetherness.

'Please don't call them that,' the young woman said again. 'You have to call them Beautiful Ones, which is what they deserve to be called. They are friends of my parents. They all go to different houses every evening, wherever there are Uglies.'

'What about the ones that aren't Powerful Ones?'

'They go into the forest, where the other Uglies live. When they find them, they perform the evening ritual in the forest with them.'

'And they do this all the time?'

'Oh yes,' she said. 'That's what the ritual is all about.'

He tightened his arms around her until her breathing slowed in his soothing embrace and her body relaxed against his. He found her mouth with his and she gasped when he pressed his lips against hers, pushed against his arm encircling her. He held on to her and she relaxed again when he started nibbling her lips and licking them with his tongue, then slid his tongue into her and began probing her passionately.

And then it was as if she had always known what to do as long as there was someone to prompt her and lead the way. She eagerly responded to his kiss, put her arm around him, and pulled him to her. He took her breasts into his hands again and revelled in their silky softness and their sensuous contours, and this time she moaned quietly to herself. Step by step he guided her through a series of mutual explorations and she responded eagerly and enthusiastically to everything he did.

Her body was a sensuous playground of gentle curves, soft lines, titillating scents, her third nipple surprisingly enough generating an intriguingly unique kind of arousal. Her hands quickly learned how to fondle and stimulate him as he kept caressing and stimulating her. When he penetrated her again, they began rocking together, she thrusting against him with equal vigour as he thrust against her. He soon felt her body straining against his as her orgasm took hold, and this time she didn't hold back. Writhing and gyrating on her mattress and clawing at him with hungry fingers, she screamed with unabashed delight as they swayed rhythmically through their earth-shattering orgasms until they were dizzy from their exertion and completely satisfied and fulfilled.

Keeping their arms around each other, they floated through the afterglow of their union, smiling contentedly, until he felt her body go limp in his arms and she drifted off to sleep. He just kept holding on to her, feeling the gentle softness of her body against him, deriving new comfort from her presence. Lying there beside her, he tried to come to grips with what had so suddenly and unexpectedly happened to him and what he was doing in her strange world, wondering desperately if he would ever be able to escape.

After what seemed like hours, he finally dozed off himself and fell into a deep, nightmarish sleep, plagued by ghastly, hauntingly disturbing images that wouldn't leave him alone. And probably never would...

Something About Mary
by J S Black

How could I not smile at Casey? After all these months of
being holed up in her workroom, never allowing me so
much as a glimpse no matter how many coffees I took her or
begged, here she finally was, beaming with pride and
moments away from unveiling her latest creation.

'Ladies and gentlemen, I give you ...' Casey announced
grandly, although I was the only person present in our
living-room, 'Mary!' Casey proudly pulled away the purple
silk sheet that had covered the shape upon our sofa and in
my disbelief at what was unveiled I felt the smile fall from
my face.

'Larry,' Casey asked worriedly, 'what do you think? Do
you like her?' I'd seen much of Casey's work but never
anything quite like this. Mary, or so the creation had been
named, was a life-sized figure of a woman dressed in a long
silken gown of black and deep green the luxurious colours
of which served only to define more clearly the creation's
pleasing curves. But impressed as I was by the figure's
shapely thighs and full breasts, it was the face that had
silenced me. Long, straight black hair cascaded around the
white face made alive by eyes that held my gaze with a life
of their own and although the face wasn't without its
imperfections, which strangely added to its realism, my first
thought was that this might be a joke played upon me by
Casey and one of her arty friends.

'It's uncanny,' I said quietly, my brow furrowed as I scrutinised the construction lounging on our sofa. Glancing towards Casey I saw her proud smile waning and chose my words more carefully, 'I mean she's so lifelike, I've never seen anything quite like her,' and I wasn't lying. Casey seated herself next to Mary, the smile now returning to her pretty little face.

'Look Larry, I've constructed Mary so that we can move her into any position we want, she's fully jointed ...' Casey demonstrated by moving Mary through a series of poses as though she were manipulating an unconscious guest. 'I won't bore you with all the details but I've used the body of a mannequin as a base and upon this I've used latex, fibreglass, plastic tubing, dowels, ball and socket joints, polyurethane ...'

'OK, OK, I get it,' I said, while not really getting it at all. Casey observed me with amusement when I began to move about the room while keeping my eyes upon Mary, testing something. 'Casey, no matter where I go her eyes follow me, they watch me.' They freak me the fuck out, I thought.

'Mary's the playmate we've desired, Larry, we can use her, we can fantasise, for us she can be real and you need never feel jealous of her.' Casey gazed upon the figure next to her and I found the adoration in her face towards her creation distasteful somehow. And despite Casey's words I felt the small ball of heat that was my jealousy began to stir somewhere deep within me.

'Why Mary?' I asked a little too sternly and immediately hoped that Casey hadn't noticed. Casey turned her gaze from Mary to me, her face calmly vacant and in a gentle voice she said, 'Larry, please don't feel jealous towards Mary, I made her for us both.' She was silent for a moment but her eyes never left mine. 'And there's something I want to tell you about Mary, something that I didn't quite figure on.'

'It was never my intention to make her look like the

Mary I knew back in my university days,' Casey told me. 'She just began to appear out of the materials I was using, Jeez, Larry, if I really thought about this I could be as freaked about her as you are, more so really.'

The bright San Francisco autumnal sun had slipped away to a murky evening and after a late evening supper we sipped Blue Devils in our cosy candlelit room, snuggled together on our favourite couch. Mary reclined in the two-seater across the room from us. Under the glow of candlelight she appeared more alive than when she'd first been unveiled and I felt that we were rudely discussing a guest.

I took a sip of my drink. 'So, do you wanna tell me a little more about Mary, the real one I mean.' I nodded in the direction of Mary's doppelganger. 'I bet that would just freak her the hell right out.'

Casey took a sip of her drink before answering. 'Well, Mary was both interesting and ... *unusual*. She was deep, you know, and her interests were things we didn't really understand but that didn't matter because we were drawn to her all the same.'

'She looks like a Goth chick to me,' I said with a smirk.

'Well, I guess she was,' Casey agreed with a smile. 'She definitely seemed more European than American, if you know what I mean.'

I looked at Casey's face, beautiful in the candlelight and knew that she was thinking deeply. I suspected that she wasn't telling me everything and her silence prompted a burning question from me. 'So, did you like her, Casey. I mean did you ...'

'Desire her?' Casey looked at the figure sitting across the room from us. 'Yeah, Larry I did. I had one hell of a crush on her.'

'You were lovers?' I had to ask the question, but I probably didn't want to hear the answer.

'No, never.' Casey gave an incredulous laugh, 'I just

didn't have the nerve back then to voice my feelings I guess …'

'But what if you had done? How do you think this Mary of yours would've reacted?' I asked, struggling to conceal my scorn.

'I don't know, Larry, I guess that's always been at the back of my mind somewhere.' She looked from me towards her figure of Mary, which returned her gaze as though fully aware of the conversation taking place.

'Christ, so all the time that we've been together this woman you adore so much has been floating around in your head,' I said vehemently.

'Larry, it isn't like I've been thinking about her every day, and don't you have memories too?'

'I guess so yeah,' I answered and realising how petulant I was sounding I endeavoured to move the conversation forwards. 'OK, so tell me a little more about her, what made her so unusual?'

'Well she said lots of stuff, Larry, maybe we should just change the subject.'

'Well, that's kind of hard considering she's as good as sitting across the room from us,' I said. 'Come on, I want to know who we're messing with here, what sort of stuff did she used to say?'

'OK.' Casey took a sip of her drink, 'Mary used to say that lust was one of the most powerful desires known to man, that lustful energy was something to be harnessed and used, but never really gave an explanation to this and if she did I guess it kind of went over my head at the time.'

'I think she was right about the lust thing, the rest sounds like mumbo-shit to me.'

'Well, whatever, look, all you need to know is this; a doll could never replace you so how about we move on from this now huh?' Casey snuggled closer to me on the couch, lifting up her knees so they were across my lap. I rested a hand upon her exposed thigh, Casey's smooth skin serving to soothe me and I felt instantly better despite my resentment of Mary, real or unreal. I just hoped that the real one didn't show up any time during my life with Casey. Casey placed her drink down upon the table; her cool lips were at my cheek, my ear.

'Want me to mix us more devils?' I asked, noticing her empty glass.

'No, not just at the moment,' Casey whispered into my ear before planting a soft yet audible kiss followed by a delicate tongue flick, something she knew melted me every time.

I glanced in the direction of Mary, hoping she had slipped from her sitting position to at least look like someone asleep and inanimate.

Mary was looking directly at us.

Directly at me.

I reminded myself that Mary was nothing more than plastic and all the other crap that Casey had mentioned earlier. Casey, though, was real and her hand rested now upon my cock through the thin material of my slacks. I tasted Blue Devil upon her lips and briefly upon her tongue pushing between my own lips and my own lust began to rise as I returned her kisses, my hand deep in Casey's lush hair as I held her close. Casey gently squeezed the erection growing beneath her hand and I moved my own hand over the expanse of her smooth naked thigh, her soft skin like silk under my appreciative touch.

I released a groan of pleasure into Casey's mouth when I felt her small hand begin to tug at my zipper and my kisses became more intense, more demanding as my arousal grew.

Casey pulled away from me, breaking our kiss. Her eyes held my own as she turned her attention to my belt, her smile enchantingly beautiful in the glow of the candlelight. I stole a glance over Casey's shoulder, not used to seeing another person in the room as we made love I needed to assure myself that the figure of Mary was still indeed just that, a contrived figure produced by Casey's own hands.

As before, Mary was looking directly towards me and in the shine of her eyes I thought I saw emotions that I was all too guilty of feeling; anger and jealousy.

'Casey wait ...' Pulling Casey's hand away from me I pushed her away in one swift movement. From the opposite end of the sofa she looked at me in shock and confusion.

'What's the matter? What did I do?' She searched my face for answers. I looked from Casey's concerned face to Mary's. The doll had fallen into a slumped position, her head tilted to one side lifelessly and yet her glassy eyes appeared to look through me as only the dead eyes of a doll could.

Holding my arms down firmly against the bed on either side of my head, Casey lowered her moist heat fully down the length of my cock and although her ferocity had taken me by surprise it didn't lessen my yearning for her enveloping warmth.

In the candlelight I watched Casey's lovely face above me as she ground herself against me, her eyes closed as she concentrated on her movements and the pleasure it gave.

'Does it feel good, babe?' Her voice was little more than a harsh whisper.

'Yeah,' I looked up towards Casey's face once again to see her looking to her left, the intensity in her eyes now for the benefit of someone, some*thing* else.

Mary was seated in the wicker chair next to our bed, carefully positioned there so as to observe us. I looked to my right and in the candlelight it appeared as though a third person was in the room watching us, those intense eyes bringing life to her otherwise waxen face in the yellow light, watching us as we fucked.

Casey's movements quickened along with her breath as she rode me hard towards her approaching peak. She held me down more firmly and a groan of sheer pleasure escaped her lips when her orgasm powered through her lithe body and still she continued to stare at Mary, her eyes locked on to the doll's, as though seeking approval there.

And despite my annoyance, despite my growing jealousy I felt the erupting warmth signalling the onset of my own orgasm when Casey it seemed had passed the peak of her own.

'I'm coming ...' I spat the words knowing I'd be able to hold back no longer, such were the power of Casey's thrusts upon me as she ground as much pleasure as she could from her orgasm. Quickly, Casey climbed off me, finally releasing me from the bed and I wondered what she intended. Although I was aware of the "watching" figure to my right I was nevertheless too preoccupied with my own release to pay Mary any attention. I let out a groan of pleasure of my own when I felt the sensation of Casey's warm mouth upon my erupting cock to relish the sensation of my powerful spurts caught by her welcoming mouth as I bucked my hips and yet Casey was sure not to release me until I'd fully spent for her.

'Oh boy.' I managed a smile for Casey who looked up the length of my body towards me. She hadn't swallowed my spend but was holding it in her mouth and I guess I must've looked confused again when climbing up off the bed, she moved towards the figure of Mary still seated in the wicker chair to my right.

'What you doing?' I asked as I admired Casey's slender form and beautifully smooth skin glowing in the candlelight, reaching for the figure of Mary. Casey placed Mary down next to me on the bed and silently I watched, wondering what she intended.

Despite my jealousy I still found it erotic to watch Casey lower her face towards Mary's, her lips meeting those of the doll's. I watched as she slowly released my spend over Mary's unmoving lips to run in silver streams down over those lips and smooth cheeks. I knew that Mary's lips weren't fully sealed, that Casey had given her the smallest of openings that was a mouth and surely some of my semen was entering that mouth now.

'You know I'm broad minded but this is freaking me out just a little now, honey,' I said as gently as I could, not wanting to upset Casey who withdrew from the doll, a seam of glistening come still connecting them.

'I'll go freshen up and get us drinks,' she told me, smiling a smile that didn't quite reach her eyes and then she was gone, leaving me alone on the bed with Mary.

I observed Mary's face in the candlelight, her features so realistic, so *creepy* but something else momentarily stopped my breath.

Sounds, so faint as to be almost inaudible were emitting from her mouth.

Leaning closer to the doll's face I heard the small "popping" sounds created by my juice in her mouth. I watched more closely, my brow furrowing as I tried to understand what was happening here in our bedroom. I watched my semen form into a small bubble upon Mary's lips before popping and knew that this was the sound I'd heard only moments ago.

The doll was breathing.

I awoke to find myself alone in bed and feeling the coolness of the other side I knew that Casey had been gone some time. I glanced at our bedside clock, 1.34 a.m. Maybe she couldn't sleep, maybe she'd gone to get herself a drink or read downstairs for a while, reasonable thoughts but I just wasn't buying them.

With a sigh I pulled myself up off the bed and padded out of the bedroom into the dark hallway. A dull light emitted from under the door of the guestroom where I'd asked Casey to keep the doll now that I didn't want it anywhere near me. I considered returning to bed but knew if I did I most likely wouldn't sleep.

Treading carefully in an attempt to be quiet in this creaky old house of ours I managed to reach the door and reached for the solid brass handle. The door let out a gentle creak but if the occupants of the room had heard then they chose not to take notice.

In the gentle light of one small corner lamp Casey lay on the bed, her arms wrapped around Mary who not for the first time appeared to be so very real in this dull light. I knew that if anyone were to witness the couple they'd be forgiven for assuming they were being treated to the sight of two women on the bed, each entwined in the other, closer than I myself had been with Casey for some months, regardless of sex.

I considered whispering Casey's name, to wake her and ask that she come back to bed but the words never left my lips; I knew I'd be intruding here, that I wasn't welcome. Gently I closed the door before making my way back to our bedroom alone.

Awake, I lay in our bed with troubled mind. It was something I'd seen in that room just a few steps away from me. Casey and that damn figure she'd constructed, *Mary*. Their arms wrapped around one another, *their* arms, Mary's arms around Casey's slender figure, *holding her*.

'Tell me about Mary, the real one I mean because if I'm honest with you, Casey, that thing in the other room is freaking me the fuck out!' I'd been waiting for Casey, having been awake for most of the night I was in no mood to be fobbed off. She looked at me with sleepy eyes and seated herself opposite me at our table. I placed a coffee in front of her and waited for her to speak.

Casey raised her face to look at me. She appeared tired, tired of me.

'We were members of Mary Wolfe's select group and would perform … *rituals* with her, she'd allow us to enter her dark world, although never really fully, she never fully opened herself up to anyone, including me.' She took a sip of her coffee and without looking at me continued, 'Something happened, something dreadful ...' She was silent for a moment, her brow furrowed.

'Yeah?' I encouraged.

'It was rumoured that she killed the man who stole her lover from her but because a body was never found she was never held to account.'

'Christ ...' I muttered.

'And it got worse, Larry,' Casey sighed. 'One foggy evening Mary leaped off the Golden Gate bridge, right here in the city but guess what? Her body was never found either and some doubted she'd even leaped at all but whatever happened, Mary hasn't been seen since.'

'And you expect me to have that thing in our bedroom?' I said in disbelief.

'That *thing*?' she echoed. 'That thing, as you call it, took me months to construct, she's my masterpiece, my playmate!' Her anger seemed to intensify with each word until she was glaring at me from across the table. 'Look, I'm going to be late for my meeting in the city if I don't get moving. We'll talk about this later tonight, OK?' Her voice had softened but there was still determination in her eyes.

'Sure,' I told her.

'You're jealous of a doll, Larry, a fucking doll!' Casey, as I'd expected, was furious with my actions. Having returned from a not too successful day in the city she'd suspected immediately that all was not well.

'It's staying there, Casey ...'

'Her name's Mary, Mary! How fucking hard is it?' In all our time together I'd never seen her so angry.

'Whatever you've chosen to call it, it's staying in the cellar until I decide otherwise.'

Casey looked at me, the fire gone from her eyes to be replaced by something far colder.

'You're being ridiculous; I'm going to get her out.' She

began to stride out of the room but my next words stopped her.

'I've locked the door and have put the key in a safe place so forget it,' I told her flatly.

Slowly, she turned to face me; 'You're jealous of anything and everything that I love, Larry, well let me tell you, this was one thing you should've left well alone.' Her voice was strangely calm and with what I took to be a smile, she turned and left the room.

The scraping sound coming from somewhere below me in the house, roused me from my troubled sleep but fell silent once I opened my bleary eyes, causing me to doubt I'd heard anything at all. To my left the sleeping form of Casey appeared still and doll-like under the faint moonlight coming through the window.

I intended getting out of bed, to at least head out on to the landing to listen for further sounds but I felt so tired, more so than I can ever remember being and listen as I might I nevertheless drifted back into sleep, unable to resist, as though something were pulling me back …

… to awaken to further sounds once again.

Casey's half of the bed was cold.

More sounds were coming from below, scraping sounds followed by loud thumps that the perpetrator made no attempt to conceal. Suddenly alert I reached into the cabinet next to my side of the bed to pull out the small tin where I'd placed the cellar key and knew before I'd opened it that the key was no longer in my possession.

'Casey!' I shouted her name as I leaped from the bed, headed across the room and out through the door into the dark hallway, where I stood motionless, listening.

Minimal moonlight shone through the small window at the far end of the hallway and to the left of the window the wooden stairway led down to the living area of the house and below this level, the cellar.

The loud clomping footsteps came from the solid wood stairs just to the left of the hallway, moments away from reaching the landing on which I was standing and I froze where I stood, my eyes wide as I desperately tried to see into the gloom.

Two figures emerged from the stairway and into the hallway, their features silhouetted by the moonlight coming in from the window behind them. Side by side, as though each supported the other, they slowly ambled towards me.

'Casey, is that you?' I spoke into the darkness as I scrambled for the light switch.

'Of course it's me.'

I felt relief to hear Casey's voice but there was something wrong, she sounded strangely excited. I flicked the switch and light filled the hallway. Casey and Mary walked slowly towards me and although Casey held on to the other in support, Mary's legs moved unaided as she took slow steps towards me.

'What the hell ...' My head swam with confusion, was this some kind of joke?

'Look, Larry, look what Mary can do,' Casey said, her voice betraying the pride she felt.

I looked from Mary's legs to her face. Those eyes looked directly into my face and there was life in those eyes and something more ... anger ... *hatred*.

I wanted to back away, to shut myself in our bedroom but found I couldn't move. While Mary's legs had found life mine it seemed would no longer respond.

Mary's footsteps quickened, each step resounding upon the wooden floor as she stepped ahead of Casey and began to raise her arms in her eagerness to reach me.

Dancer in the Dark
by Scarlett Blue

I looked the client in the eyes and he was entranced immediately. Some are easier than others, and sexual excitement leaves all the channels open and lets me get in straight away. Luckily for me this is an area I excel in.

'You had too much to drink tonight, you don't remember much, but you'll feel fine tomorrow. You'll buy your girlfriend some flowers and take her out somewhere nice. And throw that shirt away, it really doesn't do much for you.'

I rubbed the puncture marks on his neck as I spoke, holding his gaze as they closed up. There would still be a mark, but nothing too noticeable. I dropped the eye contact and licked the last drops of blood from around his collar, and, stepping back from him, picked my knickers up off the floor and started to get dressed.

He stammered, no longer under a supernatural trance but still under the powerful hold that all women have over men.

'Can I have another dance?'

'Of course, baby.' I lifted my leg on to his thigh, digging my glass heel into his flesh and proffering my garter. He knotted a twenty into the black elastic, lingering his touch on my leg as he did so, and staring at my barely covered pussy under the skimpy mesh.

I lifted his chin and looked into his eyes again.

'I think I'm worth a bit more than that, don't you?'

He smiled. It was almost natural, almost as if he really wanted to empty his wallet and give me just over a hundred pounds for three minutes work.

I kicked his legs apart and started to grind. As if by magic a heavy rock song came on. And of course it was magic. Did I mention I've got the DJ under control without even having to look at her? Even for a human she's exceptionally weak willed. Submissive. Enjoys being dominated. I only have to think her name, Chantal, and she's mine.

The client's eyes roved over me as I peeled off my bra again, and pushed my breasts in his face. I straddled him and pushed my pussy against his crotch, feeling his cock pressing against his jeans in the futile hope that it might get inside me. I pulled at his shirt and scratched his chest, but avoided drawing blood. It was 5 a.m. dawn was coming and if I ate too much I'd get sleepy before my shift was over.

I stood up and backed away from the client, leaving him bereft with a moan of longing as the physical contact ended, which turned into a moan of pleasure as the visual gorging started. I rubbed my breasts, and turned around, spreading my legs. I bent over, in no hurry, and pulled the skimpy thong aside, slipping a finger inside my pussy. He leaned and tried to lick me and I looked over my shoulder and hissed, showing my fangs. He backed off. It was reckless of me but he was so intoxicated he wouldn't remember anyway. Humans are fucked up.

I pulled my knickers down and faced him, throwing my foot over his head, my pussy inches from his face. Boring play things they are but their admiration does something to me and I felt pangs of the other hunger. Not with him, though. The song ended and he asked for more but I was bored. I looked deep again.

'You really want to go home now. And remember to take your girlfriend out tomorrow.'

He left. Happy, penniless, and rather stupid. I walked into

the main club, garishly bright after being in the private dance room. The Barbie dolls were all still hard at work trying to squeeze the last few notes out of the wallets of the drunk, the desolate, and the dirty. A man in the corner locked on to me straight away. I do stand out a bit, being pale, obviously, with dark hair in a sea of blonde and tan and little neon outfits. I'm not the only vampire in this club, but I'm the only one who looks like one. Black, PVC, lace, tattoos; why mess with a stereotype when it looks so good?

I caught his gaze and my thoughts drowned out the music.

Come with me.

He stood and walked towards me. Six foot six, broad shouldered, stubbly and rough, he looked like supper and a dirty fuck all rolled into one. I like to leave them with some memory of sex with me, just so no mortal will ever measure up. Cruel, possibly, but for so many men I'm the best they've ever had, and who could resist that accolade? And this one looked like he could be the best *I'd* ever had. I caught his scent as he followed me into the private room and pulled the tasselled curtain across. Musky and masculine, coupled with an unhurried and confident way of moving. My teeth and nails tingled, and I was getting wet. I wanted to hurt him, to feed on him, eat him, and have him inside me. I felt greedy, and slightly out of control. I knew I had to be careful, as any screams – mine or his – would have security in here, and I'd have to wipe several memories at once, which can get tricky.

The man sat himself on the couch, confident to the point of cocky, and handed me a fifty. I pushed it away and climbed on his lap, slightly faster than I meant to but still within the realms of human movement. He was hard but somehow didn't have that urgent air about him that men with an erection usually have. His hands strayed to my legs, and up, on to my back, pulling me to him. I don't usually go for this touchy stuff, but his hands were strong and

100

overpowering. He pulled off my bra and I was so hot for him, his hands running over my breasts, then up and into my hair, pulling me close.

I pushed his head back and sought his vein, licking to start with, then nicking his skin just slightly, testing him. It tasted of a memory I had pushed down so deep, of my own transformation. If my blood hadn't already been cold, it would have run cold at tasting that.

Before I knew what was happening he was out of his seat. I was flung onto the couch, face down, him holding me easily, and for the first time in a hundred years, I felt vulnerable. And bittersweet it was. My initial rage at being manhandled gave way to an old feeling, one lost for so long – that of being a woman in the arms of a man. But it was fleeting, and with all my energy I fought him, and we flew backwards through both sets of curtains into another booth. I landed on top of him.

'What the fuck are you?'

He smiled, and kissed me on the mouth. It was heavenly, if I can be permitted to use such a word.

'Wouldn't you like to know?'

And with that I was in his clutches completely. He moved faster and stronger than a human but he was too warm for a vampire and he was definitely pulsing. As he tore at my clothes his blood ran stronger, throbbing at his wrists and neck.

My hands slipped inside his clothes. If anything he was even warmer than a normal person. And definitely harder.

I was bent forwards over the couch and he pulled my legs apart. He tore the flimsy lap dancer underwear away as if it were nothing, and started licking my pussy from behind. He was hungry, gripping at my legs and pulling me wider. In one motion he was off his knees and entered me roughly, making me scream out. His thrusts were lightning fast, his hands gripping handfuls of my hair, and I came hard and wet and so did he.

We sprawled forward, tangled, onto the couch, and for a split second, there was that feeling again; feminine, protected. I pushed it away and looked into his eyes and held his thoughts in my gaze.

Tell me what you are.

'That won't work on me either.'

Well, this was new. I briefly considered the dangers of tangling with unknown, incredibly strong and totally irresistible supernatural creatures at 5 a.m. on a Sunday when I should have been getting to sleep, but, well, irresistible is the key word in that sentence.

'So, I take it you drink?' I asked him, showing just a glimmer of the tips of my fangs.

'I thought you'd never ask.'

I moved at vampire speed to gather up my stuff in the changing room. A couple of girls emerged from sharing a joint in the toilet cubicle, and though I was moving too fast for them to see, they felt the draughts and heard the scuffles, and commenced a fervoured discussion about the poltergeist that supposedly haunts the club. I really should be more careful.

The club was almost deserted, save for a couple of regulars and tables full of girls counting their money. As I passed the DJ booth I looked at Chantal, and she knew she was to follow me. It was cold and frosty outside and the multi story car park was deserted, apart from him sitting on the bonnet of my black Audi.

I blipped the central locking and hissed at him.

'Don't sit on the car.'

He smirked at me, climbing into the passenger seat. Of course, with the range of vehicles I've had over the years I'm an excellent driver, and we screeched down the levels. Chantal was shivering in a cheap fur coat at the pedestrian entrance, and walked towards the car with a blank expression. She climbed in the back and I switched the heated seats on for her. I'm not a complete sadist.

Without any human struggling or fussing, he slipped into the back seat and enveloped Chantal. His hand went up her skirt and her head went back. I pulled on to the motorway and adjusted the rearview mirror. I could still see the marks on her neck from last night. He was licking them, and her legs opened wider. He pulled her knickers off with one hand and started fingering her pussy, his fingers circling over her clit, and I squirmed in the driver's seat. I fed off her so often we were sort of connected. His hands moved to her breasts and pulled down her dress and bra. She looked perfect, with her little dress bunched around her waist, her tits bare apart from the edges of her furry coat which was falling away from her shoulders, her woolly winter socks, her legs open and her pussy on show. He had her in a total frenzy, thrusting against his hand, pulling him closer.

Then his fangs appeared. He pushed two fingers inside her as he bit down on her throat. It was so smooth, she arched her back, gushing onto his hand and letting her head fall away to allow him to feed. My knickers, what little there was of them, were soaked.

I pulled up outside my building. The sun was coming up but it wasn't so bad in winter. Steps led down to my basement flat, chosen for its ability to block out most of the light. I walked ahead and the man – or whatever he was – carried Chantal in his arms, her clothes still hanging off. A taxi dropped off a group of young men a couple of doors down and they had a good look at her, hot and young, naked in all the right places, lolling unselfconsciously in his arms.

In spite of my intense arousal, the daylight was starting to get the better of me.

'So, when do you sleep?' I asked him.

'Whenever I like.'

He carried Chantal through to the bedroom.

The coffin thing is bullshit. I can sleep anywhere during the day as long as there is no natural light creeping in. My bedroom has no windows, and the heavy black velvet

103

curtain over the door sees to any sneaky rays from other parts of the flat. I lit a candle and started to undress. It was probably the fiftieth time that night I'd taken my clothes off, but this time I moved naturally. Chantal was on the bed and he removed what was left of her clothes before starting on his own. I got my first proper look at this strange and beautiful creature as he stripped to his underwear in the flickery dim light. He was fair skinned, but not vampire pale, and very muscular.

He lay down next to Chantal and I could see a firm bulge appearing in his boxers.

'A little nightcap, perhaps?' he asked, pulling back her hair to expose the untouched side of her neck. She moaned, leaning in to his touch. In all these years she is one of the most sensual, willing, beautiful victims I have ever encountered.

I straddled the girl, and we smiled at each other. There was a fine line between where my magic ended and her masochism began. I kissed her collar bones and he bent over me, kissing my back. I could feel his erection pressing against me and I pushed back onto him, inviting him in. Chantal squirmed under me. She wanted some as well. He read the signs and moved back, and his head was between her legs, and mine. Our pussies were on top of each other, and he licked from one to the other. I nicked her skin and the blood burst forth, warm and full of love. She was almost laughing with pleasure. I knew how to make a nice clean cut, and as he licked her to a climax her heart beat faster and I fed harder to keep up. My own orgasm built up as I filled up on blood, and it spilled down my face as my juices spilled down his.

He wanted to fuck me again but the day was sapping my energy. I told him to wait until nightfall for me, but Chantal opened her legs like the little slave she was, and the last thing I remember before falling asleep was him on top of her, and her expression of complete abandon as he fucked her, vampire speed.

It gets dark early in winter, more time to play. I woke with a start, completely alert. He was up, moving around. Hot as he was, I didn't trust him. I put on a kimono. Strange habit really. I'm a professional stripper and an almost emotionless vampire; I was alone in a flat with two people I'd had very messy, noisy sex with; and of course I don't feel the cold, but I still adhered to the convention of putting on a robe. Some human stuff is hard to shake.

He was wearing just his trousers, a very good look for one with a torso like his, and was drinking coffee. Just when I thought I had him figured out.

'I had your girl prepare you breakfast,' he handed me a wine glass full of blood. 'She's taking a shower.'

I took the glass. 'Cut the shit. You drank from her, and now you're drinking coffee? I'd be down for a week if I touched coffee. What are you?'

He smiled. Chantal walked out of the bathroom in a little towel.

'Well?'

She was looking from me to him and back again, completely oblivious to what was actually going on.

'Drink,' he said. 'Then, I think you'll remember, I'm on a promise.'

He headed for the bedroom. What could I do? I knocked back the blood Chantal had shed for me before her morning shower. I could feel her pulse as it coursed through me, and the memories flooded back of last night in the club, in the car, in bed.

I followed him.

He wrapped me in his arms and kissed me deeply. I tried to stay focused, to concentrate on analysing what it was that was so different. Human men I liked, but they were a means to an end. Other vampires, while a rare treat, were cold, unfeeling. My body always responded but my emotions never did, but with him I was feeling almost human myself.

105

I pulled away.

'If you don't want me I know someone who does.'

He gestured towards the door where Chantal stood, the towel on the floor at her feet, leaning against the door frame with her hand wantonly between her legs and her wet hair hanging in her face. I could hear her heart throbbing, and his, and the rhythms were briefly in synch, but gradually moved apart until it was like one deafeningly fast beat.

I gave in, vowing just one more time before I put my mind to finding out what he was all about. His hands squeezed my flesh and he pulled open the kimono, biting my breasts with his blunt teeth. Without preamble he unzipped his trousers and pushed inside me. Chantal sank to the floor, her legs wide open, rubbing her pussy and breathing loud and fast as she watched us.

My orgasm was approaching as his body rubbed against me with every thrust. Revelling in the feelings I rolled my head back on the pillow. His fangs snapped to life and before I knew what was happening, my vein was open for the first time since I was made vampire. I screamed, hissed and thrashed, but he was too strong, then an intense feeling of peace and acceptance flowed over me, followed by wave after wave of orgasm.

I don't know if I slept, but it was a few minutes before I could speak. Just when you think you know it all, something like this goes and happens. Chantal wandered over, carrying her handcuffs.

'Please …' she said, glancing towards the shackles on the wall.

'So she does speak!'

'Yeah,' I smiled. 'When she wants something. Would you mind? I'm not sure I'm ready to move after that. And don't think you're getting away without explaining now!'

He took Chantal's hand and led her to the wall where she willingly let him tie her, hands up above her head, and legs wide open. She wiggled around as he headed back for the bed, shaking the chains, trying to entice him back.

'She is a fuckable little thing isn't she, and so well behaved. Congratulations on finding such a lovely pet. Come and drink and I'll tell you everything.'

We sat in front of her, and took a femoral artery each, sucking the blood from her thighs. He rubbed her bare pussy gently to keep her calm as we fed.

'I'm a half breed. My father was vampire, my mother was, is, human. I've never met him. He was a real Lestat by the sounds of it. Flew in the bedroom window and overpowered her, that kind of deal.' We both laughed. 'I eat and drink like a human most of the time, but if I drink blood I get vampire strength for a few days.'

'Right,' this was making a lot more sense now. I couldn't believe I hadn't managed to figure it out. 'So how old are you?'

'I'm 50 something, but my body is that of a 30 year old. I do age, you see, but a bit more slowly than a human. The more blood I drink, the slower I age. When I was younger and first got the thirst I was totally disgusted by the whole thing, so I aged like normal. But now I'm a bit more, I don't know … liberal.'

Chantal moaned as he slipped a finger inside, curling it forwards, while licking up a trickle of blood on her leg.

'And … if I drink vampire blood, the ageing slows down even more. If I drank from you every night I could live as long as you will.'

I took a long drink from Chantal's thigh, then opened my legs, exposing my cool naked body and the juicy vein at my own thigh.

'Well, so long as if I've got her around to keep my strength up, I think that can be arranged.'

The Call of the Night
by Tabitha Rayne

Leah shivered as the warm liquid trickled down her inner thigh. She breathed in, smiling to herself as she pressed a finger into the tender wounds. She looked at the stain spreading over her tattered skirt and pressed harder, hoping to summon the fear and euphoria of only a few hours ago.

Leah watched the chill of the night rise from the earth in a fine mist as the first rays of daylight flitted through the branches. Only hours ago she had been innocent. Unworldly – no, un-otherworldly. She wondered whether she should mourn the passing of this innocence but felt the sublime trickle of blood lick its way down her flesh once more. No, she was glad she had been initiated into this night time world. She felt tired but knew she must make the most of the sun for soon, she would be like Maudra.

Leah had taken a late stroll to shake off the annoyance of having to move back in with her parents after a job and relationship had soured leaving her homeless, heartbroken and penniless. It had been OK, her parents were honeys, but she was a woman with her own ambitions and wants. Very big wants. Very noisy wants.

Dusk fell as she walked up the path to the woods just outside town. She didn't notice a dark-haired woman watching her from behind an old tree. Leah was immersed in her own thoughts when a cloaked figure suddenly appeared right in front of her.

'Sorry?' Leah cocked her head towards the tall, dark-haired woman. 'What did you say?' Leah was stunned when the face remained as still as glass but a voice spoke.

'I didn't say anything. Hush now, there's no need to speak.' The voice was as rich as velvet but as sheer as silk. It took Leah's breath away and she obeyed and fell silent. Leah stared into the woman and was mesmerised by her wolf-like piercing eyes. She felt compelled to touch her and reached out a trembling hand.

'Not now.' The voice seemed to slap Leah's hand away. 'Come.'

Leah was in a strange state, she couldn't think if she was dreaming or drugged but she knew that this beautiful and fearful creature had her under some sort of spell. She followed willingly, a heat rising in her lower belly counteracting the chill of the voice. The warmth spread as she felt a hand pressing in to her lower back urging her forward. She gasped and glanced behind her but nothing was there. The hooded woman never looked back.

'Keep up,' said the voice and the hand pressed more firmly. Leah thought she felt it slide lower and a flush of desire welled in her stomach. She let out a tiny murmur.

'I said quiet!' snapped the voice once more and the sensation of a second hand clamped over Leah's lips. She breathed dramatically through her nose and kept her hands by her sides. She knew now that she would have to surrender to this being and it turned her on furiously. She pressed her thighs together as she walked trying to catch the fabric of her skirt between to give her some kind of friction. The ground was getting rocky as they made their way through the thickening trees and darkness and she tripped to the ground, grazing her knees on the gravelly path. As she struggled to get up, the hand at her back slid down and pushed on her buttocks until she was upright once more. It stayed there and Leah felt her arousal blaze as the fingers massaged her arse cheeks while she walked. She arched her back a little and exaggerated her swagger to show the hands she was enjoying it.

To her joy, the fingers began to knead her buttocks, squeezing her panties and skirt into her flesh. It was exhilarating and Leah shifted her gait to open her legs. The force kept rubbing and pressing and Leah's pussy began to twitch in anticipation for a stray finger or two.

As the thought formed in her mind, the cloaked woman looked round with a wicked smile. The pressure of the hand on her mouth intensified and Leah tried to bite at it through her squashed lips. At once the figure flew at her and she was thrown backwards to a tree. She felt a chill to her soul as the woman pressed right up against her.

'Behave,' the voice hissed, 'all in good time.' But Leah caught the woman's eyes flit to her chest. She breathed in to push her breasts higher forcing her stiffening nipples into her captor's view.

It worked. Leah watched the wolf eyes drink her in. She felt the presence of another phantom hand rip her blouse open and tug her breast free from her bra. She watched her own nipple harden as it was rolled and tweaked by invisible fingers while the woman watched.

Leah began to sense a shift in power and opened her legs. The hand that had been working on her arse worked its way down the back of her leg to the hem of her skirt. Her skirt slowly slid up over her thighs and behind like a gentle lover would. Just as she was getting used to these tender caresses, the hand over her mouth released her long enough for Leah to catch her breath. She gulped in oxygen and let out an excited giggle. The hand gripped her at once under her jaw and pinned her by the neck to the tree. Leah's own hands shot up to try and prise the digits apart but the strength was supernatural. She held on and suddenly the hand up under her skirt roughly grabbed her panties and ripped them off casting them to the ground. Leah felt hot and horny and opened her legs wider to expose her naked pussy to the night. It had the right effect and Leah stared at the woman staring at her.

'What's your name?' she whispered as seductively as she could. She felt the warmth from her breath reach out to the white face of the woman and she seemed to suck in the vapour of the words.

'Maudra.' This time her eyes met Leah's.

'Show yourself to me.' Leah was shocked by her own boldness and even more so when she saw Maudra's delicate ethereal fingers toy with the golden catch of her cape.

The hand between Leah's legs slowly and lusciously began to stroke and part her lips. Leah could imagine her moist juices glistening in the moonlight and it made her ache to be touched.

Maudra's cape fell to the earth and there stood the most beautiful sight Leah had ever witnessed. Maudra's flesh was as pale and luminous as moonlight itself and she was as poised as a ballerina. Her breasts were perfect and Leah's mouth watered as she watched the tiny buds pucker, desperate to be touched. Leah felt the fingers at her pussy slowly begin to probe into her entrance. She began to twitch as her want started to pulse through her clit and engulf her pussy and arse. 'Stroke yourself,' she commanded and her eyes widened as Maudra slid her hands onto her abdomen and up, cupping both breasts and squeezing her nipples. Leah mirrored her movements and was soon massaging her own tits along with the hands. It felt sublime to be clasping and unclasping and massaging what felt like a thousand fingers. Suddenly a hard shaft shoved deep into her. Her legs wobbled and she staggered a little but the hand around her neck held her fast. Her pussy walls bucked and twitched as the phantom hand thrust in and out again and again.

'Harder!' Leah shrieked as she felt her juices engulf the fingers and spill out onto her thighs. She put her own fingers to her lips and sucked on them to get them good and wet

111

before diving them down into the cleft of her pussy onto her clit. The fingers seemed to be expanding and filling her more deeply than she'd ever been penetrated before. Maudra was watching everything licking her lips and exposing her teeth. Leah felt the rush well deep inside her cunt and closed her eyes to concentrate on her rising want.

'Stop!' the icy voice commanded. All motion ceased and Leah stood panting and frustrated still pinned to the tree and impaled on the hand. She could have wept and tried to grind the satisfaction she craved from the fingers that were still deep inside her.

'I said, be still!' Maudra's eyes had turned black and sinister and Leah felt all the life drain from the air around her. The world was engulfed in stillness and silence as Maudra stood with her arms aloft. Leah's heart raced and all the hairs on her body stood on end. She watched as Maudra sank exquisitely to her knees before her, moonlight striking her perfect skin. Maudra flicked her long hair over her back and looked up at Leah. Leah began to shake as she watched the darkness in her eyes grow in intensity. 'Now for the main event.'

Leah held her breath as she heard a wicked laugh emanate from the surrounding forest. She was terrified but completely and utterly turned on. She clenched the hand tight within her pussy and waited for what was to come. Maudra began to smile, slowly and carefully exposing her eye teeth. They were sharp and piercing and Leah went limp at the sight. Maudra placed her hands between Leah's thighs and pushed them apart even further. 'Mmmm, you've done well, my darlings.'

Leah knew she was talking to the ghostly hands and knew now that she had never been in control. Maudra smoothed out the skin on Leah's right inner thigh, stroking and caressing it with long black fingernails. Leah shivered feeling the hand inside her begin to pulse and grow again.

She let out a low groan from deep in her throat as Maudra

flashed her one last smile and sank her teeth into Leah's flesh. Leah tried to struggle but the fight left her as a feeling of utter sublimity took over her being. The blood and warmth drained from her body, but was replaced with a surging dark desire. The deepest and most terrifying arousal overtook her and the thrusting in her cunt matched the suckling at her thigh.

Harder and harder Maudra drank and Leah lashed her fingers into her hair and pulled her deeper and deeper into her giving herself to this dark creature of the night. Again and again the hand fucked her and she felt her life drain out of her and her come rose and crashed over them both in a pulsing shrieking crescendo.

Maudra pulled out of Leah and let her head fall back on to her shoulders, blood smearing her lips and dripping on to her pale, pale chest. The hands left her too. She wiped her face with the back of her arm and rose up to face Leah. Leah grasped her by her hair and violently pulled her to her lips. She kissed the mouth of the vampire that had almost taken her life and sucked greedily on her tongue and lips. She traced the sharp spikes of her suckling teeth and winced as she felt them slice into her probing tongue. Leah tasted the tingling iron of her own blood on Maudra and it turned her on once more. She reached down roughly and dove her hand between Maudra's legs.

Maudra staggered as Leah quickly found her target and roughly shoved three fingers deep into the vampire's hot wet cunt. Maudra pulled away from Leah's kisses and threw her head back. Leah kissed and nibbled and bit at her neck, ravenous for her flesh. She stooped down and began licking and nibbling between Maudra's succulent pussy lips. She tasted of wickedness and blood and Leah was hungry for her. She thrust her tongue and fingers harder into the vampire again and again until she felt the surge come and engulf her in heat and liquid. Maudra collapsed to the earth and wrapped herself back up into her cape.

113

'How can I be like you?' asked Leah when they'd got their breath back.

'You can't be like me.'

Leah thought Maudra looked sad, but it was fleeting. 'There's no one like me.' She smiled wickedly. 'But you have changed. You are not an innocent any more.'

'Can I come back?'

'Yes.' Leah looked to the horizon where the eerie blue of morning hinted over the night. When she looked back, Maudra was gone. She tucked her blouse back in to her skirt and tried her best to smooth down the tatty fabric.

She lifted her face to the rising sun and with her breath misting in the morning air, began to walk home.

House of Seven Inches
by Michael Bracken

The real estate listing said "fixer-upper" but the two-storey house looked more like a "burner-downer". It had been empty for years and was located just south of the middle of nowhere, but I bought it anyway.

My first call was to a plumber, intending to follow it with calls to an electrician and a roofer after I received the plumber's estimate. The plumber and I were standing in the kitchen when he said, 'The last owner was one of your kind.'

I turned and glared at the weathered old man. He was my grandfather's age and smelled of cheap tobacco and cheaper beer. 'And what kind is that?'

He held up one arm and let his wrist go limp. 'You know.'

'And what happened to him?'

'He …' The plumber stopped and looked like he was searching for the right word. Finally, he said, '… disappeared.'

'You mean he moved away?'

The old man shrugged. 'One day he was here. The next day he wasn't. After he missed a couple of payments and his phone was disconnected, the bank sent a man out to look the place over. A couple of months after that the bank repossessed and put the contents of the house up for auction. I got the missus a real nice set of china.'

'He just walked away?'

'Your guess is as good as any,' the plumber said. 'Sheriff Johnson looked the place over, said there were no signs of foul play, but the previous owner ain't turned up and he ain't come back.'

I looked around, not certain what I expected to see that was any different than what I'd already seen. The kitchen was in no better shape than the rest of the house, and it needed serious renovation before I would ever feel comfortable.

The plumber patted the front pocket of his blue work shirt where he'd put the notebook he'd used while I'd explained all the work I wanted done, and said, 'I'll do some figuring tonight and drop my estimate by tomorrow.'

I walked him to the front door and stood on the porch watching his pickup until it disappeared around a curve in the road. Then I returned to the kitchen and used half a can of air freshener to eliminate the man's lingering scent.

For the next several months I had men in and out of my house, some of them quite attractive but none of them approachable. They replaced the roof and the windows, rewired and replumbed where necessary, and remodelled the kitchen and both bathrooms to my specifications. I replastered the walls and refinished the hardwood floors myself. Soon there was nothing left to do but paint, furnish, and decorate, all things I could do on my own, and I soon realised just how isolated my new house was.

I had sold my condo in the city shortly before the housing market cratered, and I was among the first wave of employees to accept my employer's buyout offer, getting out while the going was good. Most of my money was invested in things that weren't badly hurt by the stock market plunge, so I could survive comfortably for several years without additional income. I had hoped to return to my first love – writing – and thought I needed solitude to write the novel that had been nagging at me for several years. What I most assuredly did not need was the drama Kyle brought into my life, so I had left him behind when I moved, certain that he would quickly become someone else's drama queen.

Even so, it was difficult to forget Kyle completely. When he wasn't talking, he had the sweetest mouth I'd ever stuck my dick into. I was thinking about that one evening in the shower, after a long day spent painting. The warm water relaxed me, I had a handful of liquid soap, an erection I could have used to pound nails, and I hadn't been with a man since moving to the country several months earlier.

I knew what I had to do and I did it. I closed my eyes and took my cock in my hand, remembering the last time Kyle had been on his knees in front of me. We'd spent the evening at *Throttlebottom's*, a dark little bar where most of our friends hung out, and we'd returned to my apartment a little more toasted than usual. As soon as I pushed the door closed, I pushed Kyle back against it. I covered his lips with mine and then drove my tongue into his mouth. He sucked on it and sucked hard. He was just as horny as me and we stripped off our clothes, tossing them aside until we were both naked.

With my hands on his softly rounded shoulders, I encouraged Kyle to his knees. He kissed his way down my chest to my belly button, found my treasure trail, and followed it to my neatly sculpted nest of black hair. He cupped my balls in one hand and wrapped the other around my cock shaft. Then he took my swollen purple cockhead in his mouth and painted it with his tongue.

He was taking too long, so I grabbed the back of his head and thrust my hips forward, sinking my cock into Kyle's mouth until I could feel his warm, boozy breath tickle my crotch hair. Then I pulled back and thrust forward again.

My hips began moving with the memory, fucking my fist as I remembered fucking Kyle's face. Faster and faster, unable to restrain myself.

Then my breath caught, my entire body stiffened for the briefest of moments, and I spewed come all over the shower wall. Unable to catch my breath immediately, I leaned against the newly installed tiles and let the warm water cascade over my body until I could finish bathing.

When I stepped out of the shower a few minutes later I caught the unmistakable scent of Old Spice, reminding me first of my stepfather and then of my scout master, neither of whom had understood me but both of whom had encouraged me not to hide behind a societally imposed facade. I smiled.

Then I realised someone had been watching me shower. I wrapped a towel around my waist and called out, 'Who's there?'

When I received no response, I hurried through the house, checking every room for evidence that someone was in the house with me. There weren't many places to hide – I'd finished painting but had not yet furnished most of the rooms. I looked under my bed, opened all the closets, and even looked inside the dryer. I also checked every door and every window and found them all locked from the inside.

Although I was still bothered by the feeling that I'd been watched, I returned to the bathroom to finish pampering myself. By then the scent of Old Spice had disappeared, replaced by the floral scent of my body wash and the barely perceptible odour of my own come. I shaved, I tweezed, and I moisturized, not letting my personal grooming falter despite my dating drought.

Then I tucked myself into bed with a thick paperback and read until I was too tired to keep my eyes open. I fell asleep with the hall light on, just in case.

By the time my living room furniture was delivered two weeks later, I'd forgotten about the creepy feeling I'd had that night. With more furniture in the house it felt more like a home and I felt more comfortable in it. At that point I still lacked furniture for the office, so I had half a sheet of plywood resting on two sawhorses to hold my laptop computer and my printer, and I sat on a three-step aluminium stepladder. The novel was going nowhere – I'd written the first page a dozen times – but I wasn't deterred. I knew I would start my real work once I finished work on the house.

Late one afternoon I sat at my makeshift desk, a number two pencil in my hand and a yellow legal pad in front of me, stared out the window at the back yard, a vast tract of untended grass and overgrown shrubs that desperately needed my attention, and pondered the umpteenth rewrite of my first page. My mind drifted, first to the job I'd left behind in the city and then to Kyle. It had been months since I been with another man and several days since I'd handled the problem myself.

As I thought about Kyle – about his golden, shoulder-length hair, his pale blue eyes, and his full lips – my cock began to react, causing my pants to tighten at my crotch. I adjusted myself with my free hand.

I was surprised when I caught a whiff of Old Spice and felt a moist pair of lips on the nape of my neck. I spun around quickly, knocking my legal pad to the floor.

There was no one behind me. I was alone in my office.

After I retrieved my legal pad and returned it to my makeshift desk, I wiped my fingers against my neck. They came away damp. I considered my fingertips for a moment before convincing myself that I had been sweating and that what I had actually felt was a trickle of sweat rolling down my neck. My daydreaming about Kyle had made me imagine something else.

I pushed myself away from my desk and left my office. I knew I was alone but I checked every room just in case. I found no one else in the house and nothing out of place. I grabbed a beer from the fridge and stepped out on the back porch to drink it. My back yard looked even worse from downstairs than it did from my second floor office, and I knew I would need to tend to it soon.

I drove into town two days later and made my first stop the town's only hardware store. I selected a variety of tools to help me deal with the overgrown yard, and was staring at a display of hoes when I heard a voice behind me.

'You the one that bought the Samuels' place?'

I turned to find a weathered old man leaning on an aluminium walker. He made my plumber look like a youngster.

'Yeah,' I said. 'I am.'

'Heard you been fixing up the place.'

'I'm doing what I can.'

'Don't get too attached.' He coughed into his fist.

'Why's that?'

'You won't be there long,' he said.

I looked a question at him.

'Your kind don't stay around here.'

'My kind?'

'City folk.' He coughed into his fist again. 'You and your city ways. You all want something you can't find around here.'

'I'll be fine.'

'That's what the last guy said. But he didn't last long.'

The old man glared at me and I glared back. He blinked first and then shuffled away without further comment.

I took my selections to the front counter where an acne-scarred teenager rang up my charges. After I paid him, he said, 'Sheriff Johnson bothering you?'

I glanced toward the rear of the store but the weathered old man and his aluminium walker were out of sight. 'That was the sheriff?'

'He used to be, years ago,' the kid said. 'My dad says that back in the day Johnson ran the town with an iron fist. He still thinks he does, but most people ignore him.'

I attacked the front yard first, collapsing into bed each evening with sore muscles and a sense of satisfaction. Nearly two weeks after my conversation with Sheriff Johnson, after I had finished with the front yard and planned to begin work on the back, I caught a glimpse of myself in the full-length mirror mounted on the back of my bedroom door. I was in the process of stripping off my clothes and I stopped to examine myself. All the hard work on the house and the yard had changed me.

Where once I had been soft in the middle, with no noticeable muscle definition, I had developed the kind of body I had once admired on others and I was especially pleased that I sported a taut abdomen with clear signs of a developing six-pack. Hard physical labour had done for my body what years of gym membership had not. Kyle would be surprised by the change, as would my other friends, but I had no desire to return to the city, even to gloat.

After I shoved my dirty clothes in the hamper, I showered, pampered myself, and crawled into bed. I no longer slept with the hall light on, and the room was nearly black. The little bit of moonlight that usually filtered in through a gap in the drapes was hidden behind storm clouds that had been threatening to break loose all evening.

I was almost asleep when I felt weight on the bed behind me and caught the scent of Old Spice. My eyes snapped open. I knew there would be no one in bed with me if I rolled over, just like I knew there was no one else in the house. I wasn't about to climb out of bed and tromp through all the rooms to prove it. I closed my eyes.

The weight shifted and I opened my eyes again. I felt a hand on my left hip under the covers and still I didn't roll over. The weight shifted again and I felt someone press against my back. Warm lips brushed my neck. A thick erection that must have been seven inches long nestled in the crack of my arse. The hand on my hip slid down to my crotch and cupped my balls. My cock began to swell.

Nearly a year had passed since I'd been with another man and occasionally taking matters in my own hands had done nothing to relieve my sexual frustration. I squeezed my eyes shut and convinced myself that I was having a particularly tactile dream.

The hand cupping my balls moved to my cock and I felt thick fingers make a fist around my rapidly stiffening shaft. The fist gripped my cock firmly and then moved up my shaft, stopping when the encircling thumb and forefinger reached my spongy soft helmet head. Then it moved down until the heel of the hand pressed against my pubic bone. The fist continued moving up and down, slowly at first and then with increasing speed.

As I was being fist-fucked, I felt a pair of lips travel around the back of my neck, gently at first, and then with increasing urgency. More than once I felt teeth nip at my neck. My breath began to come in little gasps as my orgasm drew closer and closer. Then, unable to restrain myself, I caught my breath and held it as I fired warm spunk all over my sheets.

Before I could catch my breath, the weight shifted behind me, and the hand holding my spasming cock released its grip. The hand moved between my thighs and encouraged me to lift my left leg. When I did, I felt the cock nestled between my butt cheeks slide down until the cockhead pressed against the tight sphincter of my arse. My entire body was relaxed following my orgasm, and the cockhead slipped into me with minimal resistance. Then, with one powerful thrust, the entire cock was buried deep within me.

Hips pulled back and pushed forward, the unseen cock driving into me hard and fast, and I pushed backward to accept every powerful thrust. Kyle had never fucked me like this, had never taken me in the middle of the night and had his way with me, and I moaned with unrestrained pleasure.

Lightning flashed outside, illuminating the entire

bedroom through a thin crack in the drapes. For a split second I saw my reflection in the mirror mounted on the back of the bedroom door and I saw the covers bunched up as if two people were in the bed.

And then, with one last powerful thrust that buried the unseen cock deeper inside me than ever before, the cock stopped moving. I thought I heard a man moan with pleasure, and I felt a rush of warm air against my ear. But, at that same moment, thunder rolled across the night sky, completely obliterating any other sounds I might have thought I heard.

Then the storm clouds opened up and rain pelted the house. I felt asleep listening to the rain, convinced that someone was spooning me from behind, yet knowing full well that the only thing behind me was my imagination.

A few days later I discovered an old well on the property. It was little more than a hole in the ground, the low rock wall encircling the hole mostly collapsed, the boards covering the hole rotted away, and the entire thing covered by overgrown brush. I was tromping through the brush and would have fallen into the well if something hadn't stopped me at the last moment, something that felt like a hand pressing against my chest.

I didn't know who else to call, so I called the plumber and told him what had happened.

'You found the well, did you?'

'You knew about it?'

'Every house that old had its own well. Most of them are sealed to prevent accidents.'

'Do you know someone who can take care of it for me?'

'I'll send my nephew over tomorrow,' my plumber said. 'He's a licensed contractor. You'll like him.'

The plumber's nephew, a wiry man a few years younger than me, arrived early the next morning. My hair was still damp from the shower and I was nursing my first mug of coffee as we walked out to the well.

He aimed the beam of his flashlight into the hole and rubbed his chin. 'Before we can seal the well,' he explained as he looked me over in an overtly sexual way, a way that no other man had since I'd moved into the house, 'we have to clear out the debris that's fallen into it. I can call a couple of guys and get started on the job this morning.'

We haggled over price for a few minutes before I gave him the go-ahead. He snapped open his cell-phone as I headed into the house. I was hanging curtains in the dining room and didn't think anything about what was happening in my backyard until my plumber's nephew pounded on my back door.

'We got a problem,' he said when I joined him on the back porch. He touched my forearm with the tips of his fingers. 'There's a body down the well.'

My backyard became a crime scene and was soon overrun with sheriff's deputies and nosey townsfolk. The elected coroner wasn't a medical doctor – he was a funeral home director – so the remains were sent to Dallas for examination.

The remains were quickly identified as Nick Samuels – the house's previous owner – and Samuels was given a proper burial after an autopsy determined the cause of death. Samuels had been shot once in the back of the head and his body thrown in the well.

There's no statute of limitations for murder, so the new sheriff arrested the old sheriff and his aged cronies. In their day a jury of their peers might not have convicted the three men, but times had changed and more than half of the jury consisted of the type of people Sheriff Johnson and his cronies had worked to keep out of the county. The trial lasted a week and the jury deliberated less than an hour.

My testimony was minimal, confirming that I owned the

property and that I had discovered the well where the body was found. They never asked and I never mentioned the presence in my house all those months when I was renovating it.

Six months after the trial ended, after I had put the finishing touches to the house, I visited the cemetery and stood beside the previous owner's gave. As I told Samuels everything I had done to the house, I felt someone take my hand and I caught a hint of Old Spice wafting past me. I didn't glance to the side but kept my attention riveted on the headstone until I finished my tale.

As I finished, the hand holding mine squeezed tightly for a moment and then disappeared.

I returned home, grabbed a legal pad and a pencil and sat on the back porch.

I was finally alone in my house.

Maybe it was time to start the novel. Maybe it was time to call the plumber's nephew and find out if I had correctly interpreted his intentions.

Incubus at Your Service
by Maggie Morton

My friend, Lynne, had never gushed this much about something in her life. She'd been going on about this cleaning service she'd discovered for the last 15 minutes, and that had me rather surprised, as she was extremely un-effusive, especially for a woman. I knew to treasure whatever small compliments she gave me, because I probably wouldn't be hearing another one for ages.

'Oh, you just *have* to try them,' she continued her avalanche of compliments. 'They're the best.'

I was hoping it was just that she was a little sloshed, but my higher reasoning skills told me she'd only had half a beer, and we'd already eaten a large meal at a Mexican restaurant down the street from the bar.

'Here,' she said, opening her purse, and removing a business card. 'Trust me,' she said, then, 'Oops, look at the time, I've got to run. Love you, Nell!'

I picked up the card, read it: *'I & S Cleaning Services, to fit your **every** need.'* The cardstock it was printed on was a rich, dark burgundy, which for some reason made me think of bordellos and sex. God, Nell, you really need to get laid, I thought, then tucked the card into my purse and headed home.

That night, I dreamt of the most gorgeous man I'd ever seen. He had luscious, ebony hair which brushed his perfectly shaped shoulders – strong shoulders, the kind that would rest against you perfectly. He had a very seductive smile, richly pink lips that curved up in a promise of more, more, more! He had strong, sinewy arms, the kind that could hold you down for hours, the kind you'd *want* to hold you down for hours. He had a voice that rippled over your flesh, caressing all the best spots with each word. He had ... and then my alarm went off. Goddamn it! I flipped the covers off me, in a serious huff, and started grumbling to myself under my breath. I glanced around the disaster that was my bedroom, took in each and every pile of dirty clothes. God, what a disaster. I found the cleanest shirt and pants I could and started getting dressed for work. After I had pulled on some clothes, I stumbled into the kitchen. And then I screamed.

There was a man standing at my sink! Wearing only an apron! Washing dishes! Well, that third part wasn't the scary part, but seriously, what kind of psycho breaks into your apartment and washes your dishes while you sleep?

Was he trying to lull me into a false sense of calm? 'Oh, I'm going to wash all your dishes and make your apartment all pretty, and *then* I'll kill you!' Oh God. Oh *fucking* God.

I tried to catch my breath after my initial shock. There was no way I could fight off a man his size, with those broad shoulders and that perfect back and those buttocks that just made you want to spread them and tease his little – wait, what was I doing? I had to hide, I had to call the police, I had to ... and then he turned around, and I gasped. He was the man from my dream, identical in every single way.

'I've lost it. I've lost it, haven't I?' I muttered, turning my eyes downward. I barely heard him approaching, so his fingers on my chin surprised me a little. He tilted my head upwards, making eye contact with his lovely, full-lashed, emerald eyes, a huge improvement on my pale, dirt-brown ones.

'You have very pretty eyes,' he murmured, his voice rippling over my skin, stealing away every last ounce of fear and worry as I felt it find each place on my body that I most liked touched.

I shuddered, but in a very, very good way. 'Who ... who are you?'

'You wouldn't be able to pronounce my real name, so just call me Adrian.' He smiled at me, a smile that seemed full of things yet to come – and I do mean "come" because it was the most sexual smile I'd seen in my life.

'Where did you ... what ...?' Apparently words were still having a hard time getting from my brain to my mouth. Not only was he completely gorgeous, but I'd dreamed about him. This was all too weird. And too hot, my libido stupidly added. Yum.

'I'm from *I & S Cleaning Services*. I'm an, um, incubus.'

'Right, and I'm the Queen of England,' I said, eyes wide.

'I don't think she's ever felt the amount of pleasure an incubus could bring to a woman,' Adrian said, his words finding their way beyond my outer layers of skin and causing pleasure in places I hadn't even known I'd had until that point. 'Normally, our services just include cleaning in a sexy get-up, and we aren't allowed to feed off our clients, except in their dreams, but I can tell that you would be a feast, one to keep me full for an impressive amount of time,' he said, the word "impressive" wrapping itself around my clit and squeezing just a little.

'Uhng,' was all I could say, and I found I could barely stand as his voice's caress of my clit became more and more intense. Finally, finally I found my way back to the English language. 'You ... I'm still dreaming, aren't I? That has to be it. Pinch me, please, dream-incubus-man.' Then I realised I was having trouble standing, my knees wobbling, and Adrian caught me just as I started to fall.

'You're not dreaming, my dear, although I do take that as a compliment, if it's intended as one.'

'Yes, a compliment, to the most gorgeous man I've ever seen.' Then everything went black.

***

When I came to, I was laid out on my couch, and he was sitting in the chair across from it. And finally, reality was actually registering as reality. 'You ... thank you for catching me,' I said groggily. 'And for, um, doing my dishes.'

'You're welcome. It's Nell, right? I didn't get a chance to tell you, but your friend Lynne hired *I & S* as an early birthday gift, and she's covering for you at work today. You have me all...day ... long,' Adrian said, his final three words making me happier than anything anyone had said to me in a long time. Maybe I should stop looking a gift horse in the mouth, I found myself thinking, and maybe I should be kissing Adrian's mouth, while I'm at it, my thoughts continued, a decidedly mischievous grin finding its way on to my face. 'So, you don't usually actually do anything besides enter the women's dreams? The women whose houses you clean?'

'Nope. But when I entered yours, I could sense how...how hungry you were, for human contact, for sex, to put it bluntly.'

For once I didn't mind someone putting something bluntly. I did find myself blushing, though, a little embarrassed – or maybe more than a little – that this complete stranger knew I hadn't had sex in a very long time. I hadn't even had a date since I broke up with my last boyfriend, a fact that a few friends had tried to change, since it'd been at least five months since we parted for good. And we hadn't had sex for ages before the break-up, part of the reason for it. Not a fault on my part, but on his – he was too busy screwing our roommate to care whether I was getting *my* itches scratched. So I'd moved out and given up sex for the interim. And now here was this absolutely gorgeous man, offering himself to me, and I was half-worried I wouldn't even be able to remember what to do.

'Oh, you'll remember, I can tell you'll be a little

129

firecracker in bed.'

'You ... you can read my thoughts?' I started at this realisation.

'Only the ones pertaining to sex, and usually only if they're related to me. I'm sorry, I didn't mean to be rude.' A gentler look passed across his face for a moment, a flash of kindness, perhaps, and I found myself feeling a little less sexual towards him for a few moments, a little intrigued, surprisingly, as to what else there was to him besides his enormous sexual presence. The word "enormous" led to other thoughts, and I averted my eyes.

Adrian chuckled. 'Well, you're wondering what's under my apron now, are you?'

'Um, yeah, I guess I am,' I said, surprising myself. I wasn't usually that honest – or forward – but hell, he already knew what I was thinking. For all I knew he also knew how turned on I was, how I just wanted to climb into that lap of his and get things started. He must've heard that thought too, because as I sat up, he got up from the chair, and walked over to me; with a very visible hint that I wasn't the only one getting turned on tenting the front of his apron. Suddenly I was feeling shyer than I've ever felt in my life.

'I don't usually, I mean, I never ...' I was trying to tell him that I didn't usually bed down with people I'd just met, but I trailed off, as he slowly laid me back down again and straddled my legs.

'I don't usually either. Being an incubus doesn't mean I seduce women day and night, you know,' he said, voice low, his face coming closer and closer to mine. 'But I can tell you this much – I don't think either of us will regret it.' And then I found myself closing the last few inches between our lips, his mouth meeting mine, and it felt like no kiss ever had before.

I got lost in his lips, in the steady pressure of them against mine, so lost that it could have been hours we kissed for, or days, even. His mouth was skilled beyond all belief, his plush lips wet and forceful, and I could feel my desire flowing from me to him, my mouth to his, and I knew that he was feeding on me, and I didn't care. Thoughts flitted across my mind, thoughts of all the things I wanted to do with him, in this time we had together, and I felt his lips twitch into a smile at them occasionally, a sure sign that he liked whatever I was picturing.

His hands, just as skilled as his lips, slowly stripped me of my clothing, piece by piece, until the only thing either of us was wearing was his apron, just the barest hint of fabric stopped him from sliding the incredibly firm cock I felt pressing against my stomach into my willing pussy – it had never felt so empty in my entire life, and I had never been as hungry for a man to enter me as I was in that moment.

'Please ...' I moaned into his parted lips, 'Please ...'

'Wait just a second,' Adrian said, and he reached behind my ear, pulling a condom out from behind it. I'd never seen that magic trick result in a condom before – I guess they were the grown-up version of a quarter. I certainly wouldn't have traded it for even a hundred dollar bill in that moment.

Adrian stood up, stripped off the apron, and finally I could see him in all his glory. I stifled a "hallelujah", but just barely. Instead, out came, 'Oh my God ...'

'You approve. Good. I would have hated to have you turn me down once we reached this point.'

'Oh, no, I wouldn't turn you down after seeing that,' I said, my lips flowing into a grin. His body was possibly the most beautiful thing I'd ever seen, and I'd been to the *Louvre* when I was sixteen, the *Sistine Chapel* on the same trip. Even Michelangelo couldn't have created something that beautiful, that perfect. And his perfectly shaped, just-the-right-length cock was just icing on the cake.

'Here,' Adrian said, handing me the condom, 'I want you to put it on me.'

I took it from him, tore open the package (my favourite package I'd ever opened), and pulled out the condom. Then

I got down on my knees, my face right in front of his cock, and I slowly, slowly slid it onto him, a sigh coming from his lips, and one from mine as well. Once he was completely encased, I did what came naturally – I parted my lips and placed them around the head of his cock, swirling my tongue around it. I didn't know where incubi got their condoms, but the flavour was mouth-watering, rich and sweet, like honey and cream, and its taste did nothing to quell the shudders that taking him in my mouth caused, each one coursing down my body in lovely, sensual waves.

I looked up at his face, my mouth still surrounding his hardness, and his eyes were rich with promise, the green in them darker, a slight glow coming from each of them. 'You are a feast, indeed, Nell,' he said, his voice thick, his words flowing over me and touching each part of my body in a strong rush of heat and pressure. I couldn't take it any longer – I got up from the floor, took his hands, pulled him back to the couch, pulled him on top of me.

'I want you inside me,' I said, surer of that than I had ever been of anything in my life. It wasn't a want, it was a need, and so I found myself growling at him when he didn't enter me instantly, when he just teased my opening with the tip of his cock, rubbing it against my clit, almost sending me over the edge. Then, after what seemed like an eternity of almosts, he slowly slid it in, and nothing up until that moment had felt even close to the amount of pleasure that coursed through each and every inch of me, merely from him entering me. I hadn't realised up until then that even the tips of my hair were capable of feeling orgasmic. I'd heard of full body orgasms, and maybe that's what this was, but words alone didn't seem like enough to express exactly how it felt. If I'd been capable of thought, I would have been thankful for my apartment's thick walls and ceiling, because I was incapable of silencing myself as well, incapable of tampering back the sounds I was making in response to the feeling of Adrian fucking me.

'Yes, yes, Nell, don't quiet down, don't hold back,' Adrian murmured into my ear, his lips brushing against it, and then, when he began sucking my earlobe into his mouth, I came again. I was lost in the sea of sensation, only knowing how each touch of his, each thrust felt, nothing more. The orgasms didn't lessen in their intensity, either, they cascaded over me, rippled under my skin, in building intensity. I just let myself feel, and so it was a complete shock when I realised that Adrian was no longer inside me – he wasn't even on top of me any more.

Once I realised that, I snapped back to reality. Instead of being on top of me, he was sitting against the couch, holding what looked to be a very ornate, silver flask. It was open, and I watched as he took a deep swallow from it. My skin was still humming from my last orgasm, and words were very hard to come by, but I managed to get out, 'What ... what are you drinking?'

'Ah, well, I was so spent after our first session that I figured I could use some refuelling. This is the drink of my people, and we drink it to keep up our virility. I've never felt that spent after sex before, you should know. I was certainly right about you being a firecracker.'

'Li'l ole me?' I joked. 'A firecracker? Thanks. I would guess that's high praise coming from an incubus.'

'*Mighty* high praise, actually. I could shower you with compliments, but I'd rather just get inside you again.'

'I think that could be arranged,' I said, smirking.

'First, though, as much as it pains me to say this – I need to finish cleaning your apartment. I hope you won't take this the wrong way, but it's a disaster!'

'I, um, yeah, you're right, it is,' I said, and laughed. I hated to admit what a slob I was, but there was no getting around it.

'Tell you what – let's make a deal. For each and every dish you clean after I leave, I'll give you an orgasm next time I come by. And next time it'll be free of charge, you

133

little firecracker you.' Adrian grinned and ruffled my hair.

During the rest of the week, I cleaned each and every dish, just as he'd asked. And when he showed up that Friday night, I didn't regret cleaning a single one. Especially after the 20 or so orgasms I received over the next few nights.

Adrian helped me put together a plan for keeping my place a little tidier when we weren't busy being naked, sweaty, and entangled, and admittedly, I was a little sad when he said he had to get back to work on Sunday morning. But when I got out of bed after he left, surveying my spotless bedroom, and went out to my spotless kitchen and made some coffee, there was a note on the counter – a sheet of pale pink paper with a heart drawn on it, inside of which was written,

Call Adrian at 1 (696) 555-6969 for a good time (any time you want one, sexy).

I laughed and put the paper on the front of my fridge. All day, I enjoyed looking around my sparkling rooms, and that night, smelling the slight remaining scent Adrian had left behind in the bed, I decided I had to do something really special for my friend, Lynne. Like send her some flowers and a thank you card. Or buy her a yacht.

Just after I fell asleep that night, I started having the same dream I'd had that Monday. Only this time, the dream didn't get interrupted by an annoying alarm clock. And this time, Adrian handed me a rose, and said, in that amazing voice of his, how happy he was to see me again, before he took me in his arms. Right before he entered me, he smirked, and said, 'You washed all your dishes tonight, right?'

'Yes, of course!' And then he slid his delicious length into me, and I said 'yes' again. And again. And again.

Skyggen
by Giselle Renarde

As dusk came on like a gentle dew, Mirjam sat on the upper terrace of her rustic vacation villa. Sipping local berry wine, she gazed down at the villagers sauntering up the steep incline outside her door. The distance she'd put between herself and urban anxieties made Mirjam feel as though she'd stepped into the past. She could certainly get used to this life.

A yellow bird tore across Mirjam's line of vision, drawing her gaze to the terrace across the street. Her heart jumped in her chest as she jumped out of her wicker chair, splashing wine down the front of her sundress. After a stunned moment of concentrating on the sight that had brought her to her feet, she laughed. It wasn't at all what she thought. She could have sworn she'd caught a glimpse of a dark ghostly woman on the terrace across the street. Feeling rather sheepish, she realised the form was in fact her own shadow cast outward by the firelight illuminating her villa. In fact, when she looked very hard, she could see the neighbouring villa was entirely uninhabited. No furnishings, no people, no life. With an intoxicated chuckle, she shook the wine from her dress and stepped inside to change.

When Mirjam took coffee the next morning, she was stunned to find the villa across the way bustling with activity. Movers brought in the kind of gaudy, overpriced furnishings so often purchased by rich people with no taste.

Friends brought baskets of fruits and confectionaries. All activity seemed centred around one woman, who coasted from room to room like a shadow.

After Mirjam's vacation ended, she returned to her life in the city. At first, she thought it was the readjustment to urbanity that had her feeling out of sorts. But, as time passed and her system seemed never to conform to the old way of doing things, she wondered precisely what had happened in that holiday villa to change her personality so drastically.

Suddenly, she couldn't stand the career that had keenly held her interest for so many years. She gave up gambling for charity work and alcohol for spiritual involvement. She took up yoga and meditation, took on a vegetarian diet, and still she felt in some sense incomplete. Though her body was healthier than ever, her conscience grew heavier by the day. She became pale and thin. The evil career was killing her, she decided, and so she quit.

She'd seen every doctor, who'd attributed her condition to ennui and a whole host of other intangible diseases. They prescribed every medication imaginable, but Mirjam no longer believed in the usefulness of pills. She knew her health had deteriorated for some mysterious internal reason, and could not be restored until she knew the cause. In the meantime, her cheeks grew gaunt and her muscles weakened. As her physical condition deteriorated, Mirjam's mind brought her back to the daytime heat of her provincial villa and the firelight at dusk. She smiled as she recollected spilling wine across her dress that day she was spooked by her own shadow. Her stomach quaked.

As Mirjam laid her head to rest one evening, a commotion in the hallway outside her apartment jolted her awake. She couldn't make out the words spoken, but one of the voices seemed particularly familiar. Perhaps she'd steal a peek through the peephole, to find out what the ruckus was all about.

The very moment Mirjam crept out of bed, her front door burst open. Her heart stopped. She tried to scream, but her voice lodged itself so deep in her throat she nearly choked. The figure in the doorway didn't look much like a cat burglar, but Mirjam knew in her toes this woman was something else. Her skirt suit was accented with ruffles and patterned in every shade of Gauguin's palette. Her platinum blonde hair was almost entirely covered by a hat so flamboyant she had to duck her head under the doorframe to pass inside the apartment. In that ridiculous get-up, she looked like a cross between Carmen Miranda and a gangster's moll. The costume quality of her clothing somehow soothed Mirjam. In comparison, the eyelets in her white cotton nightgown seemed considerably less risqué.

With a look of considerable annoyance, the blonde rolled her eyes and set hands on hips. 'Do you know how long it took me to find this place?' Was her voice always so nasal, or only when she was irritated? 'I've been tearing all over this damn city looking for you! I went to your house, but you'd sold it, so I went to your office, but they told me you quit your job! And now here you are, living in a bachelor apartment on the wrong side of the tracks? Mirjam, darling, what's got into you?'

Mirjam clung to the housecoat she hadn't managed to throw over her shoulders. 'Who ... who are you?' She tried to place the woman from school days or work days, but how could she have forgotten a woman so brash and buxom?

The woman crossed her arms in front of her big breasts and tapped her toe against the vinyl flooring. 'You really don't know me?' she asked, slamming the door closed with her rear. When Mirjam shook her head, the woman took a step closer and said, 'It's me – Skyggen!'

Held in place by some supernatural force, Mirjam shook her head.

'Skyggen,' the woman repeated. 'Your shadow! Didn't you miss me? Don't you dare tell me you didn't miss me.

Oh, look who I'm talking to! You probably didn't even notice I was gone.' Skyggen's toothy grin made her comments seem more mocking than self-effacing.

'My shadow …' Mirjam uttered. The puzzle pieces began falling into place, though yet remained unfocused at a distance. 'On holiday you left me. You took the villa across the way.'

'Oh, I'd had enough with this trash heap of a city! I wanted to stay in the sun.' Skyggen dropped her body into the one chair in front of Mirjam's television. 'No offence, honey, but I was sick of being beaten down by your force of will. I wanted to stay, so I stayed.'

Mirjam sat on the edge of her bed and gazed at her shadow's manner of dress. 'It looks like you've done very well for yourself.'

Sticking out her bronzed left hand, Skyggen showed off a rock too big to be real. Though this detached shadow of hers appeared gaudy enough to wear paste, Mirjam had a niggling feeling the diamond was real. 'You're getting married?' she asked. Before she'd lost Skyggen, Mirjam would have felt a pang of jealousy at times like these. *Was it fair for her shadow to obtain these things Mirjam only coveted?* Now, Mirjam dismissed all negative thoughts. She felt numb … and somewhat nauseous.

A nod of affirmation wasn't enough for Skyggen. She had to go on and on about it. '… and this won't be just any old drive-through wedding! We're planning a seven-day celebration for the whole village. Oh, the villagers love him … well, love him and fear him. You should see how they cower. I tell you, we can't walk down the street without being given gifts of all kinds: fruits and gold and chocolates …'

There was an absence at the base of Mirjam's happiness for her shadow. She felt her joy ought to be balanced out by some emotion on the other end of the spectrum. Envy, though sinful, would have brought down her saccharine high.

'That's wonderful,' Mirjam replied through gritted teeth. Her jaw seemed to have locked again. She had to massage the pain from her cheeks before saying, 'I'm so happy for you. When is the wedding?'

Skyggen grabbed her hands and squeezed. Her eyes glared with such intensity Mirjam feared her for a quick moment. 'That's why I've come here, honey. I've felt so guilty for leaving you all alone! I just couldn't go through with this wedding without you by my side. Of course I'll pay your expenses. I mean, look at me! I'm richer than rich!' With a Hollywood kiss for both cheeks, Skyggen brought Mirjam in for an unemotional hug. 'You're like a sister to me! How could I get married without you?'

Mirjam wasn't sure how to feel. Even as she boarded the plane, she had a strange feeling about this whole affair. She believed Skyggen was her lost shadow, but she had a suspicion the flashy woman was being less than truthful about something

Onboard, Mirjam's heart swelled when she found herself seated next to a handsome young man. True, her beauty had deteriorated since her shadow split, but certainly she was still capable of flirtation. He was adorable, this boy with dimples and floppy brown hair. Better yet, he seemed intrigued as Mirjam introduced Skyggen and told him the bizarre story of their separation. 'Meanwhile, I had no idea why I felt so weak and incomplete. It all makes sense now, but it was very frightening at the time.'

'I imagine so,' the boy said, smiling at Mirjam ... or was that smile meant for Skyggen?

'Yes,' Mirjam went on. 'I used to work an executive job in advertising, but after Skyggen left, I couldn't bring myself to do it any more. All the lies we told! It made me sick – physically. As if a deodorant could make a woman more beautiful, or a beer make a man more attractive! We were brainwashing a nation.' She shook her head. 'I had to

139

quit.'

Skyggen squeezed Mirjam's hand so hard it hurt. 'You know,' Skyggen said to the boy, 'I was the one who got her that job in the first place.'

'That's true,' Mirjam confessed. 'I didn't want to do it, but a little voice in my head persuaded me to lie on my resume. I claimed I had a Master's degree, when in fact I dropped out after my first year of undergrad. That's partly why I quit: I couldn't bear all the lies.'

'And ever since, her fortune's dwindled. When I found her, she was living in a ratty old bachelor apartment with barely a stick of furniture in it.'

'That's so sad,' the boy said. *Did he mean it?* Who could tell, with the goo-goo eyes he was making at Skyggen.

The shadow woman noticed the boy's flirtation – that was certain! She leaned her big boobs across Mirjam's lap and patted his thigh. 'But I've come back for my little dear,' Skyggen said. Despite the plane's subdued lighting, her diamond sparkled like a star as she worked her way up to the brunette boy's crotch. 'Now I've got everything in the world, and I'm going to take care of my girl.'

The boy wheezed when Skyggen grasped his package. 'That's very generous of you,' he whispered, looking around at the plane full of sleeping passengers.

'Yes,' Skyggen cooed, rubbing his erection through his trousers. 'I can be very generous.'

Without another word, Skyggen rose to her feet and pulled the boy down the passage by his hard cock. He seemed to go willingly.

With a despairing sigh, Mirjam sat back in her seat and tried to sleep. At least she could look forward to the leisurely village pace and the country's dry heat. A vacation would do her good.

Skyggen's fiancé wasn't all what Mirjam thought he'd be. Knowing he was rich and powerful, she'd pictured a handsome young fairy tale prince. A surge of *shadenfreude* coursed through her veins when she met the short, husky man. Perhaps in Skyggen's presence, Mirjam's strong emotions were returning to her. She was a *tad* jealous Skyggen would be living in her soon-to-be-husband's veritable castle looking out over the sea.

Rising to greet them, Skyggen's fiancé offered a chivalrous bow. He was a military man, it seemed – his khaki uniform was the giveaway. 'Skyggen, my love! I haven't slept a wink since you left.' Pulling her close to his body, he planted a sensuous kiss on her lips. When he let up, she giggled. He released her from his arms and she fell to the floor, sighing as the military man looked to Mirjam. Embers of a deeply-lit fire burned in his eyes. He latched to her gaze and introduced himself. 'I am Valon. You must be my Skyggen's shadow.'

I must be her shadow? Mirjam shook her head just as Skyggen burst between the two. 'That's right,' Skyggen said. 'Remember how I explained that Valon thinks it's bad luck for a woman to be without her shadow? Remember I said he wouldn't marry me if my shadow wasn't present at the occasion?'

Skyggen gave a broad smile as Mirjam pronounced a long drawn-out, 'No …'

With a loud laugh, Skyggen said to Valon, 'Shadows are so forgetful! Excuse us for a moment.' Pulling Mirjam past an ensign and into the hallway, she whispered, 'All right, so I didn't exactly tell you the truth. Long story short, he thinks you're my shadow. He'd never marry me if he thought I belonged to somebody else.'

'Nice foundation to build a marriage on,' Mirjam shot back. 'You cheat on him, you lie … Skyggen, you are a terrible person!'

'Yes,' she hissed, 'but it's better to be a terrible person than the world's greatest shadow!'

Mirjam nearly jumped in response to the long-forgotten

141

sensation of adrenaline coursing though her veins. Grabbing Skyggen by the shoulders, Mirjam gave her a good shake. 'But you *are* a shadow! I've been dying since you left me, and you don't even care! You don't about anything but yourself.'

Mirjam hadn't shouted once in all the time Skyggen had been away. It felt good, but she was so loud about it Valon came running. 'What is going on out here?' he asked through a thick accent.

Grabbing Mirjam by the hair, Skyggen pulled her head back. 'She's belligerent!' Skyggen shrieked. 'She threatened to convince you I was actually the shadow and she was my mistress. Every word that comes out of her mouth is a lie!'

Skyggen surely could have gone on, but she stopped speaking when Valon untangled her fingers from Mirjam's hair. Glaring at Mirjam with dark but fiery eyes, he wrapped his hand around her arm just above the elbow. A thrill ran through her. 'Wilful mare,' he growled in a voice full of lust. 'Let me show you your place.'

As Valon dragged Mirjam along the corridor, she realised why he seemed so strangely familiar: she'd seen him on the news back home. Skyggen's Valon was *the* Valon, the overthrown despot living in exile. This tyrant was the man Skyggen had chosen for her husband? Mirjam examined his square jaw and shimmering black hair as he tossed her inside a bed chamber. Her heart leapt. The room was barely furnished, but there was a bed to cower upon as Valon lingered in the doorway. Skyggen stood behind him. Watching the two standing like that, it hit Mirjam that, married to Valon, Skyggen would always live in the shadows. As much as Mirjam wanted to spite the part of herself that had fled, she felt a warm sense of sympathy for Skyggen.

When Valon marched into the room, Mirjam's heart nearly stopped. He tore off his uniform in what seemed like one smooth motion and threw it into the blazing fire. The rising flame was almost as spectacular as his big cock resting on a cushion of black hair and balls. It seemed to both bounce and harden as he strode toward her. Mirjam's blood pumped fast through her body when he reached down and grabbed the collar of her blouse with both hands. 'You planned to tell lies about my Skyggen?'

The fear was more arousing than any pleasure Mirjam had experienced. But she'd be lying to say *yes*, so she said, 'No, I wasn't going to lie.'

She could see in his eyes what he would do next. And then he did it: he held firm to both sides of her blouse and tore it down the front. Buttons flew across the room as her breasts swelled. He grabbed her white lace bra and ripped it from her body. 'Tell me the truth,' he said, throwing her clothes into the fire.

'I am,' Mirjam squealed. She hoped he wouldn't believe her.

And he didn't. His thick fingers tore through her skirt and panties as she looked on in mortified excitement. 'What will you do to me?' she asked. Her pulse throbbed between her bare legs. She wanted to hear the words.

The expression in Valon's eyes was not that of anger, but of fierce passion. He left Skyggen in the doorway as he flipped Mirjam on to her stomach. Her legs hung off the bed. Her feet planted on the floor. She whipped her head around just in time to catch him thumping his cockhead against her ass cheeks, leaving trails of precome in his wake.

When Mirjam squirmed with wet anticipation, Valon mistook her longing for wilfulness. He grabbed her hips and pressed his fingers so deep into her flesh, she knew she'd see bruises later. 'Skyggen,' he called. 'Get over here and hold your shadow's hands still.'

Mirjam put up no fight as Skyggen leaned across the bed to grasp her wrists. She shot Skyggen a crafty smile, as if to say, 'Ha! Your man is about to fuck me, and there's nothing you can do but stand by and watch.' But Skyggen didn't seem put off by the situation. Judging by her keen grin, she might even enjoy the spectacle. Perhaps Mirjam had found something she could respect in her shadow: openness to new experiences, a complete lack of jealousy, and the heart to love a tyrant.

Squeezing Mirjam's ass cheeks, Valon slid his thick tip along the wetness of her lower lips. When Mirjam moaned, Skyggen squeezed her hands and released a giggle of affinity. That cock knew what it wanted, and it wanted to pummel her. He launched himself inside. His shaft tore through her wet pussy, lodging deep within. He rested for a moment inside her warmth before quickly pulling out. Mirjam sighed when he left her body, and Skyggen threw her face into Mirjam's open hands.

Valon pounded her pussy again, like a rocket straight inside. His cock felt so huge, she opened her legs wider. That, Valon took as intention to escape. Wrapping one of his legs around hers, he pressed his heel down on her toes to keep her in place.

'Hold her wrists,' he howled to Skyggen. But Skyggen released Mirjam's wrists and held her hands instead. In a strange sense, Mirjam felt closer to Skyggen now than she'd felt throughout the trip. They were one, were they not? Form and shadow, land and ocean, known and unknown? Skyggen, that gaudy blonde, was Mirjam's unlived life. And now, as they held hands on the bed, Mirjam lived that life.

She'd never done this before. Yes, she'd made love, but she'd never been fucked by a stranger – let alone the exiled dictator engaged to her shadow! As Mirjam bucked back against Valon's raging cock, the fire warmed her legs. Valon pummelled her like she knew he would, and Mirjam took it all in. It hurt. It panged against the mystery inside of her, but she loved it. She thumped her ass back against his hairy front.

'Your ass is excited,' Valon hissed. 'I see your hole pucker and beg.'

Mirjam's stomach clenched. She knew what came next, and she recognised its inevitability, but the idea made her cringe. 'Please don't hurt me,' she yelped. The statement itself made her skin tingle.

'Don't worry,' Skyggen said, petting Mirjam's arm. 'It hurts at first, but you'll get over it.' When Mirjam pressed her nails into Skyggen's skin, the shadow woman chuckled, 'Relax, sweetie. It'll be all right.'

Valon pulled his cock from Mirjam's pussy. When he set his tip at the entrance to her asshole, it was still dripping with her juices. Her stomach felt fluttery and her legs went weak, but Skyggen held on tight. Valon reached inside her snatch. With two fingers, he brought out more juice and slathered her asshole with the stuff. She felt slick to the touch. As he pressed his cockhead past her assring, Mirjam grasped Skyggen's hands. She tried to contain her scream, but she simply couldn't. It hurt. It hurt, but to an acceptable degree, like getting spanked again and again – the site was sore, but it was impossible to stop. She knew, as in all things, if he kept going the pain would subside. Life was like that.

Her ass blazed as he entered her. He eased in at first. Yes, he was forceful, but he wasn't rough about it. At first. Once he'd sunk his cock insider her hole to a degree that pleased him, he eased it out again. She clawed at Skyggen's hands, but Skyggen only smiled fondly at the view. Valon pushed his palms flat against Mirjam's ass cheeks before pushing them apart. She turned her head to see what he was doing. The instant she saw her body in that state, with her cheeks splayed and a firm cock between them, she no longer feared pain. Pain would heal. She wanted that cock inside her ass.

She bucked back as he thrust forward. 'Oh, so you like this, do you?' Valon growled. His voice was sexy in a reviling sort of way. She wished his voice could fuck her cunt while his cock pelted her ass. Why couldn't she have everything at once? Christ, she didn't even have a shadow any more – she deserved *something*! But her pussy sat longing while Valon went at her asshole. That empty space ached with jealousy of the crack that was too full, and soon to get fuller.

From the tone of his moans and sensual mutterings, Mirjam could tell Valon was going to come. Though he was the first actual dictator she'd encountered, she knew his type. He would pull out, leaving her broken and sore and full of come. Even so, she'd have a smile on her face. She was smiling now, in fact, through the pain and the hunger. Skyggen mirrored her expression of sheer joy. Mirjam screamed in agony and bliss, urging her ass back against Valon's prick as he reamed her. It was horrible and it was so, so good. She pushed back against him. He never eased up once he was into his groove. Valon kept at her, pressing his thumbs deep into her ass cheeks while he dug his fingers into her hips.

With an explosion of approval, Valon lifted Mirjam clear off her feet and plunged his cock deep inside her ass. Clinging to his prick, she shrieked and pressed her eyes tight shut. Held aloft by Valon's strong hands, her feet dangled over the floor. She started to slip. She tried to dig her fingernails deeper into Skyggen's hands, but she somehow lost them. When she opened her eyes, Mirjam found herself clawing at the bedcovers. Had Skyggen abandoned her? Or was she hiding under the bed?

Setting Mirjam's feet on the floor, Valon pulled out, but he didn't leave. He took a few steps to the side as Mirjam rose upright and gazed across the room. Now she could see. She could see Skyggen's brightly-coloured clothing strewn across the floor on the other side of the bed.

'Look up,' Valon said, pointing to the cream plaster. He seemed in awe. 'Look at the wall.'

As she did, Mirjam realised that, for the first time since she'd come to this country on holiday, she cast a shadow. It wasn't perfectly black, she noticed, but a shade of dusty grey. It was taller than Mirjam, and its reach exceeded her grasp. 'Skyggen,' she mouthed. The word was silent.

'So you were telling the truth after all,' Valon mused, watched her naked body against the fire. 'And Skyggen was the liar.'

Mirjam reflected for a moment before answering, 'I suppose so.'

When she spotted Skyggen's eccentric hat on the floor, she was overtaken with glee. Rushing past Valon on the pads of her feet, Mirjam picked it up and set it on her head like a vintage costume. A keen grin broke across her lips as she turned to look at Valon. He'd lost his fiancée to Mirjam; he'd need a new one. He'd need a woman who could fill her shoes. 'Well?' Mirjam asked, cocking Skyggen's feathered hat. 'What do you think?'

Lord Nano's Nemesis
by Slave Nano

'I trust everything was to your satisfaction, your Lordship?'

I have emerged from the upstairs boudoir where I have spent a pleasurable couple of hours indulging my sexual urges in the company of two of Madame Linda's finest whores. When I am in Leeds on business I always visit my favourite brothel at the sign of the Black Bull. I find it the ideal way to relax after dealing at the Corn Exchange to avail myself of the distractions of the city.

'As usual Madame Linda you run an exemplary house. I swear that you have the most buxom and willing whores in Leeds. It's always a pleasure to do business with you,' I answer.

'And it's a pleasure to be of service to you, my Lordship,' Madame Linda replies.

I have indeed had an exceptional time as I emerge dishevelled with my wig askew after satiating my carnal desires on Madame Linda's young girls. The whores eagerly comply with any lewd suggestion I make. They have no qualms about taking a gentleman's cock in their mouth and sucking it, having their arses penetrated or having a gentleman come over their faces or over their delectable breasts. To see one's come all over a buxom whore's tits is certainly a delight to a gentleman. My God, these sluts are paid well enough for it! My guineas will provide them with a supply of gin and opium for several weeks. A voice calls out to me from across the tavern.

'Lord Nano, come and join me for a game of dice.'

It is Sir Douglas Baron, a friend of mine, who also frequents Madame Linda's establishment. He is an important cloth merchant, who has made his money making up uniforms for local militia troops. He has companions with him at the table; two foppish young rakes. I suspect that Sir Douglas has a fancy for such men but I am not one to judge a gentleman for taking whatever indulgences he pleases.

'Well met, sir. We are of the same mind, my friend. We both like to indulge in whoring and gambling after some successful business,' I exclaim.

'How long are you staying in Leeds?' asks Sir Douglas.

'As soon as I've fleeced you and these young rakes at dice. My private carriage is ready to take me back to my country estate. I hope to be at home before nightfall,' I reply.

'My Lord Nano, you must be careful. There are many highwaymen on the roads these days and the risk is greater if you travel outside of daylight hours.'

'Sir Douglas, I do believe you worry needlessly,' I reply.

'Lord, I have word of a new threat on our roads. I have reports from constables of a female highwayman who targets wealthy gentlemen of good stock like ourselves. She comes silently out of the trees dressed in black like some kind of demon. Yes, a highwaywoman, I know that it's hard to credit. She goes by the name Nemesis. And it is not only golden guineas and jewellery that she is after. Apparently, she is on some kind of mission to humiliate men, especially wealthy ones who enjoy their pleasures. I do hear reports that on one occasion she left a gentleman hanging upside down with his balls tied to the branch of a tree!'

I must admit I find this tale enormously amusing. Then one of the young rakes speaks up.

'Yes, I've heard another story about this female devil. I

149

heard it reported that, because one gentleman angered her, she actually bit his manhood off, spat it out on the ground and then nailed it to his carriage door!'

I have never heard anything so absurd. I laugh out loud at the bizarre stories of the two men.

'Sir Douglas, I can understand a young wretch like your friend here believing such tittle tattle but a man of substance and breeding like yourself, sir, I am most surprised that you indulge in such fanciful tales. I do believe you must have the pox, sir, and that it has addled your brain,' I laugh.

'Sir, I am a Justice of the Peace; I assure you that these strange accounts are true and that constables all over Yorkshire have been on alert to find this highwaywoman but she has eluded them for many months now. There are even those that say she is not human at all but some kind of phantom. Heed my advice, Lord Nano, and proceed cautiously on your journey home.'

'Pah! I do not believe I will be waylaid. It is no matter. I have tarried long enough on my pleasures and must be on my way. My man and my carriage will be awaiting me at the coaching inn.'

It was dusk by the time my carriage left the turnpike road and entered the country lanes that wind their way through the woods to my country estate. I am half asleep from my exertions in the boudoir of Madame Linda's brothel when I am jolted out of my daze by the sudden movement of my carriage as it veers off the lane into a clearing in the woods. I lean out of the window of my carriage to reprimand my man for such reckless driving only to see that he has left the reins of the horses and is running into the woods. The imbecile. I will not tolerate such insubordination in my servants. I am still some way from home and consider that my only option will be to remove the harness from one of my horses, leave the carriage, and ride bare back to my residence.

I am contemplating this course of action when I sense

movement of a horse at the edge of the clearing. I look out of the window of my carriage and in the hazy light of the dusk as it shines through the canopy of the trees, I see her. At first the features are indistinct, all I can see is a female figure dressed entirely in black on a white horse. She is indeed a ghostly and phantom-like presence framed by the trees in the waning evening light. So, were Sir Douglas's tales true after all? Is this the mysterious highwaywoman who calls herself Nemesis?

As they approach and the horse and its rider come out of the dusky mist their figures become more distinct. I notice that the woman is riding with one hand and in the other is carrying a pistol, which is aimed at the window of my carriage. I have my sword stick with me, but I am no expert at using it, and it is no match for firearms. My man carries a pistol with him but he has run off into the woods like a coward, obviously scared by the ghostly rider in black.

By now the horse is close to the carriage door and the female rider dismounts with effortless grace. I can see her clearly now through the window of my carriage. She is a marvellous figure of a woman; tall, statuesque and commanding. My eyes are drawn first to her legs and her magnificent black riding boots reaching up to her thighs with silver spurs at their heel. She is wearing a long black dress coat, tailored to display her shapely figure and her ample bosom perfectly, its collar decorated with a delicate gold braid. Underneath her jacket she wears a crisp white shirt and ruff visible at her elegant neckline. On her head she wears a tri-corner hat decorated with gold braid matching the pattern on her coat and a long brown pheasant's feather. Her dark hair is swept back into a pony tail that trails down her back. She wears a red neckerchief that is raised to cover her mouth so that my attention is drawn to her piercing blue eyes that fix their gaze on me.

Her horse is a magnificent creature too; a pure white mare, perfectly proportioned. On her nose there is a black marking that looks to be in the shape of an "N". Whoever this woman is, she is no ruffian. Her whole demeanour exudes class and distinction. Despite my predicament I cannot help but feel aroused.

I am now mindful of the stories I heard earlier today and start to feel an anxiety mixed with my feelings of sexual arousal at this splendid figure of a woman. I know I should be seeking some means of escape from my plight but I am transfixed into inaction by the sight in front of me. The door of my carriage is flung open and the highwaywoman, Nemesis, stands before me. She gestures at me with her pistol to alight from my carriage. Finally, she speaks in a clear icy voice that sends a chill down my spine but yet commands my full attention.

'Well, what have we here? Lord Nano I believe, yet another rich, idle, whoremonger who needs teaching a lesson. My name is Nemesis. You may have heard of it, my reputation is spreading wide; tales abound of the mysterious dark woman who appears out of the mist to divest men of their wealth ... and their dignity. My mission is to expose men, to have them humiliated and submit to me. My motto is not "Stand and Deliver", but "Prostrate and Submit". Obey my commands and you may survive your ordeal. Disobey, and you have heard my name, retribution will be swift and complete.'

My good reader, having heard the tales recounted in the Black Bull and now having cast my eyes on this formidable woman, I dare not disagree or resist.

I merely say, 'I understand you entirely, Madame.'

'Good, first of all, pass over all of your money and valuables.'

I meekly hand over two bags of guineas, remove my jewel encrusted signet rings from my fingers and then my gold pocket watch.

'Of course, there would have been more money if you had not spent so much in the brothels in Leeds. Yes, don't look surprised. I see everything. I know who you are and what you have been doing; misusing young girls for your pleasure. Now you will undress and stand naked and exposed in front of me.'

I feel compelled to obey her command without a murmur of protest. I remove my white dress coat embroidered with delicate patterns of coloured silk thread, my fine linen shirt with ruffed collar and cuffs, my Italian leather buckled shoes and then my breeches and knickerbockers. Finally, I remove my wig to expose my shaved head. I stand before her, naked. The act of undressing in front of this magnificent specimen of a woman has given me a huge erection. If I expect this to impress her then I have sorely deceived myself.

'So I arouse you, do I?' she asks.

'Madame, you have a wonderful body, such an ample bosom and you look so splendid in your magnificent leather boots,' I say, believing that I am passing her a compliment.

From the expression in her eyes I immediately realise that I have made a grave error. There is indignation and anger in her voice.

'Lord Nano, I am not one of your tavern whores who you can have for your own pleasure. Your erection is an insult to me and needs to be corrected.'

She pulls a riding crop out from her saddle bag and with one skilful accurate motion lashes its tip across my erect cock. I flinch with the pain but she does not stop. She gives me another five swift strokes until my penis is throbbing and no longer erect.

'Get down on your knees and worship me. Lick my boots.'

I get down on to the ground obediently and, as she holds the pistol to my head, I work my way up her thigh high boots with my tongue. The feeling of kneeling before this powerful woman is both humiliating and erotic. After my tongue has licked all of the leather clean the highwaywoman is satisfied and orders me to sit against a nearby tree.

With rope gathered from her saddle bag Nemesis works quickly to tie me securely to the tree. Her skill with the ropes means I am soon so tightly bound that I am unable to move and I realise I am entirely at her mercy. My body is tingling with a mixture of fear and a strange kind of excitement at what she might do to me.

She presses the barrel of her pistol tightly against my chest. I feel my heart racing at the tension. Will her retribution be as extreme as she has said, and as I have heard? She runs the end of her pistol up and down my chest, then against my forehead and, finally, across my face. I can feel the cold metal against my skin.

'Take it in your mouth and suck it like you are sucking on a young rake's cock for my pleasure,' she orders.

The pistol slides into my mouth and I nod my head forward to take more of its shaft in. There is a cold metallic taste in my mouth, but I daren't stop and risk invoking her displeasure. She pushes the pistol slowly in and out, each time going deeper.

She leans over and whispers in my ear, 'Now you see how I have complete control over you, that your life is in my hands. One gentle squeeze of the trigger and I can take your life away. That is how close you are to death if you displease me. Don't doubt that I am capable of doing this.'

I have no doubt of this at all and keep sucking energetically on the pistol until eventually she is satisfied that I understand my predicament and that her control over me is absolute.

Nemesis goes back to where my clothes are lying in a pile on the ground and takes up my knickerbockers and holds them up gingerly by her fingers.

'I expect these are fresh with stains of piss and come from your earlier debauchery. Open wide.'

I open my mouth, she rolls the knickerbockers tightly in her hand and then pushes them firmly into my mouth. I can feel the bitter taste of dried piss in my mouth. Then she takes off her neckerchief and ties it tightly around my head so that my knickers are pressed firmly into my mouth. I have been looking up and watching her intently as she works to secure and gag me. Suddenly I jump with the sensation of being pricked but my body can only force itself against the ropes holding me to the tree. The spurs from her boots are being run up and down my thigh.

'You don't think I wear these for riding do you? I know that my fine white mare can ride as swift as the wind when needs must. Why would I need spurs to dig into her flesh? No, these are to inflict pain on the likes of you. These are to teach you not to have a hard cock in my presence and to ensure you know what your place is. Lord Nano. That title means nothing now. You might as well be the commonest knave whilst you are in my presence.'

All of the time that she is making this speech she is digging her spurs deeply into my cock and pressing down, putting the weight of her body down on it. The pain is excruciating. I try to scream out to relieve my suffering but my voice is muffled by my gag. The sharp silver spurs dig into my flesh. I can feel the surface of the skin on my cock and balls being pierced and drops of warm blood on my skin. After some minutes the pressure is eased and the spurs are withdrawn.

I am still tied to the tree and await whatever terrors this Nemesis still has in store for me. The reports of my friends that this woman is a cruel demon have proved very true but what is about to pass will amaze and shock you my good reader. The highwaywoman has retrieved some lengths of thin rope from her saddle bag. She takes one piece and secures it around the sac of my balls, the knot pulled as tightly as her strength will allow. She takes a second length and ties it around the shaft of my now flaccid cock. Once again the knot is tightened. She takes both ropes in her hand and jerks them vigorously. I let out a muffled yelp as my cock and balls are stretched to their breaking point. The cruel woman laughs in my face.

'Tell me, my Lord Nano, you must have many horses on your estate, do you consider yourself a skilled a horseman?' she asks.

I nod my head to indicate yes

'Tell me, would you consider yourself to be more skilled with horses than I?'

I nod my head from side to side. I dare not claim to be more proficient at horsemanship than her for fear of severe consequences. Nemesis pulls sharply again on the ropes and a shot of pain surges through my balls.

'Yes, you had better trust that I am indeed the most skilled horsewoman in the county. Do you see my splendid horse? She is a magnificent creature and my most faithful companion. Her coat is as white as my soul is dark. Wonder at her sleek white coat. Admire the powerful muscles on her hind legs. She can gallop with a force that would tear limbs off a man's body yet, when treated skilfully, her movements are gentle and graceful.'

I can only grunt in acknowledgement. My mouth is dry and I am dreading what her speech is hinting at. She crouches down in front of me with her icy cold eyes fixed on me, the flicker of a cruel smile on her scarlet lips.

'Shall we see how skilful a horsewoman I am and how well trained my lovely mare is?'

Nemesis stands up and takes the two strands of rope; she deftly ties both pieces on to the mare's bridle, one either side of her head. She swiftly mounts her white mare. As she does the horse takes one or two small steps forward. It is only a gentle movement but the ropes tug on my cock and balls with a strength that no man could muster. I feel my manhood being stretched. I feel the sweat of fear running down my brow. She leans forward and whispers into the mare's ear and then turns her head around to call out to me.

'What does it feel like now, my Lord, for a woman to

have complete control over your pathetic manhood. Shall I call on my mare to gallop as swift as the wind as if pursued by constables and rip your worthless cock from your body? Or shall I get her to take a few playful steps forward to make you suffer, but leave your cock intact? Are you scared? You should be, because you will understand now what I am capable of and that I will wreak my vengeance for all the women you have abused for your own pleasure.'

My body is shaking with terror. I believe this female demon is capable of what she boasts and that I am powerless to stop her. I brace myself for the very worst. I hear the command, 'Ride on!' The white mare takes a few slow steps forward, the ropes pull taught and then the pain starts. The pressure is stretching my cock and balls to the limit of endurance. I know the horse is taking only a gentle trot but the agony is extreme. I feel that at any moment, or with each new step the mare takes, my balls will be ripped from their sac. It may only have been a few moments but the agony seems to last an age before at last, and to my immense relief, I feel the pressure ease as Nemesis pulls the reins to stop her mare. My head is reeling and I feel I am at the point of passing out but all I can hear is her laughing at me, laughing at the pain she can inflict.

Nemesis dismounts and stands towering over me, the tops of her leather boots level with my eyes as I lean gagged and tied against the tree, my whole body aching with the strain of having my cock and balls stretched. She gazes down on me with contempt and a satisfaction that I have been truly humiliated.

'You have been lucky today, you have caught me in a generous mood. You will at least return with your life and your worthless piece of manhood intact. You will have learned a lesson that my feminine power can control you and that I can exact the most savage vengeance on behalf of my sex..'

I raise my head to look up at her and admire her awesome

presence.

'You will not forget this day. The day you were exposed as a whoremonger. You have had your worldly wealth and dignity taken from you. Know that my presence is everywhere and that I am watching you and, if you do not mend your ways, you have had a taste of what the retribution of Nemesis tastes like. I have one last act to carry out on you.'

She pulls out a playing card from her coat pocket and holds it up to my eyes.

'The Queen of Spades, my calling card, a symbol of my dominance over you and all men.'

She leans down, pulls the tip of my penis apart and inserts the edge of the card firmly into the end of my cock. At that, she stands up, takes the reins of her white mare, mounts her and trots slowly towards the edge of the clearing, a wondrous vision in black and white that becomes enveloped in the misty night air and disappears from sight.

Ghost With the Most
by Lynn Lake

The last thing I wanted to do for Halloween was go out to a party. After last year's bobbing for rotten apples in a drafty "haunted" barn had given me a truly frightful case of pneumonia. But my husband can be very persuasive, when he's whining.

'C'mon, Barbara, it'll be fun – this time.'

'Can't we just go out trick-or-treating as an angry divorced couple?' I deadpanned.

'It's a ghost party! A one-sheet-to-the-wind affair! A spook soiree! You'll love it.'

I swallowed a forkful of lasagne and stared across the table at the cute little redhead. His blue eyes were twinkling like the stars outside. But much like the prospects of interplanetary travel any time soon, I remained unconvinced. 'A what?'

His grin brightened even more. 'Everyone has to dress up like a ghost, wear one simple sheet … and maybe a few accessories. It saves money on expensive costumes that way. And all the money saved goes to charity – the Scare the Kids Foundation.'

'If you want to scare a kid, just show them our bank account.' I chewed moodily on a hunk of lettuce. 'And just what costume have you conjured up for yours truly?'

His twinkle turned to a wink. 'You're going as sexy ghost – the ghost with the most!'

A tingle of interest shot through me, down in between my legs. I tongued a tine, gazing at the handsome devil-may-care. 'Boo!'

October 31st was cool and damp, with a fresh layer of snow on the ground. Not exactly the perfect weather for dressing down as Cassandra the Slutty Ghost.

But Greg was not to be deterred. He'd lovingly contoured a simple white sheet into a spirited costume that was tight across my chest and tapered at my waist, short across my thighs. He'd made holes for my heavily-shadowed eyes and a Cupid's bow opening for my red-painted lips, ear holes from which silver hoops dangled from my shapely lobes. On my feet: shiny, white, knee-high leather boots.

I was putting the "ho" back in ghost. And to top, and bottom, it all off, Greg insisted I wear nothing underneath the thin, skin tight bed sheet. My nipples almost poked holes of their own in the costume, my butt cheeks just about spilling out the bottom.

We stared at me in the mirror.

'You're scaring me stiff,' hubby laughed, sliding his arms around my waist from behind.

He wasn't scared, just stiff. I felt his excited erection press in between my barely-covered buttocks. His hands glided up my stomach and onto my breasts, lips kissing my cottoned neck.

'Don't overdo it,' I warned, 'or you'll stain your own sheet, become the ghost of Fuckpad Motel.'

His costume consisted of the obligatory linen cut with eye and mouth holes, slits down the sides for his arms, a black tie painted on his chest. He had black shoes and black socks on, and was supposed to be the ghost of Enron, or Lehman Brothers, or some such defunct company.

Presently, he was just an aroused apparition pumping his appendage into my butt cleavage while tuning in the great beyond on my nipples. I tilted my head back onto his

160

shoulder and went, 'Woo!' as his tongue slid into my ear and twirled about. There was a dampness rising in me not of the grave.

'Oops, better get going!' he suddenly yelped, looking at his watch. 'You're gonna knock 'em dead, honey!'

He flew out of the room, leaving me floating.

The party was being held at an old red brick mansion on the other side of town. The place backed on to the river, was fronted by acres and acres of snow-covered lawn. It had been someone's home in the hoary past, but was now home to a women's university club, available to be rented for parties and charity events.

It was swarming with ghosts, materialising out of cars and levitating up the stone steps of the mansion, into the marble-floored reception area. There were regular ghosts, holy ghosts, Casper ghosts, green ghosts, ghosts of Christmas past, present and future, a "ghost of a chance" (fuzzy dice around its neck), and somewhere in the sea of bedclothes, the host ghost himself. Greg and I threaded our way through the shrouded masses, over to a bubbling punchbowl set up on a table literally groaning with Halloween treats.

And as I stood there waiting for my husband to ladle me out a cup of witch's brew, I felt the disembodied eyes of a whole raft of other ghosts on my hot-sheeted body. My nipples had picked up an extra quarter-inch from Jack Frost nipping at them on the long walk up the driveway, and they and I stood out like a whore in heaven.

Greg noticed, and grinned. 'Let's see if we scare up some place a little more private,' he suggested, that mischievous twinkle back in his eyes.

We departed the crowded room and made our way down the main hallway. Then turned off into a narrower, darker hallway. I didn't even have time to say 'Eek!', before Greg pulled me into a closet and closed the door. The party had

161

suddenly gotten a whole lot more intimate.

His mouth met mine in the pitch-black, and I flung my arms around him, giving him the gho-ahead. We hungrily kissed one another, two spirits communing. He pressed up against me, his cock throbbing into my belly, his hands creeping up my chest, clutching and squeezing my breasts.

Greg shot his tongue into my mouth. I spoke in tongues back, twining my slippery mouth organ around his. He kneaded my tits and pumped his cock, the pair of us frenching with a fearsome intensity, before the overexcited apparition dropped his head down and mouthed one of my nipples through my sheet, the other a yearning bud.

I shivered with delight, as he tongued and sucked on my stiffened nipples, dampening the cloth and my pussy. I ran my hands down his woven back and grabbed onto the firm mounds of his butt cheeks, groping them.

He grunted hotly into my chest, mouth full of buzzing nipple. I wanted this lascivious ghost to haunt my pussy, but now. 'Fuck me!' I breathed.

He dropped a hand off a tit and I heard the rustling of linen. Then felt something meaty press in between my legs. I quickly gathered up his shroud and clutched his bare buttocks, as he plunged the cowl of his cock through my pussy lips and sunk elongated protoplasm inside me.

This was no phantom erection; it filled me up beautifully. I moaned like a sexy spectre, Greg pumping his hips, fucking me, hands all over my tits, mouth covering my mouth. He banged me up against the closet door, more than a bump in the night. I flung my arms up in rapture ... and ensnared my fingers in webbing. 'Eek!' I screamed, for real.

Greg flicked on the light switch, and we both stared up at the tangled web my hands were weaved in. It wasn't spray-on cobweb, and that wasn't a rubber novelty spider creeping down its skein towards my wriggling digits.

Greg jerked my arms down and we fled out of the closet, he going one way down the hallway, me the other. I didn't

162

stop running, and wiping my hands off, until I'd flown up two flights of stairs and through a bedroom and out on to a balcony.

I breathed deep of the cool night air, panting like the ghost of Lassie. A wrought-iron railing ran around the small, third storey window landing, and I held onto it, staring out at the hushed, snow-blanketed landscape glowing in the light of the moon.

Finally, I got my breath back and my legs back under me. Just as some clouds scudded across the face of the moon, dimming the luminous surroundings considerably. I was about to turn around and retrace my steps to the party, when all of a sudden a pair of strong hands grasped my heaving breasts from behind, and a strong cock pressed into the goose bumped flesh of my buttocks.

'Maybe later, Greg,' I murmured. 'When I've had another four or five drinks from the witch's tit downstairs.'

But the man wasn't to be deterred, grinding his erection into my butt cleft and roughly squeezing my tits. I tried to turn around to face his lust head-on, but he kept me pinned forward, pushing me bodily against the railing. His fingers crawled up to my nipples and pinched them. A thrill streaked through me like the stroke of midnight, and I warmed all over with the heat of his passion.

His mouth found my earlobe and nibbled, then bit. He thrust his tongue into my ear, and swirled; hands kneading my breasts, fingers rolling my nipples, cock churning my cheeks. I tingled from ghostly tip to toe.

And as my ardent lover erotically worked over my inflamed body, I lazily looked down upon the snowy scene below. Ghosts had gathered beneath our balcony, their white faces tilted upwards, watching our amorous antics. The clouds parted and the moon beamed, illuminating our exhibitionism for them.

Fortunately, the spooky voyeurs couldn't see right through our costumes and identify our faces. But their rapt

163

attention served to heighten the delightfully wicked sensations I was feeling, Greg pinning me to the railing for all to see, fondling and frotting me with an urgent intensity. 'That's the way, baby!' I cooed.

He bit into my neck, and I moaned. He speared in between my legs and up against my pussy, and I gasped.

I'd never felt him harder, longer, thicker, more roughly impassioned, the sexy exhibition obviously turning him on to new heights, as well. He rocked me back and forth in his arms, the railing creaking. It could've broken, and we could've fallen through – and floated, for sure.

His hands barged through my arm slits and onto my bare breasts, and I squealed with otherworldly joy, melting like a spirit into the ether under the man's mauling hands. 'Fuck me!' I hissed. 'Fuck me right here out in the open with all those horny ghosts watching us!'

He instantly pulled his hands off my tits and gripped my hips, jerking me back a pace, bending me over. I clung to the railing and spread my legs, arched my back and wiggled my bum, a white flag of total surrender to the studly spectre.

He showed no mercy, shoving up my skirt and plowing his cap into the dewy black fur of my pussy. His aim was uncanny, splitting my lips and driving deep into my tunnel, every inch of his hard-on surging inside me. Until he banged up against my bottom, then began banging me in earnest, stroking in and out of my steaming cunt.

My body and the railing quivered in rhythm to his powerful thrusts, as he fucked me with his fulfilling cock. I stared down at the ghostly assemblage below, biting my lip, my eyelashes fluttering. There were at least twenty or more peeping phantasms now, watching our every sexual move.

But I didn't care if those imitation wraiths really could fly, right up to our perch to get a close-up vision of the action. All Hallows' Eve is the night for wickedness, and there's nothing more wicked than having costumed sex in front of a ghoulish gallery.

Greg slowed his stroke, gliding his cock back and forth in my pussy, slow and sure and sensuous. I rutted my bum against his groin when he was buried full-length, wallowing in the swollen, shimmering sensation. Then, when he pulled slowly back to the tip of his pole, I clenched my pussy muscles and clutched his hood between my lips. Until he sunk shaft deep inside me again.

He upped the tempo, fucking me faster, harder. The guy had obviously been working on his technique, waiting to unveil it just for this special occasion. Because his slow-to-medium-to-fast rhythm was stretching me to the limit, making me flare like a candled pumpkin. What a delightfully dirty treat to give his best girl on Halloween!

My head spun and body burned, the rattling railing gone damp in my hands. As Greg cocked me in a controlled frenzy, our silent audience of attendant ghosts watching. He slammed in and out of me, hitting my G(host)-spot head-on with every deep-pussy thrust. I shuddered on the end of his pounding cock, heated heady orgasm welling up from the velvety friction point and rushing through my trembling body.

'Yes! Yes!' I shrieked.

There was wooing and hooing from down below, certainly no booing, as Greg drove me almost completely over the edge, wave after wave of joy radiating through me. I came like I'd never come before, again and again.

Until my man pulled out, and I clung to the railing, dancing like a skeleton with the aftershocks of ecstasy, my sheet soaked. I sucked cool night air into my gasping lungs. Then I slowly rose up, and saluted the crowd by lifting my arms in my sheet in a "boo-like" manner, giving them a final glimpse of skin, a flash of figure.

I turned to take my lover's hand, so we could return to the party.

But there was no one there.

I stumbled inside the bedroom – empty.

I staggered down the hallway and the two flights of stairs, encountering no one living or dead along the way. I found Greg in the marbled reception area, chatting away with a bearded ghost. The rest of the spirited guests were talking and drinking and laughing, filling the room with white noise.

'There you are, honey!' Greg yelled, grabbing my sheet and steering me over to the bearded ghost. 'This is Dr. Phillips of the University Paranormal Department – a PhD in PSI. He was just telling me about the actual ghost that's supposed to haunt this house. Tell her, Doc!'

The man adjusted the pince-nez on the end of his cottoned nose. 'Yes, well, as I was saying, this mansion was originally built in the early 1900s, for the mistress of Lord Edmund Beaverton. She was a skank, to be sure, even by Edwardian standards. She used the house for the purposes of ill-repute and non-stop partying, while giving his Lordship the decidedly cold shoulder.'

The professor fondled his beard, stroking the whorled strands slow, then fast. 'And it is rumoured that his Lordship, suffering from one colossal case of blue balls, yet haunts this house in search of comely maidens to, uh, relieve his pent-up earthly desires.'

I glanced nervously over at Greg, as we drove home from the party.

'Have a good time, honey?' he asked.

'The best,' I murmured.

'Good. I knew you would.'

'Um, Greg … you explored the mansion, didn't you? I mean, you went up to the third floor, out on to one of those bedroom balconies – didn't you?'

He looked at me, his blue eyes twinkling like the stars. 'No. Why?'

I gulped.

'Good Lord, honey, you look as pale as a ghost! You

166

didn't see Lord Edmund, did you?'

I stared out at the luminous, snow-shrouded landscape, a shiver running down in between my legs. 'No, I didn't *see* him ...'

Flaws
by K D Grace

'I don't do love spells,' Sally Haddon said.

Mick gripped the arms of the chair with white knuckles. 'Your website said you specialize in sex magic.'

'Love spells aren't necessarily sex magic.' She crossed long legs and smoothed the flounces of a burgundy gypsy skirt over shapely thighs. She was a far cry from the old hag he'd expected.

'But you don't understand. Darlene isn't like other women. I believe – no I'm certain – we're meant to be together.'

Sally moved to stand beside him, taking his chin in her hand, turning his head from side to side as though she were inspecting him for flaws. He thought she had given him a static shock from the Turkish carpet, but the energy coursed through his jaw, down over his stomach to surge in his penis, which suddenly felt tight in his trousers.

'Have you had sex with her?'

He tried to pull away, but she held him firmly, her gaze like iron. 'I haven't … We haven't … But I want … '

'When was the last time you had sex with anyone?' She tightened her grip on his chin. 'I'll know if you lie.'

His heart galloped in his chest, but his straining cock didn't seem to notice the definite frisson of fear that prickled his spine on little spider feet. 'Three years.'

She pulled her hand away and nodded to his lap. 'Go

home, watch some porn, have a wank. Trust me; it's not worth the risk of a love spell.'

He shifted uncomfortably around his bulge. 'You make it sound like putting a curse on someone.'

'Not much difference, really.' She poured them tea in china cups and sat back on the sofa. 'There are so many variables in a love spell, so many factors that, if not properly figured into the equation, can backfire in very nasty ways. That you've not had sex recently will complicate the situation further.'

'If you won't help me, I'll go to someone else.'

She raised an eyebrow. 'Any reputable witch will say the same. If you find a disreputable one, well things could get really ugly.'

'Haven't you ever been in love? Don't you know what it feels like?' God, he sounded like such a whiner.

Her face softened and her grey eyes were like sea water. Slender fingers stroked the silver pentacle that hung between her breasts. Then she stood quickly. 'Come with me. Perhaps I can help you after all.'

The old Victorian house was exactly the kind of place where hc imagined a witch would live. At the top of the stairs, she opened french doors and beckoned him inside. The room was the round tower he'd seen from the front garden. Beyond tall slender windows was a profusion of foliage from oak and willow trees. It felt like his childhood tree house.

The floor was covered with exotic carpets. There was a mountain of cushions and pillows piled at the centre. The witch lit candles around the perimeter of the carpeted area. Outside sunset streaked the sky melon and mauve.

'What you need is a clarity spell.' She lit the last candle and pinched out the match with her fingers. 'I'll make you a deal. If you'll let me cast a clarity spell, if you'll let it run its course, see what you need to see, then I'll cast a love spell, if you wish.'

She offered him her hand.

'It's a deal.' He took her hand and moved into the circle. Dusk settled around the flicker of the candles. The world inside the circle of light effervesced and danced, awash in strange liquid silence.

'The boundaries between worlds are permeable at dusk. It's the time to catch a glimpse of that which we might otherwise miss. If you're lucky, you might catch a glimpse of Darlene as she really is. You might catch a glimpse of yourself as you really are.'

He baulked, standing frozen just inside the circle. 'You didn't tell me we'd be navel gazing.'

'I told you the rules. Play by them or there's no deal.'

He moved forward, swallowing the strange combination of fear and arousal he'd felt almost from the moment he entered Sally Haddon's house.

'Lie down.' She nodded to the cushions.

He did as he was told, suddenly finding it difficult to stand. As he nestled into the mound of cushions, the world around him downshifted to slow motion. The tall windows loomed over him like large gaping mouths. The candle flames roared like forest fires. 'What was in that tea?' His tongue felt unmanageably thick in his mouth.

'Just tea. It's the effect of the spell you're feeling.'

He forced a chuckle. 'No eye of newt or hair of bat?'

'This is sex magic, not Halloween.'

When he managed to focus on her again, she stood over him tall and commanding. Completely naked. For some reason, that didn't seem strange.

'Are you going to fuck me?' he asked as she knelt to unbutton his shirt. It bothered him how badly he hoped she would. Surly he should be thinking only of Darlene.

'Possibly.'

With a hand he seemed to have little control over, he cupped the witch's full breasts, his thumb lingering over the heavy press of her nipples. He wanted to taste, but he

170

couldn't lift his head from the pillows. He managed to raise his hips as she undid his trousers and eased them down over his butt. His balls felt full. His cock stood thick and stiff like the trees outside the window.

It was hard to tell what was real and what was just the result of the spell, and he was well past caring when Sally squatted over his face. She splayed her pussy, smoothed her creaminess onto her fingers and brought it his lips. Her fragrance penetrated the fog. As she slipped her fingers into his mouth, he suckled her taste, breathed her fragrance, and everything became clear, sharply focused.

'Remember now,' she spoke inside his head. 'See clearly, more clearly than you saw the first time. Remember Darlene, be with her again. Pay attention.'

He had worked late. He thought he was alone in the building until he heard sounds down the hall. He figured it was the pipes groaning. Abacus Accounting was in an old building. But pipes didn't giggle.

How could it have been only three weeks ago? His desire for Darlene filled him so completely it was as though he had never not wanted her.

He pushed back from his computer listening, holding his breath. Sure enough someone somewhere was giggling. On tiptoe, he moved down the hallway past his boss's darkened office toward the conference room, with its big window and vertical blinds, incongruous in the 19th century building.

Through the cracks in the carelessly drawn blinds, he could see the HR manager, Ted Engels, in the chair at the head of the mahogany table. Spread in front of him, like the business of the day was Darlene. She sat splay-legged, skirt hiked over her hips to reveal the exquisite pillows of her pale bottom.

She wore black suspenders with a matching bra, which Ted had pushed off her shoulders along with the black silk blouse. Movie star breasts, crowned with large peek-a-boo nipples, spilled over the rumpled lace, rising and falling with excited breath. One hand curled in Ted's mussed hair, the other braced against the table.

Mick's hands found the quickest route to his fly, releasing his heavy cock. Jealousy tinged voyeurism making his arousal sharp edged and tense. He had wanted Darlene since she joined the billing department two months ago. She was perfection, slender yet curvy, large blue eyes, ripe fruit lips displayed against a sweet cream complexion and all curtained in a lush tumble of blonde hair. He wasn't alone in his lust. All of the men at Abacus wanted her.

As Ted pulled away, Mick got a glimpse of her smoothly shaved pussy, every fold of it, every bud of it displayed for worship. There was no mistaking Ted's piety as he fumbled to free his cock while she whimpered in a little girl voice, begging him to fuck her.

But Ted was no match for a goddess. He only managed a few hard thrusts before he grunted out his wad and cursed his frustration. Caught in the throes of his release, he didn't see Darlene roll her eyes in irritation.

'I'm sorry! I'm sorry! I couldn't hold back,' he gasped when he could finally speak again.

'It's all right, Ted.' Her words were tightly wrapped in a forced smile. 'Just finger me until I come.'

Still struggling for breath, he pulled out of her pussy, plopped down in the chair and began awkwardly stroking her.

As Mick dug in his pocket for a handkerchief, about to come himself, he realised Darlene's gaze was locked on him, her mouth curled in a wicked smile. He came then, jerking and straining with less dignity than he would have preferred. She watched, licking full lips with a hungry pink tongue.

It was all so vivid, as though the witch had transported him back in time. He could even smell his own humid semen as he filled the handkerchief, knowing that Darlene

172

saw him watching her, knowing that she watched him come while she smiled and licked her lips and …

Suddenly it was as though someone had poured ice on his cock. He blinked hard and looked again. Surely he was wrong. Darlene's exquisite tongue flicked over an angry dark canker disfiguring her upper lip.

Then he was racing down the hall toward the men's room. He could feel it. He knew it was there. In the mirror, it glared back at him, a canker on his own lip, swollen and virulent. Even as he saw it, some part of him shouted in his head it wasn't real. This wasn't how it happened. Darlene was perfect!

He came to himself with a start, hand darting to his mouth, reassuring himself that it was free of blemish.

'What did you do? What did you do to me?' he gasped.

Still naked, Sally lay at his side, resting her head on her arm as she studied him. 'I've done nothing but watch you. It's your spell, not mine. What happened?'

'Nothing. Nothing happened,' he lied. 'It was just so vivid.'

She offered him a tolerant smile. 'Whatever didn't happen, didn't do your hard-on any good.'

He looked down at his penis resting insignificantly against his balls and blushed. 'It's just disturbing, that's all. I've never had magic done to me before.'

She chuckled softly. 'A clarity spell is only a minor discomfort, Mick. A love spell is disturbing.' She ran a hand down his belly, and his cock responded to her touch. 'Do you want to continue?'

'Of course I do.'

'Then let's do something about this.' She cupped his balls and gave his rapidly expanding cock a stroke. She lowered her lips to his chest and wreathed his nipples with her warm tongue until they were bullet-hard, then she trailed kisses over his stomach to where the soft down below his navel joined his pubic curls. 'This is sex magic,' she whispered against his cock. 'One has to be excited for sex magic to work. It's another way of making those boundaries permeable.' With that, she took him into her mouth clear up to his balls.

He caught his breath and arched against her. Jesus, was this a part of the spell? Could she really be making him feel so good? Whatever she was doing with her tongue, he never wanted her to stop. He curled his fingers in her hair, and noticed it was the same colour as the candle flames.

But just when he could have happily stayed in the tree house room with Sally Haddon, he heard her voice inside his head. 'Find Darlene again. Observe her. See her clearly.'

Once again he was at work. He had come to the break room for coffee. Darlene and the heavy-set secretary from billing chatted at a corner table.

He felt like a teenager with a crush. His chest ached, his balls tightened. In his peripheral vision, there was a dark shadow over her upper lip, but as she looked up at him and smiled, he was relieved to see only her perfect kissable mouth.

She spoke softly to the other woman, but he heard every word, like she whispered it in his ear. 'Ted's cock's big enough, but the man's got no stamina and no imagination.'

The secretary chuckled. 'You must really wear him out. He looks like the walking dead these days.'

Darlene shrugged. 'Told you he has no stamina.'

Mick felt his ears burn with sympathy for Ted. He wondered why he didn't remember any of this from before.

'Oh, Mick,' Darlene called over her shoulder. His heart flip-flopped. He dribbled hot coffee across the top of his hand. 'Some of us are going for drinks after work. Wanna join us?'

A dozen Abacus employees shared several pitchers of

174

margaritas that evening. Darlene ignored Ted and flirted with Ben Taylor, the head of billing. He was married, surely no competition.

But when Darlene excused herself to the bathroom, and Ben followed, Mick felt the acid sting of jealousy in his chest. When he could stand it no longer, he excused himself to the maze of hallways that led to the rest rooms. He never got that far.

A shushing sound drew his attention to the door of a store room standing ajar. Holding his breath, he tiptoed closer. He could hear soft moans and grunts. Cautiously he peeked inside.

There was Ben Taylor, trousers down, pale bare arse muscles clenching as he pistoned Darlene's upturned cunt. She was bent over, one hand pinching an exposed nipple, the other tweaking her clit. 'That's it. Jesus that's it! Fuck me hard,' she breathed.

Mick's cock felt like hot lead in his trousers as he watched.

'I'm coming!' she rasped. 'Oh God, I'm coming.'

With an expansive grunt and a quiver up his spine, Ben came too. As the pair collapsed on to a heap of tarpaulins next to a stack of crates, Darlene turned just enough to catch sight of Mick. He froze, his cock went limp. Her mouth was distorted not only by a festered canker, but by teeth grown sharp and too big for lips curled back in a sneer.

Mick felt his own distorted mouth, tasted blood where the sharp edge of his misshapen teeth grazed his lip.

He shoved his way out of the dream world and sat up like he was spring-loaded, sucking oxygen. A thin sheen of icy sweat smeared his body. 'What the hell did you do? You made her ugly. She's not. She's beautiful, wonderful.' He tasted blood.

'Give me a mirror,' he gasped, fighting back nausea. 'Jesus! Give me a mirror!'

175

Sally offered him a silver gilt hand mirror along with a tissue. 'You bit your lip while you were under. It happens sometimes.'

Sure enough, there was a small tooth mark from his normal teeth in his normal mouth. It was seeping blood. The visceral sense of relief passed, and he fumbled for his clothes. 'I've had enough. Break the spell, undo it. I don't care how, just stop it.'

'It's already broken.' She stood and slipped into a robe. Even in his agitated state, he was sorry. He'd grown used to her nakedness. He felt strangely bereft without that intimacy. She extinguished the candles one by one. Outside a heavy moon hung over the trees.

Mick drifted through the next few days in a fog. He thought about Sally lying naked, watching him dream, about the way she had cleared his head with her scent, with her taste, with her touch. He shook the memory away. He didn't want to think about her. He had known what he wanted before Sally Haddon. There had been certainty. Now there was none.

Sally promised the spell was broken, and yet the world seemed different, darker somehow. Except when he thought of her. Strange that. She was the cause of his disquiet. He should be outraged at her. Instead there were butterflies in his chest when he thought of her.

He went to the break room for coffee, but there was none. Cursing to himself, he set about making a fresh pot. At the corner table two secretaries chatted. The heavy-set one he had overheard talking with Darlene, spoke quietly. 'His wife took the kids and went home to her mother in Manchester.'

'That's too bad,' the secretary from accounts said. 'Ben loves his kids so much.'

Mick held his breath and listened.

'But he's not willing to give up Darlene,' the heavy set one said.

Mick's stomach dropped to the floor, as the secretary

continued, oblivious to him. 'Thing is, he doesn't have Darlene. You saw what she did to Ted Engels.'

The accounts secretary shook her head. 'Poor Ben. He's too naïve to see it.'

Mick left without coffee. For the rest of the day he buried himself in work. Somewhere in the swirl of numbers and accounts that kept his mind off things, he looked up to find everyone else had gone home. But he didn't want to go home. He wanted to go to Sally Haddon, but he doubted she'd be very happy to see him as rude as he'd been to her. He kept working.

'Burning the midnight oil, are we?' He turned to find Darlene standing with one hand on the perfect curve of her hip, the other blocking the exit of his cubicle.

His heart bounced in his chest, and he struggled to return his gaze to his spread sheet. 'Always work to be done.' He hoped she didn't hear his pulse hammering in his voice.

'Isn't there just.'

He could see her reflection in his monitor as she watched him. The downward curl of her lips said she didn't appreciate him looking at anything that wasn't her. He saw the impatient heave of her breasts before she pushed her way in, grabbed his chair and swivelled it around until he was looking down the gaping front of her blouse. Then she gave his cock a solicitous stroke through his trousers.

Before he could do anything more than gasp, she took his mouth, lips parted, tongue insinuating itself between his teeth. No canker, no sharp teeth, he struggled to reassure himself while she nibbled his bottom lip.

She came up for air. 'I've seen you watching me. I know what you want.' She lifted her skirt until he could see her smooth knickerless cunt. But the cubical lighting played tricks on his eyes giving her skin a rough green tint. He blinked and tried to push her away, but she spread her legs and parked her bare pussy on his lap against his crotch, which should have been bursting at the seam. Isn't this

177

exactly what he wanted? Why wasn't he hard?

She guided his hand inside her blouse against the swell of her breast, the place he'd fantasised about touching, licking, sucking. But the smooth skin he had imagined was rough, scaly. His stomach churned. As he struggled to pull free, he caught their reflection in the monitor, cankered lips, teeth grown large and jagged, skin discoloured. With an effort that nearly ended with her on her arse, he fought his way up from the chair with her cursing in surprise.

Just then Ben called from down the hall. 'Darlene? Honey? I'm ready.'

She straightened her clothes.

'The man has kids,' Mick said.

She looked up from buttoning her blouse. 'So?'

He stood looking at her once again beautiful face. 'Watching you was wrong. I'm sorry. It won't happen again.' He grabbed his jacket and pushed past her, catching a glimpse of teeth and canker in his peripheral vision. Just before he turned to go, he caught sight of his own face reflected in the monitor. It was smooth and pink except for the hint of stubble.

Sally answered the door in her robe. Before she could speak, Mick scooped her into his arms and kissed her. To his delight, she was responsive and warm. When she pulled away, he spoke in a rush. 'The spell? You're sure it's broken?'

'Positive.'

He felt an icy chill. 'Then what did I just experience at work with Darlene?'

She led him upstairs while he told her what had happened in breathless, run-on sentences. Still talking, he followed her inside the circle. As she lit candles, he savoured the air effervescing against his fragile pink ordinary skin.

'Is Darlene some kind of monster?'

'There are creatures that survive on sex, some human,

some not.' Sally slipped out of her robe, and his cock surged in response. 'Our bodies bear the flaws of our souls.' As she spoke, she undressed him. 'If we can see our flaws, we can work to heal them. The danger lies in not being able to see.'

'Then what I saw was real?'

'Oh it was real all right, Mick. Just not everyone is able to see.'

'Did you know?'

'I suspected. I'm a witch, remember?'

He looked around at the lit candles. 'Why the circle?' He forced a laugh. 'Do I need an exorcism?'

She held his gaze. 'The circle is a safe place for a love spell.'

'I don't want a love spell! Not after what's happened.' He stepped away from her nearly falling backward over the cushions, but she caught his hand and steadied him.

'Mick, the love spell has already been cast. You cast it the first moment you lusted for Darlene just like Ted and Ben did. Just like Darlene did on all of you.'

'Jesus!' He sat down hard atop the cushions fearing for a second that he might pass out.

'Love spells need no witch. They need only the power of human desire. Every day people cast love spells unknowingly. Some are harmless, some are beautiful with astonishing results. Others are devastating, as you've just seen.'

'Then what happens now?'

Sally sat down next to him and shoved his shirt off his shoulders. 'You willingly faced your flaws. That's a powerful defence, powerful enough to break Darlene's spell. That was the key. When you arrived, you were already steeped in Darlene's magic.' He yielded as she slid his trousers and boxers off and tossed them aside. 'Then while you were here, you didn't realise, but you cast another love spell.'

'Wait a minute, how could I have …'

179

She kissed him, lingering until his whole body tingled with the want of her. Then she guided his hand down to cup her pubis, and as she arched against his fingers with a soft grunt, he understood.

She whispered against his mouth. 'I assume you've come back so we can shape that spell into something a little less flawed and something a lot more yummy.'

He breathed in the honeyed scent of her as he stroked and probed her slippery folds. Just when he thought she was about to come, she pulled away and buried her face against his cock, tonguing the underside, making him squirm and writhe in the cushions before she took him fully into her mouth and moved up and down the shaft like a tight fist.

'Are you gonna fuck me?' he gasped.

'If you need me to,' she breathed.

'Oh I need you to.'

She positioned herself and he pushed into her, gasping as she wrapped her legs around him tightening her velvety grip. As they moved against each other, he understood completely what a good love spell should be. When they came together, he swore he could almost see the intricate weave of that spell glowing like a halo around their fragile, normal bodies as the magic they created spilled over the circle and out into the moonlit night.

Nymph
by Kyoko Church

'Hey ladies,' Charlotte sang out as she approached her friends in the café.

'Here she is.' Kate grinned.

'Finally,' said Becky. 'What the fuck? We thought you weren't coming.'

'Scooch,' Charlotte said and Kate moved over. Charlotte plunked herself and her bag down on the bench seating and exhaled. 'I know, sorry.' With a sly grin she leaned in and added, 'I was at Ben's.'

'Here we go,' Becky said, also leaning across the table. 'That Brit guy is sex on wheels, Charlie. Give us the goods.'

'He is intense,' said Charlotte.

'Intense,' scoffed Becky. 'You mean he's fucking hot. Don't bother with all the euphemisms, woman. Just tell us the naughty deets. For the sake of your poor married friends who are trying to live vicariously.'

'Wait,' Kate said. 'I don't know about this one yet. Start from the top.'

'OK, hold on. Let me at least get a coffee first.' Once Becky and Kate's mugs were refilled and Charlotte had her own steaming mug in front of her she took a sip and began. 'Remember that Goth club that chick I work with dragged me to last month?' The friends nodded. 'We met there. It was like, boom, instant attraction. Smoking hot, right from the second we laid eyes on each other.' The women drank in

181

every word. They loved her hook up stories. 'We were on the dance floor the whole night and, damn, grinding doesn't cover it. It was like vertical sex with clothes on. It was amazing. Off the charts.'

'Ahh!' Becky exclaimed. 'Charlotte's got a live one. Fuck, I can't wait to hear about the sex.'

Charlotte laughed. 'Yeah, the sex is mind blowing.' She paused. 'But it's more than that. I don't even know how to describe it. You know that fluttery feeling you get in your stomach when you are attracted to someone and you realise it's mutual?'

'God, I miss that feeling,' Becky lamented. 'Sorry, not about me. Go on.'

'Well, it's like that times ten. Times a hundred. It's like that on speed. I've lusted after guys before but I've never had this feeling like my head and heart and body are all connected and when I'm with him, they all come alive. They're all revved up and plugged into this other frequency he's on. I feel like I've been sleeping my whole life and he's woken me up from a dream. It's so intense it's practically tangible.' She stared off then blinked a couple of times when she realised nobody was saying anything. She looked at her two best friends. They looked completely stunned.

'What?'

Becky was incredulous. 'You're asking *us* what? Who the fuck are you?'

'Chill, Becks.'

'It's just,' Kate chimed in, 'we've never seen you like this.'

'Yeah,' said Becky. 'Where's our pump 'em and dump 'em Charlie? What is this,' she gestured dismissively, 'gooshy look you've got happening?' She pounded her fist on the table. 'Screw all that mind, body and spirit bullshit. If I want Oprah I'll turn on my TV. I wanna hear about the fucking.'

'OK. Geez. Keep your pants on.' She winked. 'Cause I

182

haven't been.'

'Now we're talking,' Becky said. 'Dish. How amazing is he?' She smiled knowingly. 'Something tells me he is an oral master. I'm right, aren't I?'

'Actually, that's one thing ...' Charlotte trailed off, her smile fading.

Kate gasped. Becky was wide eyed.

'Get out!'

They knew Charlotte's track record. She had unceremoniously dumped guys for a hell of a lot less. Any hesitancy in that department was non negotiable. Charlotte loved head. Giving and especially receiving. Her attitude had always been any guy worth her time had to be great at it.

'It's so weird,' she sobbed. 'Everything else is the best, way hotter than anything I've ever experienced. And the strange thing is, I feel like he really wants to. You know me, I can weed out the assholes who won't do it in two seconds.' She exhaled and her whole body deflated. 'This is different.

'He did the hottest fucking thing. That first night, we were on the dance floor, it was packed but we were in our own little world, completely oblivious to everything.' Her eyes glazed and she went on in a whisper. 'He took his fingers, reached down under my skirt, inside my panties and pushed them inside me. I thought I was going to come right there. Then he pulled his fingers out, brought them to his mouth and sucked on them. And fuck. The look on his face was like he was tasting the sweetest, most amazing honey he'd ever had. Like it was a sinful treat he couldn't help himself from eating.' She sighed and her friends remained in stunned silence.

'But he's never gone down on me. It's bizarre. I don't get it.'

Charlotte peeked in the window of Ben's first floor apartment and could not fucking believe her eyes.

In her desperate attempt to "figure Ben out", to make

sense of this sexual puzzle she couldn't solve, when she saw him leave the Goth club with another woman she decided to follow them and see what they got up to.

Or, rather, down to.

The thin blonde was splayed on the couch with Ben kneeling on the floor between her legs. Charlotte felt the strangest jealous but horny thrum go through her as she held her breath and watched Ben's mouth go to work on the woman's cunt. Physically the woman was everything Charlotte was not: pale where Charlotte was olive skinned, skinny where Charlotte had curves, a blonde bob in contrast with Charlotte's thick cascade of chestnut curls. But the worst discrepancy in Charlotte's mind was the woman's reaction to what Ben was doing. While Charlotte and Ben's bouts were the loudest, wettest, wildest fucking Charlotte had ever known, this encounter had all the intensity of watching grass grow. She looked like she could be getting a pedicure. She wasn't even breathing hard. Could Ben be bad at it? But no, she looked down at Ben and her own pussy pulsed as she saw him lap like a man out of the desert with a juicy piece of fruit.

What the fuck was going on?

'Charlie, where the hell have you been? I've been ringing and texting you for two days.'

He'd caught her outside her office as she was leaving for the night.

'Sorry, sweetie, I've just been so busy with work.' She'd been avoiding him since the night she saw him with the woman she now thought of as Frigidaire. She couldn't sort her feelings out, didn't know what to make of what she saw. But now that he was here, now that she was standing next to him looking into his eyes, all that emotional and physical intensity rushed back and throbbed inside her.

Which she also didn't understand. He wasn't her usual type. She generally liked her guys buff, kind of the blond

California lifeguard sort. But Ben was dark-haired and British, tall and lanky, muscled but wiry. Something about him though, made you aware of an undercurrent of heat. Something mysterious and even a bit dangerous. His dark eyes shone with a light that made it seem he was carrying a delicious secret. She couldn't resist him.

He took the subway with her to her apartment. In the elevator he pushed her against the wall, held her there with his body. 'I've missed you, my Charlie.' He nuzzled into her neck, pushed his nose into the crook of it. 'Missed the way you smell,' he murmured as he inhaled deeply. Charlotte could feel his cock pressing against her thigh and her limbs went watery. 'Please don't say you're ready to chuck me just yet,' he whispered. 'I can't get you out of my mind.'

They barely made it into her apartment before the clothes started flying off. She fell back on to her couch as Ben began pulling off his jeans when her mind suddenly flashed to Frigidaire with her legs wide and Ben's head between them.

'Baby,' she whispered as he laid the length of his body on top of her and cupped her naked mound in his hand. 'You know what I really want?'

'What's that?' he murmured and she gasped as he dipped his fingers inside of her, brought them to his lips and sucked.

'I want to suck your cock,' she said and he smiled down at her lasciviously.

'I think I could probably oblige.'

'And then maybe after,' she began, staring meaningfully into his eyes. 'You could, you know, return the favour.' Then she added quietly, 'Since you like tasting me so much.'

She watched as his eyes clouded over. 'Charlie, I would like nothing more than to feast on your gorgeous nectar,' he sighed. As he said it his hand roamed over her body, plucking delicately at her nipples, teasing them into peaks.

185

'But I can't,' he said quietly. 'Or I can, but …'

'But what?' she said, baffled. 'Ben, look, I know this was wrong of me but I saw you with that blonde.'

'What? When? Wait, have you been spying on me?'

'I didn't mean to be. I just, I didn't understand, I felt like there was something you were hiding. But I saw you going down on her.'

He was silent. He seemed to be working something out in his head. Finally he sighed.

'Charlotte, there's something I need to tell you.'

Shit, she thought. *Here we go. What freaky thing is he into?* The last guy who honoured her with a bedroom confession wanted her to let him wear diapers and call her Mummy.

'Look, Ben, that's cool if you've got some weird kink, I'm just not …'

But he interrupted her. 'I'm a nymph.'

She stared at him waiting for the punch line. But his face was stone serious.

'A … a …?' she clamoured.

'A nymph.'

A snort escaped her, a sound that could best be described as a guffaw.

'I'm sorry!' she laughed. 'But it sounded like you just told me you were a little woodland fairy.' He bowed his head in a kind of resigned, knowing gesture. She laughed a bit more but when he remained silent she said, 'What the fuck are you talking about?'

'Look, I know this sounds crazy to you. I didn't mean to entangle you in our world. When I met you at the club, you were so hot, so passionate, I thought you were one of us.'

'One of who? What the hell?'

'Charlie, just listen.' He struggled for words. 'I'm, I'm different from you. Nymphs are super-sexual beings. Our lives revolve around creating and maintaining erotic passion. We feed off sexual secretions. Nectar. To us it's a life

186

force.'

Charlotte's head spun. 'So Frigidaire, I mean, that blonde ...'

'Julie lets me feed at her well. She's anorgasmic.'

'She's what?'

'She's incapable of achieving orgasm. I can do what I need to without any ... consequences. You see, that's the problem Charlie.'

She stared at him, lost.

'I would love to go down on you, to lick and suck you. I crave your nectar. But I can't let you come. If you come, you become what I am. If you come while I'm eating you, you become a nymph.'

That night Ben went down on her for the first time. But not without some strict ground rules.

'I'll go slowly,' he told her as he caressed her and licked at her hardened nipples. 'As slowly as I can. If you get close, you tell me. Give me a number, ten meaning coming, so I know when to back off.'

'What do you mean, "as slowly as I can"?'

'As you get excited, your nectar becomes more potent. It's like your passion increases the vitality and makes it even sweeter, even more fulfilling. That's why with Julie, it's impossible to be sated. She doesn't get excited. She's only a temporary measure. But you ...' His hand pressed gently against her mound and his eyes gleamed as some of her moisture leaked out into his palm. 'You are so sweet,' he whispered as he brought his hand to his mouth and took her essence on his tongue.

Charlotte never knew there would be a difference between being licked and being tasted. Ben knelt before her, held her labia gently open with his thumbs, and when he dipped his tongue into her quim, he swirled it around as though he were licking delicious cream from a bowl. Then he placed his tongue very delicately on her clit and, true to his word, began to lick the swollen flesh very slowly. But the intensity of their union seemed at an ultimate level, her sensations felt as though they were being heightened by some unknown force. Her clit was so sensitive that, despite the slowness and the softness of his lapping, Charlotte could not help but cry out in ecstatic delirium. She felt the wetness pouring out of her and then Ben's tongue dipping down to take in her juices. Then he went back to teasing her clit. Back and forth from her hole to her clit he worked his tongue. And even as she struggled against it, she could feel her orgasm looming. He kept his tongue moving slowly, but the slowness created its own delicious frustration. She panted and thrust her hips up as he lapped. She could tell how hard he was trying to hold back from increasing his pace. As he licked he moaned out how good she tasted.

'Ben!' she cried finally. 'Seven!' He groaned, took his tongue from her hard clit and snaked it into her pussy hole.

'It's so good, baby,' he mumbled as he licked and sucked. 'Just relax your muscles.' He laved her. 'Mm, just give me a little more, sweet Charlie,' and he tongued her clit harder this time, faster. 'But don't come, baby. Don't,' he muttered.

'Ben!' she gasped. 'I'm an eight! Fuck!' He was licking her with abandon now, like he was in his own universe, gasping and mumbling his appreciation into her pussy, suckling like a starved animal.

'Oh God, nine Ben! Nine!' She tried desperately to relax her quivering pelvic muscles but it was impossible to calm her quaking body as his tongue worked it into a frenzy. He seemed not to hear her, as he continued feasting. 'Ben, if you don't stop I'm gonna come. I can't help it!'

Suddenly he snapped out of his intoxicated reverie. He pulled himself away from her, panting, his mouth covered with her juices, as she gasped out in thwarted desire.

He held her in his arms, her body quivering with need. 'Oh please,' she begged him, 'just finish me, let me come.'

'I can't, not even with my hand right now. It's too

dangerous. It could still make you change.'

'Maybe I want to change. Maybe I want to be like you.'

'You don't Charlie, trust me. You have a job, friends, a life. You can have sexual passion, feel fulfilled and do other things. I'm a slave to this. I think about nothing else. My hunger for sex is constant.'

Later, after she'd rested and he deemed it safe, he took her. With his cock like a steel rod, he slid into her and worked her to the most intense orgasm she'd ever experienced. Then she straddled and rode him to three more shuddering climaxes before she felt sated.

She came a fourth time while he worked to his own finish.

They struggled to be together. Some nights he went down on her. Unlike the first time, he managed to stay in better control, would lick and suck her until she was a six or seven and then let her rest before licking again. For Charlotte it was erotic torture. His tongue in her pussy was exquisite, an addictive bliss. But not being able to ride the orgasmic wave to its conclusion was maddening. Sometimes he licked her for an hour or more while she moaned and gasped, unable to come, but unwilling to stop. Other nights she'd decide, no oral, she just wanted to fuck and come like a normal couple.

But those nights she craved his tongue even more.

'I can't do this, Ben,' she whispered finally one night. 'It's over.'

It was Kate who told her something was wrong.

She called her at work. 'Charlotte, I saw Ben this afternoon. He looked like hell. I mean, really sick.'

Charlotte raced over to his apartment after work.

She found him in his bed, pale, thin, languid. He looked at her vaguely, his eyes unfocused.

'You were right, Charlie,' he croaked, his voice barely audible. 'I can't do this either. I can't replace you, your

189

sweet nectar. I don't want to be a slave to this any more.'

She undressed wordlessly. As she moved to straddle his head he whispered, 'Charlotte, no.' But even as he said it, she positioned herself over his mouth, he breathed in her scent and a light went on in his eyes. Gently she put her hand at the back of his head and pulled his mouth to her opening.

His tongue was weak at first, fluttery, barely moving. But as her juices flowed into his mouth it got stronger. He licked, gasping and suckling more, more. When she cried out he hesitated a moment, then, with new strength, pushed her off him and down onto the bed, diving between her legs and feasting like never before.

He fastened his lips around her hard, sensitive nub and sucked. He pushed his fingers inside her, pulled them out, licked them clean and shoved them back in while he tongued her clit hard and fast. Charlotte writhed and screamed. After weeks of soft, feathery licks and slow tonguing, she was powerless to stop her orgasm building now with the firm, fast flicking on her engorged clit and fullness of his fingers stretching her opening and working her juices out. She knew she should cry out, stop him. And yet …

'Oh God,' she screamed. 'OH GOD!' There was a roaring sound in her ears as his tongue worked her over the precipice. Then everything went black.

Charlotte woke. Her body felt different. Charged. Not only was her sex molten, pulsing, but she distinctly felt every nerve ending in her body. The blood running through her veins seemed to carry a hot, electric tension. She'd never felt more invigorated. Alive. And there was something else.

Hunger. Intense and insistent.

'It's OK, baby, I know.' Ben moved toward her, his stiff cock in his hand. An offering.

Charlotte took it and began to feed.

Skin Deep
by Kat Black

I love the smell of a summer's night in the city. Nowhere more so than here, in the club district, where the young and vibrant come to seek their nocturnal hedonistic pleasures. In the guise of a human man I come also, to hunt, drawn by the irresistible lure of life at its most decadent.

Tonight, sweat and desire saturate the humid air, drenching my senses and coating my tongue with the dark, velvety taste of sin – my favourite flavour. I draw the essence deep, sharpening the already keen edge of the Hunger, tensing every fibre of my being in anticipation of the coming chase.

Ignoring the crowds that wander the streets, I descend the stairs to a nightclub named *Skin*, where the patrons like to wear just that and very little else. Without slowing at the entrance, I cast the doorman a glance over the top of my dark glasses. His eyes pop wide as they meet the otherworldly glow of mine then glaze over before the shock of the impossible has a chance to fully register. He shivers as I pass, but sees nothing and will remember even less. Better for him that I go about my nightly business undetected.

Once inside, I slip through the shadows and stake claim to a vantage point along the rear wall. The place feels hot as hell, and if I were classified a member of the warm-blooded humanity packed tight in here, I'd already be melting inside

191

my heavy leathers. But I'm no such animal. I'm the stone-cold stuff of their nightmares, instead – the monster lurking in their midst.

If only they knew.

Behind the private tug of amusement pulling at my lips, my tongue runs over the stiletto-sharp tip of one elongated canine in anticipation. Propping a shoulder against the wall, I cross my arms over my chest and, with a patience born of centuries, settle down to wait and watch.

Under pulsing Technicolor lights, the dance-floor heaves with a press of bodies getting down to a hard-funk beat. Into the undulating mass, a fresh group of semi-clad young things strut their way, driving like a wedge through the crowds.

With Mediterranean-dark good looks, they move with a loose-limbed, sensuous grace – beautiful, desirable, and knowing how to make the best of both. Laughing, they begin to dance, teasing and titillating, and as the air around me grows heavy with lust-laced pheromones, it's obvious I'm not the only one captivated by their sultry show.

However, while the human desire is directed at all the smooth olive skin on display, my own cravings run a little deeper – to the promised pleasure of the warm spiced blood coursing beneath the surface of that firm flesh.

I find my interest piqued by the tallest of the group – a new-grown man with glossy black curls and the taut vitality of his youth evident in the lean physique revealed by the shirt he wears unbuttoned. Full of the arrogance of youth, he radiates confidence and pride, and out of instinct the alpha in me stirs, flexing its own muscles in response to the perceived challenge.

Into my mind flashes a vivid picture of the male and I locked in a desperate embrace. Grappling chest to chest, he pits every last ounce of strength against me in the battle for dominance, his attempts to keep my deadly teeth from puncturing the vulnerable skin of his throat heroic, yet ultimately futile…

The Hunger rakes its claws, nearly bending me double and my body hardens in readiness for just such a fight.

Not that there's the slightest need for things to get rough, if the truth be told. Like all of my immortal kind, I'm blessed with the talent to hold my prey in a state of hypnotic suspension, thereby sparing them the trauma they're otherwise so prone to suffer. In the case of this cocky young buck, though, I can't seem to find it in me to be merciful. Not if it means denying myself the intoxicating taste of his testosterone-fuelled, adrenaline-laced terror.

The mere thought of the sweet taste of fear has my canines throbbing and lengthening in a visceral reaction I wouldn't do anything to stop if I could. What can I say? I'm as much a slave to my nature as the next beast.

Focusing my will, I begin to send the first wisps of mental suggestion the male's way. Before long I have sufficient power of persuasion over his mind to begin directing him away from the security of his friends and toward the fire exit situated in the far corner. Reining in the sense of urgency triggered by the ravenous demands of the Hunger, I have him move slowly, steadily – subtly guiding his movements through the crowd so as not to raise suspicion. Only when he nears the exit do I emerge from the shadows and move to join him by the door, careful to keep my teeth hidden behind my predatory grin.

As I close the distance between us, I'm delighted to note that my prey has worked up a nice sweat, leaving his skin slick and salty and deliciously lickable. Docile and obedient as a pet dog, he waits as I reach up and lower my glasses. A second of eye contact is all it takes to have his dark, liquid gaze widening with terror, but before he can so much as squeak in fear, I have him well and truly bent to my will.

Leaning in close to make myself heard over the pounding beat of the music, I'm met by the piquant tang of heat rising from his body. Saliva pools.

'There's a door behind you,' I instruct. 'Turn around and leave ...'

'Excuse me.' A small female steps in from the side, barging into the narrow space between us. 'There's no way out here. It's an emergency exit only.'

The untimely distraction is minor but an annoyance all the same. 'Yes,' I say, and without shifting my gaze away from my dark-eyed treat, I weave a subtle thread of compulsion into my tone. 'But my friend here is feeling unwell. We're just stepping out for a breath of air.'

Instead of the automatic acceptance and retreat I expect, the female stands her ground. 'I'm sorry, the door is alarmed. I can't allow you to do that.'

Allow? She can't *allow* me? The sheer audacity of anyone – anything – presuming such authority over me shocks me into breaking my focus, leaving the male blinking in dazed confusion as the bonds of the thrall unravel.

Hastily refocusing, I re-establish control and, perturbed at finding myself wrong-footed by this female, forego finesse in favour of issuing her a blunt command. 'Go away.'

'No,' she returns just as bluntly. 'Not until you release this man and leave my club.'

Her resistance is no less shocking the second time around but I manage to keep my eyes locked on target and my prey tethered. Just. Never, in all my long years, have I encountered a human capable of withstanding my will the way this female seems to be doing, and I have to admit that I don't much like making the discovery now.

I ensure that my next delivery carries the weight of a mental punch. 'You need to walk away from here right now and forget this encounter.'

From the corner of my eye I see the female stagger as if from a physical blow, hands flying up to clutch her head. I feel a spurt of reassurance and satisfaction before, unbelievably, she straightens and says, 'You can't control me, I know what you're up to.'

This time she really does break my concentration as the meaning of her words ring like warning bells. I look down at the female for the first time.

She's tiny – delicate and petite, although obviously lacking the sweet, diminutive personality to match. She's dressed to party in a next-to-nothing black dress that clings to every feminine curve, but the determined glint in her eye means all business. Beneath the bravado, however, her pulse hammers, the tell-tale tic at the side of her neck indicating a high level of fear. Even so, I'm convinced she thinks she's dealing with the illegal sale of drugs or sex here. There's no way she could know what I'm really up to. If she had the slightest inkling of the truth she'd be running for her life instead of standing there daring to face up to me.

As tempting as the notion is to teach her a lesson in minding her own business, I'm not prepared to sacrifice my prime catch simply for the pleasure of a game of cat and mouse. Given her size, the female would make a poor substitute, barely big enough to quench my thirst.

And as inconvenient and astounding as it is to find her so resistant to my mental authority, there's no doubt that, physically, she's no match at all. By employing the strength and speed of my kind, I can have my tasty Mediterranean out and away so fast that no one will be able to stand in my way.

Dismissing the female from my mind, I turn my attention back to the waiting male, only to find him gone … stumbling his way back through the crowd to the safety of his friends. The Hunger roars in denial, furious at the sight of my dinner walking away.

With deliberate slowness, I turn the full force of my displeasure back toward the female. Anger getting the better of caution, I reach up and remove my glasses, wanting her to see for herself exactly how much danger she's landed herself in.

With some satisfaction, I watch the blood drain from her

face and her eyes grow huge. But instead of fainting as I half expect she might, she swallows convulsively and dares to stare right into the luminescent silver depths of my eyes.

'I know what you are,' she stutters.

In a flash I have her by the scruff of the neck and out of the fire door, utilising that strength and speed to take us well away from the clamouring sound of the alarm and any responding pursuit. Half way down a deserted alley, I swing into a shadowed doorway and push her against the door. Using the weight of my body I hold her pinned, leaving her dainty feet dangling a foot off the ground.

'You might think you know me, little girl.' I lean close and snarl right into her face. 'But you've no idea of the trouble you're really in.'

'I d … do know.' She can barely choke the words out past the terror squeezing her lungs and I have to give her points for courage. With one hand she attempts to push me away, while with the other she scrabbles around in the neckline of her top. Pulling out the end of a long silver chain, she brandishes a crucifix at me. 'I've been w … watching you for weeks. You're a vampire.'

I'm stunned that she appears to know the truth, but given her current predicament, see no need to deny it. I laugh nastily, making sure she gets a good eyeful of long, sharp fang. 'And who the hell do you think you are – Buffy the Slayer?' Wrapping my hand around the useless talisman, I rip it from around her neck and toss it away, gaze locking on the thin red graze left by the rough pull of the chain … and the pulse ticking hard and fast beneath it.

'Oh God, don't you bite me!' She struggles harder as she registers the intent stamped on my features. Her heart races flat out, pitter-pattering through the layers of our clothing to tickle against my ribs. 'I'll scream!'

She really hadn't taken the time to think this through to the end, had she?

'I don't doubt it, darling.' I clamp a hand over her mouth

and use it to push her chin to the side, stretching out the long line of her neck. Leaning down, I inhale her scent, running my face from clavicle to jaw. She smells good enough to eat. 'It's really just a question of how loud,' I say with soft menace into her ear.

With that she goes wild. Screeches muffled against my palm, she lashes out with hands and feet, elbows and knees. She scratches and hits and kicks, hair flying around her and skin growing flushed as she fights for her very life.

All of which the beast in me *absolutely* loves.

Goaded, ravenous, I go straight for the jugular, teeth piercing through gossamer-fine skin to sink deep into the hot, living rush of arterial blood.

The female's taste explodes in my mouth, exotic and lush and heavily spiked with adrenaline, and as I swallow down the first mouthful and feel the glorious heat of her spread to every cold, dark corner of my being, I know I'm never going to be able to get enough. A noise rumbles up from my chest, like a big cat's victorious growl, and I pull her even closer, sucking hard so as not to miss a single precious drop.

Even as she fights to stop her life force flowing into me, something about her struggle changes and the female begins to moan and writhe in my hold, her body heating, loosening, blossoming. With a jolt I realise that she's one of those rare humans susceptible to the erotic rapture of my vampiric bite. This interesting fact has barely time to register before she takes me by surprise yet again, and bites me back.

The effect is instant, thrilling. The sting of her blunt little teeth sinking into the flesh at the base of my thumb, combined with her sudden full-blown arousal has my own body responding with need, my cock lengthening and hardening with every new pulse-beat of blood coursing between us. Her taste tells me she's inflamed and terrified in equal measure, and the cocktail of sweet female musk and even sweeter fear blazes across my senses, igniting my basest urges to fight, feed, fuck.

My head begins to spin with the primal frenzy of it all, and the Hunger howls in delight when the female's fingers tangle in my hair, pulling my feasting mouth closer and holding me where I most want to be.

With her flailing hands now otherwise occupied, my own take the opportunity to do some exploring. Propping a thigh between both of hers to keep her pinned aloft, I run my palms down over her curves, taking in the swell of her breasts with the hard-peaked nipples, the tiny waist which my fingers can almost span, and the fertile flare of her hips.

Down her thighs my palms glide, slipping beneath the hem of her short black dress and sliding the clingy jersey up as I head to cup the rounded cheeks of her buttocks.

She's an exquisite little thing, womanly and ripe, and given the explosive way she reacts to the brush of my fingertips against her damp underwear, she's thoroughly caught in the throes of carnal ecstasy.

'Please,' she begs so nicely that my need peaks in answer to the frantic call of hers. I rip the underwear right off her body as she lifts her legs to wrap them around my hips.

'Hurry ...' she gasps, rubbing and rocking her pelvis against mine.

My sentiments exactly. Manoeuvring a hand between our bodies, I wrestle to release my engorged shaft from the too-tight confines of my trousers. Once free, I grasp her under the thighs and lift her onto me. Unable to wait another second, I drive straight up into her hot, molten core, sheathing myself to the hilt in one move.

Her cry drowns out my muffled one as I grind right into the centre of her amazing heat. Every pull of my mouth on her vein is answered lower down by a spasm of muscle clenching around my cock. She can't seem to get close enough, hands all over me, grasping and grabbing, nails raking and clawing as she pulls us together like she's trying to meld us into one.

The skin beneath my lips burns with a sexual flush and

shudders begin wracking the female's small frame. And then she's coming, fast and hard, her body bowed taut, straining between the deep double penetration of my cock and fangs. Locked onto her screaming throat, my mouth is flooded with honeyed, orgasm-spiked blood even as her body weeps its silky release over the length of my iron-hard erection.

The grasping, squeezing grip of her body sees me undone and I follow her over the edge, shattering with such force it's like a starburst in my head – blinding and burning and brilliant.

I gradually return to awareness to find the female sighing and slumping against me, pleading to her god over and over again in a broken murmur. She's weak, her pulse fluttering as her heartbeat stutters, and now that the Hunger has been satiated it's time for me to make the ultimate choice.

Given all that she knows about me, as well as her extraordinary resistance to my influence which leaves me unable to wipe the memory of our encounter from her mind, there's no question as to how this should end.

I shudder at the dragging pull of flesh over the sensitised enamel of my canines as I withdraw my teeth. The female's head lolls to the side revealing a livid burgundy-coloured bruise that darkens a good portion of her neck – evidence that I've not been at all gentle with her.

'Now let that be a lesson to you.' Her gaze is fogged and unfocused as she mutters nonsense. 'Don't think you can come around to my club and just help yourself to my customers.' Her eyes roll back and she slips into exhausted unconsciousness.

I feel a tug of genuine amusement play on my lips as I look down at the plucky little thing in my arms. I haven't a clue as to how or why something so tiny and insignificant should have the strength to resist my persuasive powers, let alone the courage to dare bait me, and I suspect that for the sake of a continued uncomplicated existence, I really shouldn't care.

But I find myself intrigued. There's definitely more to this female than meets the eye. There are more answers to find, more surprises to uncover – not to mention further womanly tastes to explore, other warm, wet places into which to sink both my cock and my teeth.

And so, against my better judgement I find myself running my tongue over the puncture wounds in her neck, allowing my saliva to help slow the bleeding before I return her limp form to the stairwell behind *Skin*.

Propping her like a rag doll against the wall, I force open the fire door to activate the alarm once more and retreat to the shadows. I wait long enough to witness club security arrive and fuss around her, feeling no apprehension about what the female might say once she regains consciousness. Who would believe the tale she has to tell?

The important thing is that I know where to find her when I'm ready to come asking my questions. And, as she's carried inside, head drooping over the arm of her rescuer to expose the delectable arch of her throat, the Hunger resurges, demanding that she be subjected to a full and thorough interrogation. Sooner rather than later.

Airfield
by James Hornby

It is night again and stars have begun their celestial dance. Here on earth a gentle night breeze rushes over fields, trees and hedgerows before whispering in through her open window. It tickles her face as she dreams of a magical night on horn-white beaches where fires crackle and music plays.

The girl before her, a few inches shorter, rises on to her toes and kisses her. She can feel the caress of the girl's cool, sweet breath on her cheek; the pressure of the girl's body against her own; pressing soft, warm. She feels the nipples of the girl through her silk dress, they are hard and erect.

A sudden roar; both metallic and prehistoric, rents the night. She jerks awake, the taste of sleep in her mouth, her vision blurred and this cacophony in her ears.

She lies for a moment, disorientated, desperately trying to identify this alien noise. It is not the owl that asks its eternal question, it is not the far away yap of foxes as they play on the moon bathed hills. It is man made thunder. It roars into the night like a fierce animal tearing itself from the earth. It roars for blood though it has none of its own, it roars for freedom though it has no soul to feel it.

Slowly, like breaking dawn, she comes to realise what it is, though she can't believe it. She can even identify this beast, sprung from the fog of time, and name it. What she cannot explain is why it is heard now, on this silent night over 60 years since it last shattered the world with its voice.

But that is wrong, she tilts her head, fanning dark hair out on her pillow, for there is more than just one. There is an entire squadron of them, challenging the night like so many hunting hounds.

The sound abruptly stops. It echoes away across the sleeping world; some stir in their beds with its passing yet most do not hear. She has heard and wonders.

From her single bed, past her desk containing the disembodied limbs of a great flying machine, past the bookshelf heavy with volumes of war and out on to the thick carpeted landing she moves as a ghost moves, stealthy, silent and yet there is no need. The house is empty and void of life except for her. She remembers when it was otherwise, when Sammy used to live there. It was a strange love they had, timid yet fierce, withdrawn yet insatiable.

Sammy was a girl from a wealthy and well to do family and the concept of having sex with other women was foreign and slightly repulsive to her. The concept may have worried her, but, after that night on the beach when concept became practice, her fears soon slipped away.

Sammy gently mocked her for her hobby. She sat in her room making airplane after airplane, a fascination taken from the nights she would sit in her father's study and watch him do the same.

And then Sammy would come in, complaining of the smell of paint and doping fluid, yet still sit primly on the edge of the bed. They would talk about this and that; the sort of conversation that leaves the gaps where the real meaning sits, unseen. An awkward silence would fall and, putting down her paint brush, rubbing her hands clean of paint, she would go to the bed, and to Sammy.

Despite her solitude, she walks silently down the stairs, past a row of expectant shoes and boots and to the door. On bare feet she steps into the night.

The night is neither cold nor warm, the seasons are on the turn and vestiges of one melt with the next. A soft breeze, a

202

lover's breath, ruffles her nightshirt. It is long and comes to mid thigh. A rock star glowers from in-between her breasts, the dip making the singer look cross eyed.

Fields lie sprawled and silver with busy networks of hedges patching them together like God's own quilt. The stitched blanket of fields could run away into infinity, or so she thinks, after it has folded over the horizon.

She has reached the old road when the sound rises again: a pack of iron hunting-dogs bay into the night. The ground beneath her bare feet trembles with their fury. One of the animals rises in an urgent scream burning away the tranquillity. It crescendos and she looks to the east where, incredibly the thing rises into the air, materialising from behind fat black trees. It is vast and glints with malevolent purpose. It turns laboriously and comes toward her.

She cannot remember stopping, yet she finds her hand gripping the wire mesh fence. She wonders if they, the spectral pilots in that vast machine, have seen her. Do they know her to be an intruder in this time?

The B17 passes low overhead, so low she feels that if she jumped she could touch its expectant underbelly like touching a pregnant woman's belly, though here it is not life that is harboured but cool, metallic death.

She turns her head; following the iron dragon and then … it is gone; vanished for the moment taking its bestial roar with it. The rest of the pack have silenced also from somewhere beyond the dark trees.

After a moment … two moments, she releases the cool metal and continues along the perimeter fence.

Dreams within dreams, she thinks as she walks. She recalls her dream before waking, clutching at elusive tendrils of memory and maybe, as is with all memory, a little fantasy.

The beach on which they had met blooms in her mind, spreading and unfurling. The sand was coarse beneath her feet, and the touch of the girl's hand, Sammy's hand, on her

203

sex was hesitant yet so good. Gentle fingers exploring. There was a wonder in Sammy's eyes that seemed to reflect all the wonders of the universe from the night sky.

Sammy's scent was that of vanilla, lavender, the tang of sweat and the sweet undertone of tobacco. As she held Sammy, running her hand over her thigh, up past her hip, over the curve of her belly and on to the comforting weight of her breasts, she could feel the skin radiating heat as if the sun, taken during the day, was seeping back out of Sammy's skin. It was a perfect moment, she had never believed in them, but here one was, clutched in her arms, sighing with pleasure as somewhere out in the darkness the whistling frogs celebrated with a song of lust and desire.

She almost passes the old gatehouse, so lost is she in thought. She is very aware of her lack of underwear and now the loving breath of the night cools moisture upon her thighs.

Beneath the moon cast shadow of the gate house and into the city she walks on silent feet.

The old prefabricated homes stand with blind windows and gaping doors. She has been here at night before, with Sammy. In this place their cries of passion could be heard by none but the most secretive of night creatures who, by their secretive nature, never tell.

They had broken into the old cinema. It had smelled of dust, thousands upon thousands of hours of habitation by airman, soldiers and their lovers. Kissing, fondling some simply holding hands. Sammy had become aroused with the concept of making love on the high stage before the old dead screen.

'Think if they were all watching,' she had whispered in her ear.

With their bodies entwined; exploring one another, tasting one another, they made the old boards creak with their lovemaking. The flickering candlelight played swift shadows over Sammy's naked body and her curled dark hair

204

which lay heavy over both of them.

Like the blushing dawn sped up tenfold, light grows about her. She is illuminated by lights of the past. Windows, no longer blank and staring, twinkle and gaze with the happiness of habitation. The old cinema glows invitingly and now a crowd appears.

Women stand hip to hip with officers; dashing in their white uniforms; the women with masses of curled hair, blonde, black, red, brown and every tone in-between. They whisper excitedly as the queue moves slowly forward.

On the front of the building, imprisoned in glass, a long dead movie star smiles at his patrons, his teeth stark in the black and white photograph.

One man turns his capped head and glances back down the street. He is alone and by the way he bites his nails it seems he waits for a date. Perhaps the officer is worried that she will not come.

The officer's eyes pass blindly over her as she stands, in this bubble in time. Something stirs within her, the fact that she is mostly naked may be the cause. Crossing her arms beneath her breasts she tugs off her nightshirt, her blonde hair tumbles down her back as the shirt comes free. She casts it away and stands naked before this group. Is it her imagination or do eyes flick to her and away again, as if they glimpse something though reason dispels it?

The waiting officer removes his cap and turns it nervously through his hands and then a smile infuses his features.

She turns to look back down the road of store fronts of which some still blaze with light, others are shut for the evening. A woman appears, running awkwardly, her high heels making little clipping noises that ring off the buildings.

The woman's hair falls in dark waves about a face with large bewildered blue eyes, a small nose and a mouth curved down in concentration. Her dress is green and the twin mounds of her breasts seem enormous, thrusting high and forward.

She watches the woman pass and feels a jolt of recognition. It is Sammy, incredibly it is Sammy, her erstwhile lover, yet lost.

The shock leaves her standing watching the woman pass and go to the officer. It is Sammy's walk, her legs, her waist, her flared womanly hips.

Her momentary paralysis passes and she moves closer to this woman who looks so much like her dead lover yet cannot be. The wind gusts, sending discarded cinema tickets spinning into the air and a chill racing across her naked skin.

The officer opens his arms to the girl he has been waiting for. They embrace and kiss deeply.

As she watches, unseen from her bubble in time, she is aware of a jealousy rising within her. Though all sense says this cannot be Sammy, this must all be some strange wandering of imagination, it seems so real.

'Sammy?' she says in a cracked voice. 'Sammy, is that you?'

Again there is but a flicker of the eyes, Sammy continues to talk with the officer though a slight frown has appeared on her brow, as if she's uncertain of a lost memory.

'Sammy?' she says again and moves closer. This time there is no response.

Now she is closer, she can see that it is Sammy, though not precisely. This woman is a little younger than Sammy had been when she died. This woman is slightly plumper, not to a great extent but her cheeks are slightly fuller, her breasts a little heavier and hips a little wider, though these were always her favourite parts of Sammy and ...

She looks at Sammy's lips as she speaks to the officer; full lips, painted red and ever so glossy. She recalls the press of those lips on her own, on her nipples, on her sex.

'Oh Sammy,' she says again, but it is to herself. This woman cannot hear.

'There is a chill in the air tonight,' Sammy is saying and

rubbing her bare arms.

'Is there?' the officer asks. He drapes his jacket around Sammy's shoulders, the white lapels making a V over her bust.

'Thank you,' she says, tugging it close about her and looking around.

'Can you feel me?' she asks Sammy. Again the eyes flicker, those blue eyes, and that plump mouth, so mischievous, even in repose, twitches.

Sammy glances back at the officer who has returned to biting his nails. Even with Sammy's arrival his air of unquiet remains.

'What's wrong,' Sammy asks as she looks up at him.

'Oh nothing,' the pilot says in a clipped English accent.

'You can tell me,' she pleads and rests her hand on his shirt sleeve. Her nails are short, her hands business-like.

She remembers the feel of Sammy's hands upon her, stroking the inside of her leg, or trailing slowly and deliciously down her back. She shivers as if phantom fingers have reached out and touched her.

'I think it is going to be soon,' the officer says with no elaboration, though it appears there needs to be none. Sammy nods with understanding and her fingers momentarily squeeze his arm before falling away.

'Come on,' she says briskly, taking his hand. 'Lets go in, you can buy me some popcorn.'

He smiles down at her and they pass under the garish arch of the cinema.

Inside it's the same as she remembers from her and Sammy's, nocturnal visitations, though now it is alive with people, colour, sound and lights. The officer, having bought the tickets, is buying popcorn while Sammy happily chatters away.

Into the velvet shades of the cinema they pass. The place is large and less than a quarter of it is filled, with few people left in the line in the foyer. They select a seat far back from the screen which is, from her experience, tiny. They slip in, one by one, the officer, Sammy and finally her, the ghost in this time, and settle into seats.

She watches Sammy as she speaks, popping knobbly pieces of popcorn between her lips. She has a nervous aspect, eating without tasting as a sort of reflex.

There is the scent of Sammy all around, the vanilla, the lavender, the scent which is her own. She wants so much to reach out and touch Sammy's lips, her pale throat, cup a breast ...

Sammy is timidly touching the officer's sleeve, but he stares at the blank screen and doesn't appear to notice her.

There, in the cinema, there is a tension. All around, lovers sit, cuddle and spin out their uncertain lives. They know this could be their last night together. Some sit immobilized by fear and what may come to pass, others live just for the moment; embracing the present and submitting to its wanton lusts.

She can see the panic in Sammy's eyes; the usual blue of a warm summer sky has turned cold like the hard depths of winter. She leans forward and presses her lips to the corner of Sammy's mouth. Her breath expels in a rush. Sammy's skin, in life, was warm, but now it is hot, though not uncomfortably so.

Maybe it is me, she thinks. Maybe it is me that is cold.

She sees Sammy's eyes flick toward her but not focus. Sammy's lips curve a little in a smile and a blush rises.

Somehow she knows Sammy feels a little better, for here and now is only created by what is around her, what happens to her, and here and now everything is fine.

'Live for now,' she whispers in Sammy's ear.

Sammy leans across and kisses the officer, hard and passionately. The widening of his eyes suggests he did not expect this, but the motion of his hands up her sides suggests he doesn't disapprove, not at all.

'The lights lower and a flickering image comes on to the

screen, jerky and washed out. From somewhere the opening bars of distorted music begin to play.

'Make love to me,' Sammy implores in a deep and desperate voice.

She is almost certain that Sammy's blue eyes flick to her.

'Are you asking me?' she enquires, but Sammy does not respond as she returns her attention to the pilot.

The officer looks surprised and gently presses her away from him.

'We can't do it here.' It is half statement half question. The officer looks awkward.

Sammy's eyes flick toward her, the unseen presence, and she knows, in that instant, that Sammy is speaking not just to the pilot, but to her too.

Unperturbed by his reticence, Sammy slides over to sit on the officer's lap, her large breasts hover buoyantly below his face. She takes his head in confident nurse's hands and presses his face into her cleavage. Over the top of his blond head Sammy looks directly at her. With a slight flush of self conscious embarrassment she crooks a finger in the air, smiling as if she knows this is a ridiculous thing to do.

But it is not. She slides across the seats to where Sammy is astride the officer. She presses her lips to Sammy's. She tastes of tobacco and popcorn with a hint of burned sugar. Sammy presses into her, lips soft and supple beneath her own.

'Yes I'm here, Sammy,' she whispers into her former lover's mouth.

Below, the officer is tenderly kissing the valley between her breasts which rise and fall with her building passion.

She rushes quick ticklish kisses across Sammy's cheek, dancing for a moment on the delicate folds of her eyelids before moving down to her earlobe which she takes in her mouth and toys between her teeth.

The officer moves up to Sammy's mouth and, unseen, she takes her opportunity.

Hands pass through the officer and yet land on the soft swell of flesh beyond. Like a blind woman she feels and traces her way across the contours of Sammy's large breasts.

She can feel the nipples, crackling against the brittle material of the corset which Sammy wears. She wants to kiss and rub those points of pleasure. She wants to make Sammy forget the future as Sammy makes her recall the past.

She kisses Sammy through the dress and runs invisible hands down the slopes of her hips to land on her thighs, which are slightly parted, the dress making a cradle of cloth between them.

She works her hand beneath the hem, between the soft and sensitive skin to find Sammy's panties. They are softly cushioned with a puff of pubic hair.

She hooks a finger beneath one elasticated edge. Feeling the motion, Sammy raises herself from the seat. She pulls the garment away and Sammy is exposed. Her dress has ridden up and the soft flesh of her legs is in direct cool contact with the vinyl seat. She feels Sammy shiver.

She reaches behind her and squeezes, gentle at first an orb of one buttock. Sammy again gasps, this time into the pilot's mouth who is fumbling for the hooks of her corset.

She applies a little more pressure to the yielding flesh, a tightening balanced on the cusp of pleasure and pain. With her other hand she seeks Sammy's sex, gently parting hair and lips. She thought that Sammy's flesh was hot to the touch before, now she feels it is an inferno in a cauldron. Yet she continues to press in with her finger, feeling that Sammy is already slick in anticipation. She teases further into Sammy, hooking her finger upward.

This time Sammy groans, low and hard in her throat, her body trembles with it.

There is an expanding and filling as Sammy's corset sloughs away leaving her in a natural feminine state, still curved, still bountiful yet realistic in her proportions.

She feels the softness of Sammy's skin, running her forefinger up the girl's spine, pressing and feeling the give of her flesh.

'Oh, Sammy, I miss you,' she sighs. Her hand still works busily inside Sammy's heat, pressing exploring, feeling her engorging. Her other hand rises to cup one round breast, her thumb flicks over the nipple, which is hard and to attention. She presses forward until her own naked breast presses into Sammy's, nipples teasing one another.

Closing her eyes against what she may see, she passes her head, lips poised, through the officer's body. It is as if he is not there at all. No sensation until her mouth touches Sammy's scorching skin. Her lips kiss across the tender flesh, around the areole and graze the stiff nipple which she presses with her tongue.

'Give it to me,' Sammy demands with her head thrown back.

The pilot is quick to act, opening his trousers and allowing Sammy to guide him in. Sammy leans forward as he enters, increasing pressure between breast and mouth. She continues to stroke Sammy's lips, in and out, occasionally drifting a finger up to stroke her bud. Each time this happens Sammy's belly contracts with the sensation.

She looks up at Sammy, past her breasts past her mouth and into her blue eyes which now shine. Sammy is staring at her, the tip of her tongue on the full bottom lip.

'Wait,' she instructs, and the officer pauses in his rhythm.

She takes him down on to the popcorn flecked floor, her legs spreading apart and encasing him beneath her as if she never wants to let him go, or this moment of pure reality.

Sammy's head turns, eyes ablaze with desire, and she looks over her shoulder. She knows what to do, maybe it is the knowledge that all ghosts have, but with what feels like a spiral through space, in a tunnel both a nanometre wide and the width of the universe, she passes into Sammy. She becomes Sammy.

She can feel the beat of her heart, thundering in her breast, rising so sweet and full of life. She can feel his hardness inside her drifting in and out, teasing and more than anything she can feel the fire in her belly, the heat rising.

Like a bomb must feel when released from a payload door, she becomes for the moment weightless. No knowledge of direction or dimension. She is a singularity burning brighter than all of the suns in the universe before …

She explodes and the world rushes in seemingly thunderous and confusing. Somewhere a man is talking through a speaker; there is the rustle of popcorn, the smell of cigarettes. She relaxes breathing heavily.

The officer whips sweat from his brow and puts a finger to his lips. They both smile.

That is when the siren begins to howl somewhere out in the night.

The officer sits up, looking confused.

'That's us,' he says, and takes his jacket back. He kisses her tenderly on the forehead and leaves with a number of other gentlemen.

'Come back to me,' she whispers.

It is night again and the stars have begun their celestial dance. Below, here on earth, a woman remembers lost loves, she remembers ghosts, she wanders in the dark...

'Ghosts,' she whispers unheard.

Also from Xcite Books

Kinky Girls

Women who act on their most shameful fantasies and embark upon the most daring misbehaviour, is still the most enduring and timeless theme in erotic fantasy, and loved by male and female readers alike. And this collection takes the idea of a kinky adventurous woman to the max. A collection of 20 original, varied, outrageous, eye-watering and utterly sensuous stories from the best new voices and established authors around today.

ISBN 9781907016561   £7.99

Indecent Proposals

A kinky collection of erotic stories exploring sexy propositions and inappropriate behaviour in edgy situations. 20 brand new stories from the best new voices and established authors around today. Guaranteed to be surprising, inventive, imaginative and talked about. The first of four new Xcite collections in 2011 exploring the themes that worked so well for Black Lace.

ISBN 9781907016585 £7.99

Threesome

Threesome – When One Lover Is Not Enough is a
collection of twenty varied stories with ménage themes.
All combinations of couplings are explored allowing the
reader to indulge in a fictional feast of ménage
naughtiness.

ISBN 9781907016554   £7.99

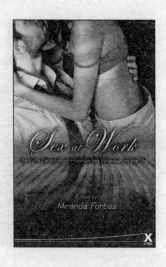

Sex at Work

Stationery cupboard trysts, conference connections and office party couplings – we all know that the workplace can be a hive of sexual activity.
In this collection Xcite have gathered together a selection of the best writing about inappropriate behaviour on the job.

ISBN 9781907016578   £7.99

Best of Both

Why limit yourself to one gender when you can have two? A collection of 20 stories celebrating the bonuses of bisexuality. From one-on-one loving to foursomes and moresomes, this anthology ticks all of the boxes, in every possible gender combination you could imagine! These bi-curious and bi-veterans know exactly what they want. They want the best of both worlds ...

ISBN 9781907761669   £7.99